P9-AQQ-031

CHILDREN of DAEDALA

Children of Daedala is published in 2018 by Switch Press,
A Capstone Imprint
1710 Roe Crest Drive
North Mankato, Minnesota 56003
www.switchpress.com

Library of Congress Cataloging-in-Publication Data

Names: Smith, Caighlan, 1994- author.
Title: Children of Daedala / by Caighlan Smith.
Description: North Mankato, Minnesota : Switch Press, an imprint of Capstone Press, [2018] | Sequel to: Children of Icarus. | Summary: "Six months alone in the labyrinth has made her strong. But the search for the exit means gambling on an old 'friend' and going against everything she's been taught to survive" — Provided by publisher.
Identifiers: LCCN 2017035922 (print) | LCCN 2017047183 (ebook) | ISBN 9781630790882 (reflowable ePub) | ISBN 9781630790868 (paper over board)
Subjects: | CYAC: Survival—Fiction. | Monsters—Fiction. | Labyrinths—Fiction. | Horror stories. | Youths' writings.
Classification: LCC PZ7.1.S6 (ebook) | LCC PZ7.1.S6 Ch 2018 (print) | DDC [Fic]—dc23
LC record available at https://lccn.loc.gov/2017035922

Book Design: Kay Fraser
Illustrations by Colin Marks
Author photo © Cecily McKeever

Image Credits: Shutterstock: Eric Isselee, Cover Right, Jacob Lund, Cover Left, photolinc, Design Element, Thomas Hartwig Laschon, Design Element

Printed and bound in China.
010732S18

CHILDREN of DAEDALA

CAIGHLAN SMITH

Switch Press
a capstone imprint

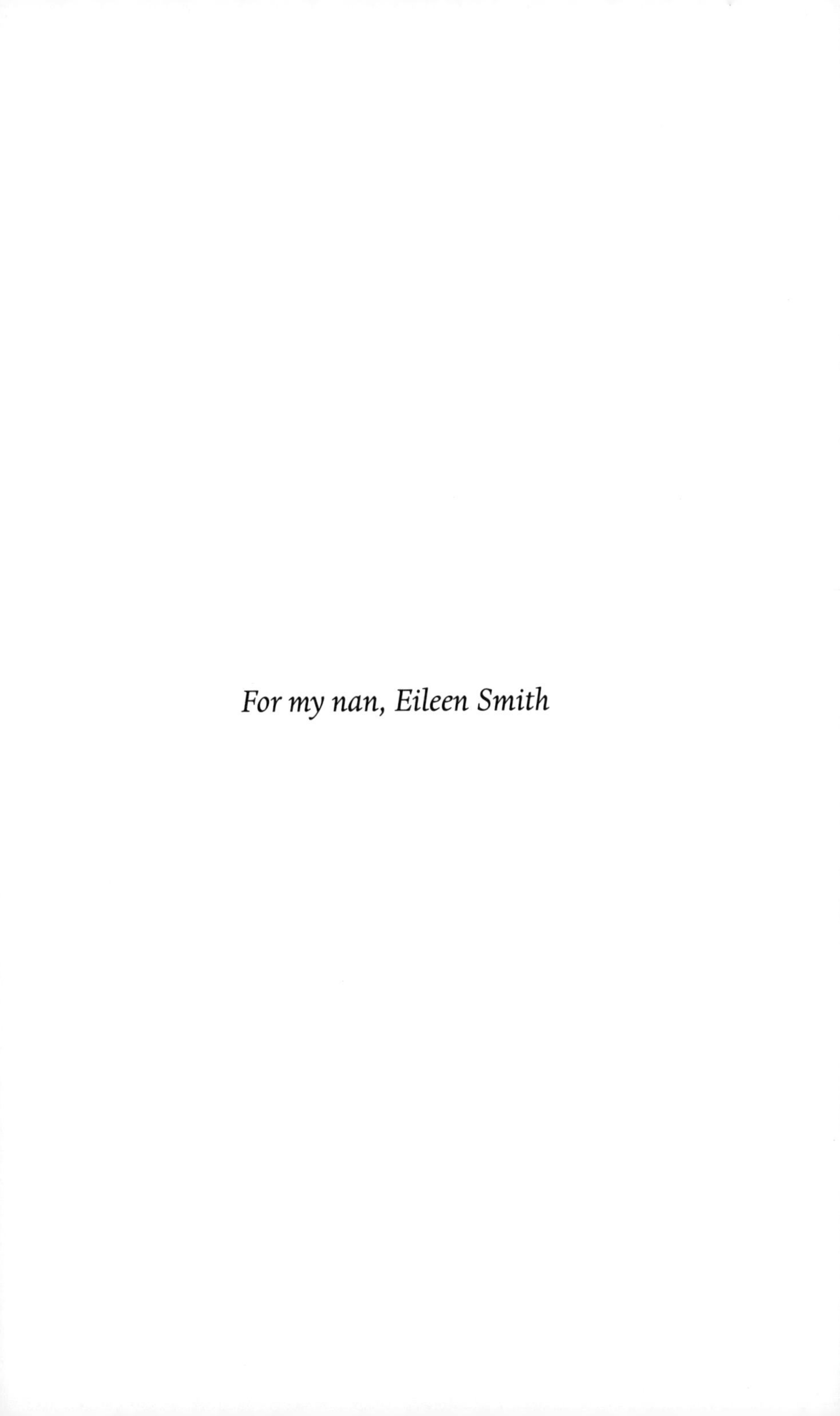

For my nan, Eileen Smith

As I turn the bell around in my fingers, it catches the sunlight, reflecting in my eyes. It's as silent as the Executioner. Perhaps a part of her remains in this bell, a fragment of her spirit that will stay forever in the labyrinth.

I don't believe that. It's an indulgent thought, and I can't afford those anymore.

DIVIDE

It's been six months since I entered the labyrinth. After my mentor, the Executioner, died, I thought I'd be alone forever. I am, but in a way, I'm not. When I'm reminded of this fact, I wish I were entirely alone.

I'm on top of one of the wider walls, having climbed up a crumbled section to access this shortcut. From here I can barely see anything ahead of me but mist. Back near my main base the sky is often clear, but the deeper I get into the labyrinth, the mistier it becomes — sometimes obscuring the sun entirely.

I guess this is where the legend of the Fey comes from. I can still remember Gus telling me about those three beings while he guarded the doors to Fates — the only *supposed* safe haven for those of us sent into the labyrinth. Gus said the Fey were spirits who could see the fates of everyone in the labyrinth, aside from one girl. When the Fey looked into their own futures to find out if they'd ever learn the girl's fate, what they saw made them disappear. It's said they turned into mist and still haunt the labyrinth today, while the fate of the girl remains a mystery. Fateless. That was what Gina called her.

Thinking of Gina is still painful. She wasn't even nine when she died, and she'd only just been reunited with her mother.

My only comfort is that, with the Executioner's death, they've been reunited again.

Crouching on the labyrinth wall, I scan the sky. I was tracking a pair of screechers — carnivorous humanoid bird monsters, which are distracted by bright colors. I was hoping the screechers could lead me to the rest of their flock. I'm not looking for a fight today, but I want to know where the screechers are going. There aren't nearly as many of them as there used to be. It could be that they're migrating, but it could also be because of the screecher-eater. I haven't encountered this monster personally, but I've seen the aftermath of its attacks. When I down a flock of screechers nowadays, I cover the bodies in poisoned paste in hopes of killing the monster. It's safer than facing something that dangerous head-on. So far no poison has been strong enough to take it out.

The screechers I was tracking seem to have disappeared into the mist. I can't hear their wingbeats anymore, let alone their screeches.

What I can hear is footsteps. The sound makes me pull my hood further over my face, gaze turning from the sky to the passageway on my left. Two boys round the corner, one carrying a wooden shield on his back, the other holding his in front of him, showing the image of a bucking horse. This boy walks ahead, peering down the path. The taller boy behind him is much more relaxed, spinning his two-handed spear in leisurely circles. He tries tossing the spear. It makes a single loop in the air before he catches it.

"Don't do that," the first boy says. "You're going to miss one day and cut off your hand or something."

"As if." The boy with the spear is looking right at me. He juts the weapon in my direction. "Look at that. We've found ourselves a Fey Bell."

My newest nickname. According to these boys, I can disappear into the mist, like the Fey. They've also noticed my bell and seem curious about it. What need does a girl out here have for accessories? Only Jack's ever had the nerve to ask — not that I answer him.

Silas, the shorter of the two boys, doesn't have the nerve for anything. He gulps before looking up at me. The second our gazes lock, he looks away.

I continue scanning the pair. No sacks. They're not out collecting, so they must be hunting. And they haven't encountered anything. Otherwise, Jack wouldn't be playing with his spear.

"Why not pull back your hood?" Jack calls. "Get a bit of sun. It's not like you've got to worry about being spotted out here."

Jack gestures vaguely to the misty air, then to his own downed hood. Even though his blond curls don't catch the sunlight, they still stand out significantly more than Silas's short brown hair. I don't touch my hood. Instead, I rise from my crouch and carry on down the wall.

"That's polite," Jack calls as I pass them. "Gammon said to say hi next time we saw you. Should I tell him you replied with a cold shoulder?"

I increase my pace until I leave the duo behind. Coming to the end of the wide section of wall, I hop down on the right side, bracing my legs for impact. After steadying myself, I dart down the adjacent hall, putting more distance between myself and the boys.

There's a group of them. By my guess, just under twenty. They call themselves Kleos, which apparently means "heroes" in Ancient Daedalic. I can't say I trust their translation skills, considering I don't trust the boys at all. They're a group of all-male Icarii, led by the oldest, Gammon, who's two years older than me. Silas, his mousy second-in-command, is a year younger than him, as is Jack. The other boys are all my age or a year younger from what I can tell.

I found out about Kleos two weeks after I started exploring the routes on the Executioner's map. Although the Executioner said the map is my key out of the labyrinth, I can't see an exit on it. The answer might be in the Ancient Daedalic scribblings in the margins, but I have no way of reading those. For now, I've been exploring cautiously, which has led me to discover two new underground bases.

I'd just found my second base and was searching the area when I ran into Gammon for the first time. He was backed by Jack and one of the other boys. When I first saw them, I thought they were scavengers from Fates, and I froze completely. That gave way to shock when I realized they were strangers. I'd had no idea that other Icarii — other children sent forth from Daedalum city in the name of Icarus — had survived this deep in the labyrinth.

"What do we have here?" Gammon asked. "A lost Harmonian wandering in Kleos' territory?"

The confusion must have been plain on my face, because Gammon's smirk widened, and he said, "Maybe not. Where do you think she's from, boys? Do we have a Fates wanderer? Has she lost her team?"

"Nah." Jack leaned on his spear, looking me over. "Her gear's too good for those losers."

I didn't like how relaxed Jack and Gammon were in the middle of the labyrinth — how they seemed at home. My hand found the bell at my throat. When Gammon's gaze followed the action, I covered the bell entirely from his view.

Jack wasn't looking at my bell. "Hey, is that a flail?"

I didn't correct him.

"I've always wanted a flail," Gammon said. "Mind giving us a look?"

My hand moved from my bell to the chain's handle.

"That's it," Gammon prompted.

I took out the chain and flicked it loose. The spiked ball slammed into the wall to my left, spewing stone onto the floor. The boy with Gammon and Jack flinched, but they remained unfazed.

"Very nice." Gammon held out his hand. "Can I hold it?"

I gave the chain one sharp yank, and the spiked ball fell from the wall, scattering more rock. Collecting the chain in my hands, I glared at Gammon, not moving from my spot.

"No? Maybe after we're better acquainted. Right, my manners." He introduced himself at that point, making sure to add he was the leader of their "proud little group." Then he introduced the two behind him. Jack grinned at me when Gammon said his name, showing surprisingly white teeth.

"And you?" Gammon asked. "What should we call you?"

By that point I'd scanned each of them and was sure they weren't carrying bows. Still, I didn't want to risk being wrong or one of them being skilled at throwing spears. Keeping my eyes on them, I started to back up.

"Going so soon?" Gammon said. "We've only just met. Don't you want to stay and chat awhile? Or maybe we could go back to our base, get comfy, and have a nice long talk. Share our stories. I really want to know where you came from and where you got that flail."

I dug in my heels. I hated Gammon's smug tone and the way he was looking at me. It reminded me of how Collin had started treating me when he learned that I wasn't his estranged sister, just a girl who looked a little like her. The rest of Fates followed Collin's lead after that, turning hostile against me before ultimately turning me out to the mercy of the labyrinth.

But instead I found myself at the mercy of the Executioner, and I never hesitate to make use of the skills she taught me.

As Gammon watched, I loosened the chain until the spiked ball was inches from the ground and started swinging. As I swung I maneuvered the weapon over my head until the circles above me were so fast the chain whistled. I watched Gammon the whole time, reveling in the way his smirk disappeared, how the boy behind him trembled, and Jack brought his spear up defensively.

"Not very friendly, are you?" Gammon said.

"If she's not with Harmonia yet," Jack said to him, "they'll recruit her in no time. Should we . . . ?"

Gammon looked me over, considering. "No. Not yet. There's still a chance for her, I think. Maybe next time we meet she'll be a bit more receptive."

At that I let the spiked ball fly. It slammed into the stones inches from Gammon's feet, sending shards of rock over him.

"Maybe not," Gammon said as I jerked back the chain. "Watch yourself, bell girl. It's better to have Kleos as your friend."

They left then, and I had to resist the urge to swing my chain further. When they rounded the corner, I finally put my weapon away.

The next time I ran into a group from Kleos was the first time I saw Silas. He and Gammon were discussing a scavenge route, so I decided to tail them and listen in. I got too close, and Gammon noticed me. Immediately, I had my notched arrow aimed at him.

"If it isn't bell girl," Gammon said, unperturbed by the arrow pointing at his skull. "Is this an assassination or your way of greeting?"

I pulled the bowstring taut.

"This is the girl I was telling you about," Gammon said to Silas before introducing him to me as the second-in-command at Kleos. "So if you shoot down both of us, you'd effectively wipe out our group's hierarchy. Of course, Jack or one of the others would eventually take over, but there would be enough anarchy for you to pick off a third, maybe half, of the group. If that's your plan, I recommend shooting me first. If you start with Silas, I'll have you on your back before his heart stops beating."

Silas had gone ashen by the time Gammon finished. His voice was squeaky when he said, "Don't give her ideas!"

Gammon grabbed Silas's shoulder with a laugh and gave him a shake. "Don't tell me you can't take a joke, either?"

"Not when we're in the middle of the labyrinth and a girl is about to attack us!"

"She's not going to attack us." Gammon looked at me. "If she were, she wouldn't have hesitated. She would have shot me while I was talking. Unless, bell girl, you like the sound of my voice?"

I wanted to shoot him so badly at that moment. I wanted to let my arrow fly just past his head and notch another while he recovered. But then I'd have had to pass him to retrieve the arrow, if I let him live.

"I guess that's a yes," Gammon said when I neither acted nor spoke. "Drop by our base whenever, bell girl, and I'll let you hear my voice some more."

Gammon turned and left, pulling Silas after him. I was furious that Gammon thought so little of me so as to turn his back. I could have shot him at that moment, and his last surprised thought would have been that I'd actually done it. That would erase every trace of his smug smile.

But I didn't let the arrow fly. Despite all the monsters I've fought and killed, I couldn't imagine killing a human.

That never stops me from pulling my weapons on Gammon whenever I run into him. I simply glare at Jack, Silas, and the others until they go away or until I pass them. Gammon isn't so easily avoided. He's very persistent whenever we encounter each other.

He's since stopped calling me "bell girl" and started calling me "Fey Bell," which has stuck. The name's even reached Harmonia, a group of female Icarii I've run into on occasion. They seem to hate Kleos, and I think the feeling's mutual. I'm not sure what happened between the two, but from what I've observed, they have a truce now, provided each group stays in its own territory.

I sometimes wonder how they both made it so far into the labyrinth. Did Fates save any of them, or have the members of Harmonia and Kleos survived on their own from the start? Despite my curiosity, I try to keep my distance from the groups. I haven't so much as seen the leader of Harmonia, although I've encountered some of the other members. The first time I met a girl from Harmonia, we had arrows pointed at each other. As Kleos has their shields and spears, Harmonia has their bows and arrows.

We entered a clearing at the exact same time and immediately drew on each other. Before either of us could decide what to do, a small group of screechers attacked. Together, we shot them down. Afterwards we collected our arrows, but I took one of hers by mistake. I realized it wasn't mine as soon as I pulled it from the screecher carcass. Although it was almost the exact same shape and size, the paste covering it wasn't black but a dark brown.

"I think this is yours," the Harmonian archer said, holding out my arrow to me. We exchanged arrows, and as I put mine away, she seemed to hesitate. Ultimately she said, "Screecher talon arrowhead?"

I hesitated a moment as well. Then I nodded.

"You're not from Kleos, are you?"

I shook my head.

"Didn't think you were." The Harmonian archer put her own arrow back in her quiver. "No girl in her right mind would join them. No boy either, at that. Look, just a heads-up, but Kleos doesn't know how to make these arrows. Don't show them, OK?"

I nodded. I wasn't about to give Gammon's group any sort of advantage. The Harmonian archer nodded as well. We stood there a moment. Then she started backing away, toward the corridor she'd come from. She turned right before rounding the corner and dashed off. Later I found out, by following a group from Harmonia, that her name is Risa. I've encountered her once more since then, but we didn't speak. We just sort of eyed each other when we passed in a corridor. We kept glancing over our shoulders after that, making sure the other wasn't drawing a weapon. Then we rounded opposite corners.

Risa's dark coloring is very similar to Elle's. When I first saw Risa, I actually thought for a moment that Elle had entered the labyrinth. After my encounter with Risa, I couldn't stop thinking about Elle, my only remaining friend in Fates. Is she as worried about me as I am about her? Maybe she's pretending I'm still around, like she pretended her brother Prosper was just out scavenging, even though he's been dead for years. Or maybe she's forgotten me altogether. That would probably be for the best. If she talks about me too much, Collin might snap.

Whenever I start thinking about Elle, or anything to do with Fates, it always comes back to Collin. It's better not to think about it at all. It's in the past, and the only part of my past that's any use to me now is the time I spent with the Executioner. Only that.

Harmonia is sneakier than I thought.

I've finished checking the area around one of my favorite mossy watering holes before a bath. It's something of a luxury, but I like being clean. When I actually enter the watering hole, I find myself faced with three Harmonia members. Risa is among them, and next to her is a girl wearing a hood. I've seen her patrolling with Risa before. I think her name is Celia.

Risa and Celia are flanking a girl I've never seen before. She has black hair cropped to her earlobes and very tanned skin. Her dark brown eyes skim me as she purses her full lips.

The second I draw my bow, Risa and Celia draw theirs. The tall girl stays where she is, as she is, arms crossed.

"You're right," the girl says, and her voice is surprisingly rich. She's speaking to Risa even though she's still eyeing me, my bow in particular. "She has good form."

"Good aim too," Risa says. Then louder, "We're here to talk, Fey Bell, not fight. Ten-minute truce and we'll leave you to your bath."

They know this is where I bathe? All this time and I didn't realize I was being tailed.

"She shouldn't have drawn on us here anyway," Celia says. "This is Harmonia's territory. We have a right to shoot those that enter uninvited."

"We shoot those uninvited from Kleos," Risa corrects. "We never decided on what to do with solo Icarii."

"There was never a need," the tall girl murmurs, as much to herself as to Risa. Her thoughts seem to be elsewhere; namely, on me. She speaks louder, her voice strong and clear. "Fey Bell, I'm Polina, the leader of Harmonia. Typically we require potential members to pass a test, but we've been watching you, and we've decided to skip straight to the offer. We'd like you to join Harmonia and become one of our sisters."

I'm furious, but I make sure not to show it. I can't tell if I'm angrier at them for following me or at myself for not realizing I was being followed.

Risa lowers her bow with a sigh.

"What are you doing?" Celia snaps.

"We've got to give her a minute to think, don't we?" Risa says. "It's hard to think when something pointy's pointing at you. Besides, at this rate, my arm's gonna cramp."

"Sisters of Harmonia don't get arm cramps," Celia says. "Anyway, what's there to think about? Every female Icarii wants to join Harmonia."

"I have to agree," Polina says, eyes still on me. "What reason could you possibly have to refuse? Unless you're allied with Kleos?"

I shake my head as I lower my bow.

"I didn't think so. Then you'll join us?"

Again, I shake my head, holding her gaze as I do.

Her jaw clenches. "Why?"

They may have been observing me, but whether they know it or not, I was observing them too. Their group has a similar structure to Kleos and, at that, to Fates. There's a leader and a second-in-command and those who do the grunt work. I don't care if their group's more liberal than Fates. They still have that pyramid of power, and I know I'd be at the bottom. I don't want that, but I don't want to be at the top either. At the bottom I could be crushed, while at the top I could fall. Either way, being in a group would spell potential disaster, as it did back at Fates. I'd rather survive on my own. And I know now that I can.

Instead of explaining this to Polina, I just shake my head. Slinging my bow back over my shoulder, I turn to leave the watering hole.

"Celia, put your bow down," Risa says. "It's over."

"She's declared herself an enemy of Harmonia!"

"She literally didn't declare herself anything."

"True," Polina says, silencing their fighting. "But we can't have those not allied with us infringing on our hunting grounds. Fey Bell, you have until nightfall to leave Harmonia's territory. If we find you here again you'll be shot and meet appropriate punishment for trespassing."

Punishment. I clench my fists.

"What if she wants to join us after all?" Risa asks.

"She had her chance." Polina's voice follows me down the corridor. "There are no second chances in the labyrinth."

I'm sitting on the top step of a shaded watering hole. The wooden bobber of my fishing pole dips gently up and down beside the sack of screecher meat, which has since sunk and risen. The Executioner taught me this trick to test for water diggers — awful snake monsters that dwell underwater and cluster in hordes. They're much smaller than their subterranean counterparts, which tunnel under the labyrinth and occasionally breach the surface to attack a fellow monster or an Icarii.

Since the meat remains untouched, that means there are no diggers in this watering hole. At the rate my fishing's going, it looks like there are no fish either.

Footsteps sound, approaching the watering hole, but I don't move. From the corner of my eye I can see who it is, and there's no point in leaving now that I've been spotted. If I did pack up in a flash and unsheathe my deadliest weapons, he'd probably take it as a compliment.

"I couldn't believe it," Gammon says, "when Silas said this was what you were doing. I couldn't imagine our feisty Fey Bell deigning to spend her time on something as peaceful as fishing, but here you are."

I want to tell him that "Fey Bell" has to eat too, but that would be acknowledging the nickname, and him, and I don't want to do either.

"You've been in our territory a lot recently." Gammon lays his shield on the ground by the watering hole. "Hoping to get a peek at me? How many times do I have to tell you? Just drop by our base when you're missing me."

Gammon lowers himself onto the step beside me. I immediately slide away from him, almost to the wall. My fishing line follows my movements, and the bobber hits the sack and dips a bit more.

"Getting shy now that we're alone?" Gammon smirks at me. "I heard you had a falling-out with Harmonia. I'm not surprised. Temperamental bunch, aren't they? Someone as sweet as you would never fit in with them."

I wonder, if I shove Gammon into the watering hole hard enough, would he crack his head on a step underwater?

"Can I take your refusal of Harmonia to mean you're going to join Kleos? We both know it's going to happen eventually. Even though we typically only let in men, you're always welcome. Have I not made that clear in the past?"

He's made it painfully clear. I wonder if the line of my fishing pole would hold against his meaty neck.

"Seems like the water's dead today. I'm surprised you stayed here so long when it's like this. Was it because you passed Silas, and you thought there was a chance he'd tell me you were here? That's really cute. You know, you can act cute more often. It's not as if the screechers will snatch you up the second you make an effort to act more feminine."

Instantly I'm standing and snapping back my fishing pole.

"Finally ready to head back to base?" Gammon says. "*We* caught some fish earlier. We could make a nice meal out of that. Can you cook?"

Gammon starts to push himself up. Before he can, I decide to act as feminine as possible and kick him hard in the back. He probably won't hit his head, but as he falls straight into the water, the resounding splash he makes is reward enough. Well, almost reward enough.

As I go, I grab his shield and toss it over the labyrinth wall.

The next day, after securing my second base, I leave Kleos' territory. Instead of re-entering Harmonia's territory, I head to the other side of Kleos. It's not that I'm afraid either group will be able to do anything to me. I just don't like the thought of Harmonia observing me, and I realize it's best to disappear for a bit and let things blow over with Polina. As for Kleos, I've had enough of Gammon for the month.

My goal is to head back to my main base, but on the way I'm trying out a different route on the map. I memorized it last night so I could start out early this morning. If I follow my chosen trail correctly, I should make it to my main base a couple of hours after nightfall, depending on how many breaks I take.

As I start out on my new path, I find myself thinking back to the Executioner's journal. I've flipped through it a hundred times. It's full of Ancient Daedalic. Although I recognize the monster terms Addie taught me back at Fates, I can't understand the rest. There's the rare sketch, and those are even more unnerving than the monster names. There are pictures of screechers drawn from different angles, as well as diggers. There are bats, horrible nocturnal creatures, the size of a child and somewhat humanoid, which travel in packs of three and rip their victims limb from limb. There are also stingers, which are giant scorpion monsters, and temple lions with their wicked sharp teeth. At the back of the journal is a sketch of the hundred-headed monster, which the Executioner could only defeat by burning it up from the inside.

There are other creatures in the journal that I've never seen before. They might be waiting for me deeper in the labyrinth, and here the Executioner has probably written the means to defeat them. But I'll never know.

It infuriates me that I have no way of uncovering the secrets of the journal. Addie would know — she knew more about the labyrinth than anyone at Fates, thanks to her studies and monster experiments. She seemed fluent in Ancient Daedalic, and the Executioner did say Sybil, the old leader of Fates, taught some Icarii the language. The Executioner even told me to go to them for help. She can't have realized Fates sent me back into the labyrinth to die. Maybe she thought Gina and I were just on a water run gone horribly wrong. If the Executioner had known what Fates — what Collin — had planned for me, I'm sure she never would have told me to go back there.

And I won't. As curious as I am about the journal, there's no way I'll risk returning to Fates. I know where Fates is now, thanks to the map, but since finding it again, I haven't returned for fear of running into the others — especially Collin. That's one of the reasons I've been spending so much time in the Kleos and Harmonia territories, since they're deeper in the labyrinth and farther from Fates.

It's no use dwelling on the journal. I don't even have it with me right now; I often leave it hidden in my main base. The Executioner's bell is another matter entirely. I've since affixed it to its own strap, which I wear around my neck. Where the Executioner always kept the bell hidden, I like having it immediately on hand, since it's become a habit to run my fingers over its surface. When I put up my hood to cover my hair, the collar covers the bell too, so I don't have to worry about it catching the light.

I also wear it like this as a reminder, because every time I look down I can see the edge of it. I don't want to forget what the Executioner gave me, from every tough lesson to this very bell.

I don't want to forget that I'm stronger now.

While following my route, I hear screechers up ahead. They sound low to the ground. Should I backtrack or fight?

It doesn't sound like there are too many of them, and I've got spare poison on hand. If, by chance, the screecher-eater resides in this part of the labyrinth, maybe now's a good time to set some bait.

As I increase my pace, I draw my bow, deciding to make this quick to save travel time. At the end of the hall there's a left and right turn. Left connects to my planned route. Right leads to the screechers.

Set the bait, get back on track. With this plan, I take the right.

I reach an open area, and the scene playing out within it makes me pause. There are five screechers attacking three humans. Two, one hooded, seem to be trying to lure the screechers to the ground to fight with short swords. The person closest, with their back to me, is trying to shoot down the screechers. The arrows aggravate the monsters but do no damage.

Ordering myself to think later, I notch one of my arrows and down the closest screecher. It slams into the ground in front of the archer, who turns to look back at me just as a screecher dives.

I shove the archer out of the way, just in time to bury my axe in the screecher's head. I grab my bow from the ground as the screecher dies at my feet. In seconds I've notched another arrow and downed the next circling screecher. Another dives at the sword wielders. I just manage to get the monster in the side of the head, sending it veering toward the final screecher. The creatures crash to the ground, and the two fighters are on them instantly, finishing them off with their crude short swords.

Turning from them, I find an arrow trained on me. The archer is glaring at me from under his bangs, gaze wary and hostile but, more than that, shocked.

"Nice shot, Ryan," the hooded girl says as she turns around, already smiling with her painfully familiar cheerfulness. That smile vanishes when Andrea sees me. *"You?"*

"Put down the bow," Ryan says to me.

I recognize him now. I can't believe I didn't at first. It's only been four and a half months since I last saw him. But he's only fifteen. I know I changed a lot between fifteen and sixteen, and I know boys change even more. Ryan's taller now, taller than me at this point, and his facial features have sharpened. His hair's grown too.

His proficiency with a bow hasn't changed. But he's not aiming at a monster like he did my first night in the labyrinth when he, Andrea, and Theo rescued my group of Icarii and brought us back to Fates. Now, Ryan aims at me.

Even if his arrows can't down screechers, I know they can pierce me easily. I crouch down and lay my bow on the ground. As I do, I carefully withdraw my chain.

"Up," Ryan says when I don't move fast enough.

As I rise I snap into action, flicking my wrist and the chain toward Ryan. The chain wraps around his legs, and he yelps as I pull him down. His arrow goes wide, and his bow clatters away from him. Andrea cries out as he hits the ground and starts running to him. I make it there first. Ryan's only half pushed himself up, the chain still tight around his lower legs, when I crouch behind him. I pull him back against me and press a dagger to his throat. Andrea draws up short, horrified.

"Don't," she begs. "Please, please don't. I don't know what you're doing here, but please don't hurt him."

Over Andrea's shoulder I notice the other Fates member approaching, not half as concerned by Ryan's position, but clearly spooked to see me. I'd assumed, when I first saw Andrea and Ryan, that it would be Theo. It's not. I stiffen and, as I do so, I draw a prick of blood against Ryan's neck. He hisses out a breath.

"Isn't she supposed to be dead?" Jay asks, but I don't think he's asking anyone in particular. I see that he, like Andrea, is still holding his short sword. If anything, they seem to be holding their swords tighter now than when they fought the screechers.

"She doesn't feel dead," Ryan snaps at Jay. He struggles against my hold as if to make a point. I press the dagger more firmly to his neck, digging my nails into his chest where I'm keeping him braced. I don't want him wiggling around in case I accidentally cut him before I decide what I'm going to do. Because at this point, I really have no idea.

I never thought I'd ever see anyone from Fates again.

"We saved you," Andrea says. "On Fallen Day we saved you from that digger, and we got you back to Fates. *Ryan* got you back to Fates. Is this any way to repay us?"

I start laughing. I can't help it. The laughter bubbles up my throat and forces its way through my lips, relentless. Following the laughter comes a voice I didn't even know I owned anymore.

"He got me back to Fates, did he?" I jostle Ryan, and he grits his teeth when the blade digs in again. I can see my laughter and words are shocking Andrea and Jay. "I guess he never told you about the part where he ditched me. Or maybe he didn't need to tell you. Was that another group plan to kill off unwanted Icarii?" My voice becomes so bitter it stings my own ears. "*Useless* Icarii?"

Andrea's voice shakes, like mine used to: "We never meant for you —"

"I want someone," I say. "A trade. For Ryan."

"Collin's never going to go with you," Jay says.

"Collin?" I stare right at Jay, and I can see that I'm unnerving him. "Who says it's Collin I want? There's a faster route to revenge right here."

I pause, watching Jay. I can see that even when he spoke about Collin he was worried it was really him I was after. At Collin's suggestion, he was willing to do awful things to me — and I'm sure he would have if I hadn't stabbed him. I wonder, fleetingly, if he has a scar.

But I'm not after Jay right now, even if it doesn't hurt to let him think I am, for a moment.

"Then again," I say, "any of you would do for some form of revenge. For a group so set on everyone doing something, there wasn't much any of you did for me."

I move the dagger, sliding it without cutting, up Ryan's neck and over his chin, resting it against his right cheek. As Andrea follows the movement, hatred starts to mingle with the panic in her eyes.

"He didn't do anything," I say, pressing the blade against Ryan's cheek. Then I point the dagger at Andrea. "You gave up and left." I slide it toward Jay. "And you . . ."

Ryan tenses before trying to break my hold. I'm prepared and brace him easily. I bring the dagger back to his neck.

"But I don't want any of you — not yet. I want Addie."

"Addie?" Andrea's confused, as is Jay, who also looks relieved that I didn't choose him. "What do you want with her?"

"My business," I say. "Addie for Ryan. That's the deal. I'll even give Addie back when I'm done with her — heart beating and everything."

Andrea's livid. "I can't believe I felt sorry for you all this time!"

"You pitied me?" My voice rises to a scream. "I didn't need pity! I needed someone to stop him!"

Silence falls after my outburst. I'm breathing heavily, and my eyes are stinging. This is making me remember. It's bringing back the old me.

I look down at myself, at the bell. I say, "Have you ever gutted a rabbit?"

"She's gone crazy," Jay mutters to Andrea. I don't comment. He can think that way if he wants. I don't care, even if I have gone crazy. I'd rather be crazy and in control than sane and powerless.

"We can't give you Addie," Andrea says. "Just let Ryan go, and we'll pretend we never saw you."

"It took me a while to get comfortable with it," I say, "but eventually I got pretty good. Bleeding them out before taking them home is best. It's fastest if you slit the throat." I ghost the dagger across Ryan's neck. "Then hang it upside down, so the blood drains properly."

I've gotten to Andrea. I can see it in her eyes. She's always treated Ryan like a little brother. He's always seen her as an older sister. Even now, with Theo gone, they're still on a team together.

"All right." Andrea's voice breaks. "Come to Fates tomorrow morning, and we'll do the exchange."

"No. At noon we'll meet at the place where Collin sent me to die. Bring Addie. If you don't, I'll gut a rabbit."

Andrea swallows. I can't tell if she wants to shout at me or cry. "Fine. Tomorrow, at noon."

"Great," I say. "Get lost."

Andrea hesitates, staring at Ryan with such concern my heart almost goes out to her. I push that feeling aside as she and Jay head for the exit. Then Jay reaches for the arrow sticking out of a nearby screecher.

"Don't you dare," I yell.

"We can't even collect our arrows?" Jay calls back.

Jay doesn't even know what their arrows look like — he's trying to take one of mine.

"If your finger touches that arrow, Ryan will be missing a few of *his* fingers when you get him back."

Andrea grabs Jay roughly by the arm and drags him after her. She glances back at us once more before they disappear around the corner. When they're gone, I find myself relaxing the smallest bit. I can't be too relaxed; I still have to deal with Ryan.

"What are you going to do now?" Ryan asks. "If you kill me, you'll never get Addie, but the moment you move that dagger I'll attack you."

When he puts it like that, it sounds like a stalemate.

Pressing the dagger against his throat again, to remind him it's still there, I move the hand that's bracing him back to my side. I unsheathe my short sword.

"You know," Ryan says, "you spoke more today than in your entire time at Fates."

I hit him hard on the head with the hilt of my sword. Ryan goes slack against me, head lolling forward so that I have to drop the dagger in fear of actually cutting him.

"Wrong," I mutter at his unconscious form as I sheathe my sword and shrug off my rucksack. "I just didn't speak to you."

I usually carry rope with me, since finding a supply in my second base. It comes in handy for tying up and transporting hunted game. It comes in handy today.

I bind Ryan's arms behind his back. Although I want to bind his feet too, I know that would slow our journey too much. After collecting my arrows and axe, I return to him and dump a flask of water over his face. He wakes up, spluttering. When he sees me and remembers what's going on, he glares. His eyes narrow further when he realizes his hands are bound.

Crouching beside him, I yank him into a sitting position. Then I pull a long rag from my pocket and fit it over his eyes.

"Blindfold?" he asks. "Why?"

I don't answer, partially because my throat is raw from earlier, partially because I don't think he needs to hear it from me. He'll figure it out soon enough, if he hasn't already: if he found out where we were going, he'd not only be able to get back to Fates should he escape, but lead Fates to me after the exchange.

Even though I don't answer him, Ryan doesn't struggle as I tie the blindfold tightly in place. Has he accepted the situation so quickly?

Pushing to my feet, I haul Ryan to his. Grabbing his bound hands, I push him forward, not letting go. Eventually he gets the hint and starts walking. Holding onto his hands as I am, I can push him forward and steer him in certain directions. We head back the way I came, down the hall I saw before. That should connect to my old route.

After a minute or so we turn again, and I'm sure we're back on the route I planned. As we turn down the next corridor, it occurs to me that Ryan might be counting the turns. If he's maintained an idea of our direction, he may be able to find his way back to Fates. He's a scavenger, after all, so his sense of direction and ability to navigate the labyrinth have to be relatively good.

"Why were you there?" I ask, relieved when my voice doesn't come out as scratchy as I expected.

Ryan doesn't reply until after we've turned another corner. He *is* counting them. "Where?"

"This area isn't near Fates."

"Collin's expanding our scavenging grounds. You could have run into him instead."

If he's trying to get to me, I won't let it work. Even though the idea of running into Collin is more unnerving than I'd like to admit. "Why wasn't Theo with you?"

"If he was, would you have picked him for your hostage?"

"No. You're smaller. More manageable."

"Thanks," Ryan says dryly.

"How did you end up fighting a flock of screechers?"

"I could ask how you ended up defeating a flock just as easily." Ryan pauses as we take another corner, then he says, "Whatever happened to you out here has made you more talkative. Haven't you learned yet that silence gets you through the labyrinth?"

"I've learned how to be an accommodating captive, unlike some people."

"The situation's different." At least Ryan isn't denying I was a captive at Fates in the end. "You weren't being pushed through a labyrinth full of monsters with no way to fight, blindfolded."

"You're right," I say. "I wasn't blindfolded."

I don't speak again for a while after that. Ryan can count turns and create a mental map if he wants. By the time we do finish our journey, I'll have him so turned around there'll be no hope of him ever getting back to Fates.

Night's closing in by the time we reach my main base. It turns out the route I mapped is actually something of a shortcut from my main base to Kleos' territory. I could have made it back sometime late in the afternoon, but I took an extra hour wandering around my familiar area to confuse Ryan. Finally, here we are and finally, here I am, pushing Ryan through the sliding wall.

As the wall closes behind us, I grab Ryan's hands and yank him backward to keep him from falling down the steps. Realizing it may be tricky getting him down the stairs blindfolded, I untie the rag.

"Am I supposed to see something?" Ryan asks.

I strike a match against the wall and light an alcove candle. I hold it up so he can see what's ahead. "Steps. Go down. Don't look back."

"We're going underground?"

I don't answer. I give him a prompting shove. He starts taking the stairs as I hold the light for him to see the steps. It's slow going, considering his hands are tied, and he has to balance differently. Eventually, we make it to the bottom.

Laying the candle in an alcove by the door, I say, "Turn around."

"I thought I wasn't supposed to look back?"

I grip his shoulder and physically start to turn him. He ultimately turns around himself, staring down at me as my hands falls off his shoulder. He really is taller than me now, if only by a bit.

"What's with the bell?" he asks. "It hasn't made any noise."

"Don't look," I say as I pass by Ryan. I glance at him to make sure he's still turned around, then pull out my base key. After unlocking the door, I grab Ryan by his tied hands and drag him after me.

While he's busy gaping around, I close and lock the door, then hide my key again and lay the candle on the crate near my bed. I'll have to make up some sort of bed for Ryan. The thought of making him sleep on the ground instead crosses my mind, and I give it some serious consideration.

"What is this place?" Ryan's voice is breathless.

I don't answer, mostly because I don't know what it really is. To me, it's the Executioner's old base, now my base. Studying Ryan's expression, I'm reminded of the first time I came here, of the awe I felt, which is clear on his face.

Depositing my rucksack in the usual spot, I begin putting my weapons away. I keep my dagger on hand, just in case Ryan decides to try something. Then I go to the pile of blankets and pull one from the top. I carry it over to the other side of the room and set it up in front of the door to the lavatory. If any foul smells manage to work their way out during the night, that's just too bad for Ryan.

Ducking back out from around the crates, I immediately get Ryan's attention. "Come."

Ryan scowls at me, but he does come over. I gesture to the blanket. "Sit."

"I thought I was a rabbit," Ryan says, easing himself down onto the blanket, "not a dog."

"At least you're not a mouse," I say, before returning to the other side of the room.

"Are you going to untie my hands?" Ryan calls.

"No." I come back to him, having retrieved my desired object. I stretch the rope taut. "I'm going to tie your legs."

Ryan isn't exactly pleased, but he's not surprised either. As I bind his legs, I stay alert, prepared for him to kick me. He doesn't try anything, which surprises me but doesn't make me lower my guard.

"Why do you want Addie?" Ryan asks. "She was mean to you, but she never did anything close to what Collin did."

"So now you admit how bad it was?" I tie the ropes tight.

"I never said it wasn't bad."

"No." I get up. "You didn't say anything. Just like the others. You, at least, I expected to act like that."

"Andrea spoke up."

"And then she left."

"To get a weapon! That's how much she was willing to help you!"

"If that's true, then why didn't she come back?"

"Because I stopped her."

Ryan looks away, and I'm glad. This way he can't see the shock on my face. I don't know why I'm shocked. I guess it's that, as much as Ryan disliked me, I never expected him to help Collin.

I know that's probably not why he did it. He was trying to protect Andrea from Collin's wrath. But he doesn't say that, and I don't ask him.

I get up wordlessly and head to the kitchen, where I start boiling a pot of water over the fire. From my rucksack I produce the packaged meat I brought with me, the last from my hunt in Kleos. Tomorrow, at some point, I'll have to go hunting again.

As the water simmers, I cut chunks of meat into it. They land with little plops before sinking to the bottom. I count each sound until there's no meat left. Twenty-three. Why is that familiar?

Oh, right. The day before I learned I was to go into the labyrinth, my friends and I were on the twenty-third floor of our tower, watching the Icarus parade. I couldn't take my eyes off the Dancers of Icarus; they were angels of gold.

The water blurs in front of me. I shake my head, hoping to shake the memories too. This is why I never strayed near Fates. It drags up everything from the past I keep so carefully buried.

Ryan's voice sounds to the right: "Do you want to know how everyone back at Fates is doing?"

I reach for the bottles of herbs, the ones that will add flavor. Uncorking them, I sprinkle the little green bits into the water.

"Kyle's still alive," Ryan says. "It wasn't a fluke that he survived his first few weeks as a scavenger. He's a quick learner."

I haven't thought about Kyle in quite some time. Although we entered the labyrinth on the same day and were saved by Fates together, we never really had much in common. Kyle was interested in going back out in the labyrinth, to fight as a scavenger. I was terrified of the labyrinth's monsters and hid away in Fates with Elle, letting Collin and the others look after me.

It's strange. The labyrinth and its monsters have become almost a comfort to me now. It's the thought of being trapped in Fates again that's terrifying.

Ryan continues, "Kyle and Theo get along really well now, and they fight together even better. They're their own team, like Collin and Prosper used to be. That's how we ended up with Jay."

I test the broth, even though I know it's nowhere near done. It's mostly just hot water, and if there's any flavor, the heat hides that. My tongue burns.

"You were curious about that, weren't you? Where Theo went? I'm surprised you're still curious about him. You know, that night, when Collin sent you off with Jay, Theo was just as prepared to volunteer for the part. And he knew exactly what it meant."

I drop the spoon, and it splashes hot water over the pot. Some hits the side of my hand, but I barely notice. I'm on my feet in an instant and in an instant more, in front of Ryan. He regards me passively.

"Don't talk like you're any better." I hate how my voice is shaking again. I wish it wouldn't. "You pushed me down, back when you hurt your leg."

"I wasn't going to do anything," Ryan says. "I was just trying to make a point. If anything, it prepared you for what Jay tried to do, didn't it? Everyone heard about how you stabbed him."

"That's what you did it for — to prepare me? You think that's any sort of excuse?"

"It's not an excuse."

"Then what would have happened if I hadn't stabbed you that night?"

"I would have bullied you a bit more, then I was going to leave you alone. I was never actually going to *do* anything. I'm not like that."

"Then why do it at all? Why were you always so cruel to me?"

"Because I thought you had potential," Ryan snaps. "I said all this to you that night. And I was right. Even if Collin was coddling you at the time, you could fight back. You stabbed me, you stabbed Jay, and you're alive, here, now."

"Not because of anything you did," I hiss.

"Even if I was mean to you, I still helped save you from that digger and the bat. You ate the food we scavenged, back at Fates. You can't say you made it this far on your own."

"I didn't." I clutch the bell at my neck. "But it wasn't any of you that helped me. The girl you say you saved died when she was supposed to. Collin's execution was carried out."

"Execution, huh? Is that what you plan to do to Addie?"

"So what if it is?" I turn from him, heading back to the kitchen.

"You know how important Addie is to Fates."

"It functioned before her. It functioned before all of you. Better, by the sounds of it."

"It did," Ryan says more quietly. "A lot better."

He doesn't elaborate on what he means, and I don't ask. We don't speak again until I bring him a bowl of broth. A small bowl, without any meat. Just enough to keep his strength up for the trek back to Fates. It's also an easier way to have him down the sleeping tonic for tonight. I want to get a few hours' rest without worrying about him escaping his bindings.

I untie the ropes around his hands so that he can feed himself. I sit close by, dagger pointed toward him, so he knows if he makes even the slightest move out of place I'll strike. As he's done the rest of the day, Ryan gives me no trouble. He just sips his broth.

"How did you make this?" he asks. "What are these herbs? Poison?"

The same thoughts I had when the Executioner fed Gina and me. I do as she would have and don't reply. Ryan starts eating again.

"Did you find this place on your own?"

Again, I don't answer. Ryan sighs. "It's going to be a long night if we don't talk."

"I prefer my nights silent." Ryan's only being talkative to try and get useful information out of me to bring back to Fates. Little does he know his night will only last another half an hour.

"You won't tell me anything about how you ended up here? Six months ago, you could hardly make an arrow right."

"Six months is a long time in the labyrinth."

This quiets Ryan for a while, since we both know it's true.

"What happened to them?" Ryan asks into his broth. His breath mingles with the steam, distorting it.

"Who?"

I didn't expect this question. At least not from him. I don't want it to be this question.

"Felix and" — Ryan's voice drops to almost a whisper — "Gina."

Felix, despite being two years younger than me, was one of the only people at Fates to stand up against Collin on my behalf. Because of that, he was exiled with me. But Gina? She had no idea what was going on. She just wanted to go outside with us and play.

I wonder if Ryan wants me to tell him that Felix and Gina survived outside of Fates, like me. Maybe even Ryan wants to hear that they're out shooting down screechers or in their own bases and that we'll meet up to trade or have a group meal.

"Felix died at the watering hole," I say, fighting back the memories of those water diggers ripping him apart.

"And Gina?"

There's a lump in my throat. I don't know when it got there. It makes it hard to speak. "Dead too."

Ryan closes his eyes. He doesn't speak for a long moment. Then he asks, "The same way?"

"No." My throat is closing up entirely. "Screechers."

"Was it fast?"

"No." My eyes are stinging. "She was wounded. It got infected. Festered."

I don't know why I'm telling him this. I'd decided never to think of it again, let alone talk about it to Ryan, of all people. But I keep talking.

"I tried to save her," I say. "We looked after her. I tried to . . . I couldn't help her. I thought I did, when I distracted the screecher and it let her go, but I was too late with that too. She died slowly, and it hurt her, and she just wanted to go home the whole time."

I press the heels of my palms to my eyes to try and stop the stinging. "I should have just tried to take her home. She was going to die anyway. I should have given her that. It's what every Icarii wants, isn't it? To go home. And Gina, I could have given that to her, but I didn't because I . . . I was . . ."

Too scared.

The words die on my lips. I shouldn't be saying any of this to Ryan. I'm glad he's silent, unsympathetic, like he always was. It's what I need to jolt me back to my normal self. I grip the bell. Hard. I never should have done this. When I saw the screechers, I should have really looked at who they were fighting. I should never have gone toward them in the first place.

I want to be on my own, or at least out of sight of Ryan, but I can't leave him with his hands unbound. I wait until he starts eating again. The moment he's finished, I grab the bowl from him and motion for him to turn around. He does. After I've re-tied his hands, I return to the kitchen, where I get my own supper. By the time I'm done eating, Ryan's out cold on his blanket. It crosses my mind to get him a pillow. I don't.

Even though I drugged Ryan specifically to get a few hours of solid sleep, it takes me forever to drift off, and when I do, my sleep is anything but solid.

The morning finds my nerves abuzz as I prepare breakfast. I hear Ryan groan, just as I add another handful of twigs to the fire. He's up.

I go check on him. His eyes are still cloudy, and his voice is groggy when he says, "You drugged me."

Since that's been established, I return to finish breakfast. When it's ready, I fill Ryan's bowl and bring it over to him, along with a flask of water. Ryan's managed to push himself into a sitting position against the wall. Another sign it was smart to drug him. If he can manage this much in a couple of minutes, there's no telling how far he would have gotten during the night.

"Is that drugged too?" Ryan asks, as I lay the bowl on the floor and unsheathe my dagger. "Show me it isn't. Taste it."

A taste probably wouldn't knock me out, but it might slow down my movements or thought processes a bit. I need to stay alert, today more than ever.

When I don't taste it, Ryan says: "Don't bother untying me. I'm not eating it."

And I'm not leaving him in my base, conscious. I don't untie him. Instead I straddle him, which startles him until I pick up the bowl of broth. He immediately clamps his mouth shut, but it's a futile effort. I force his jaw open with my free hand and tip his head back at the same time. He struggles against me but soon enough I'm pouring the broth down his throat. He tries not to swallow and ends up getting water over both of us. I stop, maybe a little late, because he starts hacking, and the last mouthful of broth spews over his tunic and mine. Mess aside, I know more than enough broth went inside him to knock him out while I'm gone.

Uncorking the flask, I hold it up to him. "To wash it down?"

Ryan glares at me but gives a single nod. He's more accommodating when I pour the water into his mouth. The second I pull back, however, he spits the water in my face. Unfazed, I wipe the back of my hand across my cheek, then take a sip from the bottle myself. I cork it and stand up, looming over him.

"Sweet dreams," I say.

I didn't just pick the meeting place to make a point. It's close enough to Fates for them to arrive on time and far enough to help me feel like I'm not waging war on someone else's stomping ground. This area also has a prize hiding spot and vantage point.

I left hours early to go to the meeting spot, because I know they'll likely arrive early as well, and I want enough time to set up. I find a crumbled, climbable wall that gets me on top of a section wide enough on which to walk. I have to jump at one point, but I make the leap easily, thanks to a wide landing zone. Walking along the broad roof, I try not to think about the water in the corridor below me and the monsters that could be swimming within.

I reach a broken part of the ceiling that reveals the hall below. From here I can see the exact spot where I watched Felix get sucked below the water. I try not to look over there. Instead, I focus on scouting the small open area where we're to meet in two hours. No sign of Fates yet — not that I thought there would be. I put down my bow and lie beside it, tummy flat against the roof. When my stomach starts to hurt I get up and crouch for a while, then risk standing to stretch my legs. As it gets closer to noon I stop standing, then I stop crouching. Eventually I just lie on the ceiling, watching and waiting. If I'm right, they should show up any minute, despite the fact we probably have more than half an hour until the meeting time. They'll want time to prepare for my arrival. If I'm right.

Which, it appears, I am.

The first into the area is a scavenger whose name I can't remember, bow up and aiming into every corner. When he sees it's empty, he waves at the hall behind him then runs ahead to the other exit, checking that corridor too. Meanwhile Jay enters, sword at the ready. Collin is behind him.

My gaze locks on Collin immediately. He's wearing a hood, but I can still see his face, the hardness in his jaw and coldness in his once warm blue eyes. A chill runs down my spine, and I clutch the bell at my neck.

Collin and Jay approach my perch, stopping right below it. They seem to be peering in at the watering hole, but they don't enter the crumbling hall.

Three more Fates members arrive. A girl runs over to stand guard with the other male scavenger, while the other two stay by the corridor they just left. I recognize Theo immediately. Aside from his hair being shorter, he looks exactly the same. He's even chatting to his partner like he'd usually chat to the other scavengers.

I wouldn't have recognized Kyle as quickly if Ryan hadn't told me about him and Theo pairing up. I can barely see his face at all from this angle, let alone the red hair hidden under his hood. He's clutching a spear, something like the one Jack uses, except Kyle's is more rusted. He doesn't handle it as leisurely as Jack does either. Kyle seems ready to fight at any moment.

No one else from Fates enters the clearing. I'm not surprised. They never intended to bring Addie along. That's probably why Collin didn't bring Andrea with him. Andrea would insist they bargain for Ryan, and when she realized Collin had no intention of doing so, she'd prove more a hindrance than an asset in confronting me.

They wait awhile, guarding the exits. Collin and Jay remain right below me. I could jump onto Collin's back from here. I could shoot him or bury an axe in his head before the others could even react. If I take them by surprise like that, I might even get away.

I don't move. Even if Collin's here for a fight, I'm not. That's why I came early.

"Are you sure we can do this?" Jay asks Collin. His voice is low but carries enough for me to hear.

"Even if she managed to take out a flock of screechers," Collin says, gesturing vaguely to the others, "this, she won't be able to stop."

"Do you think she'll bring Ryan? If something happens to him Andrea's gonna nag —"

"Ryan's probably dead. If he isn't, he definitely won't be the same if we get him back. Who knows what she's done to him by now?"

"Reassuring," Jay mutters. Then awkwardly, "Are we actually going to . . . you know . . ."

"Only if we have to," Collin says. "If we can, it would be better to bring her back alive, so that we can find out where she's hidden Ryan — or whatever's left of him."

Collin wants to capture me. I expected as much. But I know what he's saying to Jay is a lie. He doesn't want to kidnap me so that they can recover Ryan. He clearly still hates me as much as before. I wouldn't be surprised if he had another punishment in mind. I'm sure he'd kill me eventually, or send me somewhere to die, but only after his anger was sated.

I catch myself reaching for my bow. Even if I were to shoot him down and get a head start on escaping, there's no guarantee I'd manage it. This is still their territory, and even if I went down in the opposite corridor, there's a chance they'd manage to locate me. I'm outnumbered on fairly even ground. It's better to avoid a conflict, even if initiating that conflict would be so, so satisfying.

The members of Fates wait until noon, and so do I. Theo evidently gets bored, as does Jay. Kyle tries to stay alert, but his posture has worsened, and eventually he leans against one of the walls. As for me, my legs are so numb I'm sure that even if screechers descended this instant I wouldn't be able to move.

After noon, Theo calls, "She obviously isn't gonna show. Can we leave now?"

"Quiet," Collin snaps, "in case she hears you."

From my position I see Theo roll his eyes before turning back around. Jay hesitates a moment, then says to Collin, "Aren't we wasting scavenging time? Some of us could get back to work."

"Securing an insane danger to Fates isn't work? I'd say this is the most important thing any of us could be doing."

"Yeah, I know. Addie just told me to say that if you had us waiting awhile . . . not that I think it's really been awhile, but you know Addie."

Collin scowls, considering for a moment. Then he calls over the other scavenger and sends her and her partner away. Theo is indignant. "Seriously? They weren't even complaining!"

"Which is why they got to go." Collin waves Theo over to guard the other door. "That, and you two are better at the kind of combat we'll need."

By that, does Collin mean they're willing to kill other Icarii? I may have misjudged Theo's original, seemingly kind, personality, but I can't imagine Kyle, skilled scavenger that he may be now, being willing to kill another person. Not after the way I saw him handle that dying boy during our first night in the labyrinth.

They wait another hour. Finally, Theo says, "I really don't think she's coming."

Collin doesn't reply right away.

"She might have seen our guards," Theo continues. "Or maybe she decided against coming or was never planning to come at all."

For a moment, I think Collin's going to throttle Theo. Then he sighs and says, "You're right. We've wasted the morning."

"The afternoon's still left," Theo calls back. "Does this mean we can go?"

Collin offers a clipped nod. Theo's energy returns immediately as he goes to Kyle, clapping him on the shoulder before disappearing down the hall. Kyle glances back at the watering hole, and I get a good look at his face for the first time. Like Ryan, his features have matured, but they've gotten even harder. The coldness in his eyes as he stares at the watering hole surprises me. Then I remember: Kyle and Felix came from the same tower. Even if they weren't that close before the labyrinth, they grew up together. They were all each other had left of home.

After Kyle leaves, Collin and Jay stay for a moment longer.

"We should go too," Jay says. "Addie also said to remind you about checking the new corridor if you forgot. I know you probably didn't but . . ."

Collin ignores Jay's comments. "How can we relax now that we know she's still out there? She knows where Fates is. She took Ryan, and she wants Addie. This is her first move against us. We have to follow up before she does something else."

"What do you mean?"

"We have to find her," Collin says, his voice steely. "And when we do, we have to make sure she can never harm Fates again."

After Collin and Jay leave, it takes me a few minutes to massage my legs back to life. When I'm able to move again, I stretch for a while, making sure my movements are as fluid as possible. After stretching, I wait another ten minutes or so to make sure the coast is clear. Luckily, all the Fates members went back the way they came. My way down is in the opposite direction.

Luckier still, I don't run into anyone from Fates as I hurry through the labyrinth. I'm extra cautious the whole time, but at most I sense a stray junior digger somewhere in the distance. It's not in my way, so I leave it for Fates to worry about.

I spend the rest of the afternoon hunting in the area around my main base. Hunting helps take my mind off what happened this morning. At least it does at first. When it becomes clear I won't be finding any game today, I start thinking more about what happened. Not only am I disappointed at having lost a chance to have the journal translated, but now I have to worry about Collin and the rest of Fates snooping around my territory. What if they manage to find my base?

No. Even if they do stumble into this part of the labyrinth, there's no way they'd find out about the sliding wall. Even if they find me, they won't find my base, and if they do find me, I'll escape. If they prove persistent, I'll lead them into digger territory, no matter who my pursuers may be.

What I really need to worry about right now are two things: the lack of game and Ryan. The former is solved easily enough. I can survive on the food I brought with me and on labyrinth crops for a while. Then I'll make my way back to my Kleos and Harmonia bases, both of which are located in parts of the labyrinth with far more game. My second problem is less easily solved. What do I do with Ryan?

The question consumes me as I return to my base and trudge down the steps. As I unlock the door, I consider dropping off Ryan somewhere in Fates' territory and leaving him to find his way home. Can I risk that? Have I told him or let him see too much to give him back?

My thoughts are broken when, the second I step into my base, I'm knocked to the ground. Before I can push myself up Ryan's on top of me, unsheathing my axe and tossing it away. I'm lying on my side, on my short sword and chain, causing the handles of both to poke into my hip while they remain unreachable.

I throw a punch at Ryan, but he catches my fist. When I make a grab for the dagger now sheathed in his belt, he grabs my other hand too. We start grappling. In this position, I'm at a disadvantage, and soon find my back being pushed into the ground. I've turned my body enough to access my sword now, but Ryan doesn't release either of my hands, and I can't break from his grasp.

Ryan forces my arms above my head. The back of my hands scrape against the cold stone floor, a sharp contrast to the heat of his palms against mine.

"Did you meet them?" Ryan demands.

I glare at him. His hold on my hands tightens, and he pulls my arms taut until they're stretched farther than they should be. I grit my teeth against the pain.

"What happened?"

"Intended ambush," I say. "They didn't bring Addie. There was never going to be a trade. You must have known that."

"Of course I did. There's no point in trading one person for another."

"No," I say, "there's no point in trading a person who's worth more for one who's worth less."

Ryan stretches my arms again but this time I don't wince.

"We both know," I say, "if it was Addie, they would have traded you for her. If it makes you feel better, they were going to make me tell them where you were after they caught me. At least that's what Collin said. He also seemed pretty confident I'd killed you already. He wasn't all that bothered by the idea."

"You're making this up," Ryan says. "You couldn't find out all of this and avoid the ambush."

"If that's the excuse you want to use, then go ahead. They betrayed you. At least when Fates abandoned me I was brave enough to see it for what it was."

"This isn't the same!" Ryan yells. "You know nothing about Fates!"

"I know the real Fates, the one that leave people for dead. You're just another part of that."

"Is this still about the wall?" Ryan demands. "You should be over that by now."

"It's hard to get over things I don't understand. The labyrinth tests us enough on our own; we don't need to test each other. You must know that, but you test everyone anyway. Why?"

"That doesn't concern you."

He's right. It doesn't. I don't even care all that much. I'm just trying to distract him enough for him to relax his hold, which he has. Before he can realize his mistake, I twist my right hand free and punch him in the face. He reels back in surprise, and I manage to get my left hand free as well. Balancing myself with my hands, I pull my feet up and kick him in the chest. As Ryan starts to topple backward, I move to hop to my feet.

Ryan's hand shoots forward, clamping around my left braid and — unbeknownst to him — the spikes hidden in my hair. He curses and lets me go. I'm on my feet in an instant, short sword drawn. Ryan is still on the ground, staring at his bloody hand in a mixture of anger and shock.

Although I have a handle on the situation now, we should have been able to avoid this entirely. If only I'd given him a greater dose of sleeping herbs. The reason I didn't is because I'm unsure of the effect of regular concentrated doses, and on the off chance Fates did make the trade, I wanted to return Ryan in as good condition as possible. As much as I hate Fates, I didn't want to give them further cause to antagonize me. Not that I need to worry about that now.

"You had to have known," I say, "that wasn't going to work. You need me to get back to Fates, and I never would have shown you under threat."

"It was worth a shot." Ryan is still staring at his hand. The shock's faded, and to my surprise, so has the anger. "I'd like to know how you got like this."

"Probably the same way you got like you are now. Just faster."

"Why did you want Addie?"

I'll never get her now. There's no reason to tell him, but there's no reason not to tell him either. "I wanted her to translate something for me. Ancient Daedalic."

Ryan's brows crease. "What?"

"Something I found. It doesn't matter now."

"Can I see it?" When I cast him a confused look, Ryan says, "The thing you found. If it makes you feel better, tie me up before you show me."

I still hesitate. I'm going to tie him up again, naturally, but even if it won't mean anything to him, I don't like the idea of anyone else seeing the journal.

"Just show me. At this rate, I'll never make it back to Fates to tell them about it. What do you plan to do with me, anyway?"

I'm still undecided. Because of that, I'm definitely not going to show him the journal. Keeping an eye on him as I retrieve more rope, I re-tie his hands. After that's done, I help him up and push him over toward his old spot. Once there, I tie his legs again.

"You're not going to show me," Ryan says flatly. Because it's true, I don't see the point in saying anything.

As I heat up supper, I try to figure out what to do with Ryan. There's no doubt I'll have to move back to my Kleos and Harmonia bases soon. I can't possibly take Ryan with me. Blindfolded and bound, he wouldn't make the trip, and even if I did attempt that, it would only be prolonging the problem. The point is, I don't want to keep Ryan around.

Eventually, I decide to spend the next couple of days scouting Fates' territory. They'll be hunting for me now — at least Collin and his most trusted scavengers will. I'll have to be careful and plan a secure route to drop off Ryan. Until then I'll have to keep him drugged for the most part. I won't be sparing with the herbs this time, whatever the consequences. I don't plan on coming back to this base for a long time, considering the lack of game, so it's not as if I'll have to worry about Fates' wrath if Ryan isn't quite the same upon return.

When I bring Ryan his supper, he says, "It's drugged again, isn't it?"

He sighs when I kneel down beside him, not refuting his statement. He seems more haggard than earlier. "Look, I'll eat it, no complaints. Just show me whatever it is you found."

I guess I'll be force-feeding him again. As I move to get on top of him, Ryan says, "Wait! Just wait, would you? I might be able to translate it."

I blink at him. "You?"

"Do you think Addie entered the labyrinth knowing Ancient Daedalic? The old leader of Fates used to teach new members who wanted to learn. We used to think of it as a way to pass the time, but she always said it might come in handy. Collin never took the lessons. Theo took a few, but he got bored. Only Addie and I continued with it — at least, we're the only ones who did that are still alive."

The old leader of Fates, Sybil. The Executioner told me about Sybil in her letter. Collin told me about her too.

Apparently Fates was very different under her leadership. Collin hinted that near the end of her life she wasn't the best for the group, but it's not as if I believe anything he says now.

"Are you fluent?" I ask.

"Probably not. I don't know as much as Addie. But I might know enough for this, whatever this is. That's why you should show me."

I hesitate a moment longer, then go to retrieve the journal, leaving the map hidden. When I return to Ryan, I drop the book in his lap and motion for him to turn so I can untie his hands.

"Where did you find this?" he asks.

"In a destroyed room when I was scavenging."

"I've never found anything like this," Ryan says, half to himself, as he tentatively picks up the book. With gentle fingers he undoes the clasp, then flips to the first page.

"Well? Can you read it?"

"Not right away," Ryan says, almost tersely. "I told you, I'm not fluent, and I haven't practiced since . . . it's going to take me a while to figure out if I can understand it or not. At least give me a few hours."

"You have until this kicks in." I shove the bowl of broth at him.

"Which is what, half an hour? That's not even close to enough time."

"Then you can finish tomorrow." Even if I don't drug Ryan while I'm out hunting in the morning, I'm not letting him off tonight. It's one thing to return prepared for an attack. It's another entirely to sleep when he could attack me and turn the tables in an instant.

When Ryan's finished eating, I get my own meal. In what's closer to an hour than thirty minutes I find him asleep, the closed journal in his lap. I leave it on the crate next to him as I tie his hands and ease him down. After a moment's consideration I go and return with an extra blanket and a pillow.

Maybe if I make a bit of an effort he'll be less likely to attack me when I get back from hunting tomorrow.

I don't run into anything the next day. There's neither game nor monsters to be found. The only things that seem plentiful are berries and herbs, untouched since my last time here. I spend most of the day going from mossy spot to mossy spot, collecting. I've never encountered a monster in a mossy area, so it's a fairly low-risk activity.

I'd try fishing, but without monster meat I can't test the waters. The last time I tried throwing my fishing line in without testing, water diggers broke my pole. I could always use myself as bait, splashing the water and dipping my hands in, but if they're close to the surface they could catch me unaware.

After collecting, I head back to base. Although I locked Ryan in, I left him awake, without drugs, and even with his hands unbound. As I open the door I grip my unsheathed axe, prepared for him to strike.

There's no attack, so I hesitantly edge into the room. I find Ryan in the kitchen, sitting in front of the hearth. Although the book is open in his lap, his eyes are on me. Since this morning he's untied his legs but hasn't armed himself.

"Well?" I ask.

Ryan closes the book. "I can't understand everything, but I've been able to translate a few pages so far. If you want to know what they say, you'll have to give me something in return. Your knowledge for mine."

I was afraid this might happen. "I'm not telling you how to get to Fates."

"That's not what I'm talking about." Ryan picks up something from the floor beside him. I realize it's one of my arrows, the black paste almost entirely chipped off. "I want to know how you make these. The feathers belong to screechers, I know that much. What's the arrowhead made of, and where did you get these bones?"

Of course — Ryan wants information to bring back to Fates. Do I tell him the truth or lie to him? My first reaction is to lie, but then I realize there's no need. If they get the chance to shoot me, any arrow will do. Plus, even if they did manage to collect the materials, they'd never be able to cut the bone properly, let alone sculpt the arrowhead. They don't have a bronze-beak dagger.

"Any monster bone," I say, tapping a finger against the shaft. "Screechers are easiest. The arrowhead . . ." I gently touch the tip. If Ryan pushed the arrow right now he'd cut my finger, but he doesn't. "It's made of screecher talons."

"Screecher?" Ryan gazes at the arrow. "But . . . you have so many."

I figured he'd search my supplies if I left him alone and awake, as I often would when the Executioner was gone. It couldn't be helped. If I left him bound, he couldn't go through the journal.

"What did you find?" I ask him.

"Why do you coat them with this paste?" Ryan asks, ignoring my question.

"Camouflage. Don't chip it off again." I take the arrow from him. "What did you find in the journal?"

"A lot, but it's confusing. It's kind of like a labyrinth survival guide. Where did you say you found it again?"

I undo my weapons belt, heading over to the crates as I speak over my shoulder, "Read the first entry to me."

"*Read* it to you?"

Dropping my rucksack onto my bedding, I return to the kitchen and sit beside Ryan. There's just enough room in front of the fire for us to sit side by side. I remember sitting like this with the Executioner while we gutted rabbits.

With my unsheathed dagger I gesture at the book. Ryan sighs and unclasps it, flipping through the pages. He doesn't seem particularly unnerved by the dagger I have pointed at him.

"You skipped the first page," I say.

"I can't make sense of it." He skips a few more pages until he gets to the section titled *leo nemeum*. The sketch stares back at us: a ferocious lion with a dark pelt and sabre teeth. "This entire entry is about temple lions. It says their pelts are impervious to most things, with bronze beaks and their own claws and teeth being the only listed exceptions. They form packs and stick to their own territory. Other monsters leave them alone, except bats or screechers, who will go after stray cubs. If prey is scarce, they've been known to turn on their own pack. Their pelts are usually black, sometimes gray, and they have red eyes."

I flash back to the toy lion the Executioner made for Gina. Then something else occurs to me: I think about the gray jacket the Executioner always wore. I found it odd that she'd wear something seemingly flimsy over her armour. I used to think it was so she'd blend in with the labyrinth, but her armour wasn't reflective, and it was gray too. When we fought the hundred-headed monster, the jacket disappeared, just like the Executioner.

"Does it say anything about fire?" I ask.

Ryan glances at me curiously, then skims through the entry again. "It might. I don't understand all the words."

I scowl at him, and he says, "I told you, I'm not fluent."

I pull out the whetstone I brought with me and start sharpening the side of my dagger. "Keep going."

He continues, reading aloud the temple lion entry. When he reaches the end, there's a long paragraph of haphazard notes. Even though I can't read them, I can tell the writer's thoughts were jumbled.

"This is as far as I've gotten." Ryan picks himself up. "I'm going to keep going through it."

"Wait."

Ryan hesitates, and I take the journal from him. I flip to the very back, to the picture of the monster the Executioner and I fought. I point to the words beside it. "What does *hekaton hydra* mean?"

Ryan doesn't react to the image of the horrifying monster. He must have flipped through the whole journal earlier. "The first part of the term has to do with the Ancient Daedalic word for a hundred. I don't recognize the second part."

I stare at the monster's name, suddenly angry. It's not fair. It took the Executioner from me, and I don't even get to find out its name. I feel like I can't hate it properly without knowing that much.

Ryan asks, "Do you want me to keep translating or not?"

His tone is verging on testy. When I glance up, I find him waiting, hand outstretched for the book. Since he's acting irritated, I want to snap at him. Or maybe that's leftover feelings from the hundred-headed monster. Not wanting to give in to the creature's effect on me, I wordlessly hand Ryan the journal.

He disappears behind the crates, toward his bed. As I heat up the broth, I stay on guard, prepared for him to attack with a weapon he might have stolen while I was gone. He doesn't attack. He doesn't even speak to me when I bring his food over, just lays the book flat in front of him to read while he starts eating. I return to fix my own supper.

After eating and sharpening my sword, I find Ryan asleep. Even though he's out cold, I tie him up as an extra precaution, then head to my own bed, more exhausted than usual. Everything that happened with Fates and all the stress of looking after Ryan must be getting to me.

I wake up, feeling a sudden cold, and gasp, which makes me start choking. I promptly spit out the water clogging my throat. When I try to push myself up I realize I can't. Someone's pinning me. Ryan.

Of course it wasn't regular exhaustion. I should have realized that.

"Nice way to wake up, huh?" Ryan tosses aside an empty flask. "Where is it?"

"What are you talking about?"

Ryan grips my shoulders so hard I flinch. His face is inches from mine, but he still shouts, "The map!"

I freeze.

"So you *do* have it. Where?"

"In my rucksack."

"Don't lie to me. Don't you think that's the first place I checked?"

"How do you know about the map?" I ask, hoping to distract him long enough to come up with a plan.

"How do you think? It was in the journal. Where is it?"

My mind races. "In my tunic. I'll take it out so just let —"

"I said not to lie. You're not getting out of this like before. Just tell me where it is."

"How do you know it's not there?"

"I searched you while you were still asleep," Ryan says tersely, as if I should have expected this. "I'll hurt you if I have to, so just give me the map."

I slam my fists into Ryan's chest. I start beating at him, my arms shaking, but he doesn't move. "Get off me!"

"Only if you give me the map!"

"I'll never let you have it!" I scream at him. "You're just as bad as the others! You all deserve to rot here!"

"Does that mean there really is a way out? *Is there a way out?*"

"If there is, what does it matter?" I've stopped fighting him. I've even stopped shaking. "The memories will always be there. You'll never really be out."

"You're an idiot." Ryan starts trembling now. "Give me the map, and I'll use it."

My lips stay shut as I stare right past him. He's lit a candle, which is on the crate beside me. By its flickering glow I can just make out the drawings on the side of the crate: a boy, a horse, a little girl.

Ryan's still screaming at me, threatening me, demanding to know the map's location. He starts breathing heavily, and when he finally quiets to pleading whispers, then silence, his breath is the only thing that remains. I can feel it against my wet cheek, warming my cool flesh.

"You've been in the labyrinth a long time," I say. "How many people have you seen ripped apart by screechers?"

I don't think he'll answer. For a while, he doesn't. Then, in a breath of a voice, he says: "Twelve."

"How many have you seen pulled to pieces by bats?"

He doesn't reply.

"How many have you seen lose a limb to diggers, or carried off by bronze beaks, or torn to shreds by water diggers, or skewered by a stinger? Are you ever going to forget any one of those moments?"

Ryan still doesn't say anything. Even though he's hovering over me, I turn on my side, as if to go back to sleep, hugging my pillow to me. "Even if I showed it to you, it wouldn't matter. There's no real exit."

"There's no exit?" Ryan whispers. I shake my head against my pillow. He's silent for a very long time, then he scrambles off me. He rocks back on his heels at the foot of my bed, pressing his hands to his forehead.

"I'm sorry," he says, his voice broken. It's the closest I've ever heard Ryan come to crying. It's definitely the first apology I've heard from him. And then I get another: "I'm sorry."

I don't say anything. I hug my pillow and, within it, the map.

The next morning I leave early to go to the very first mossy area the Executioner showed me. After bathing I lie on the soft ground and stare up at the sky. The sun beats down on me, quickly drying my flesh and slowly drying my hair. The warmth is nice against my cool skin, although the water itself isn't terribly cold, not when it's under the sun like this.

My usual methods to keep myself from thinking don't work today. What happened yesterday makes me wonder: if Ryan could really translate the whole journal, and I trusted him enough to show him the map, would I try to escape?

Even though I want to think I would, I'm not sure. Dangerous as it may be, I know the labyrinth now. I have no idea what could be outside it.

Although I put it off in the morning, as afternoon creeps in I head toward Fates' territory. As soon as Ryan's done going through the journal I intend to return him.

I don't run into any Fates scavengers until late in my scouting. Even then, they don't see me. Andrea, Jay, and another scavenger continue at a steady pace. Instead of following the trio, I head in the opposite direction, not wanting to risk an encounter.

It's late when I finally return from Fates' territory. I tell myself it's because I want to finish scouting the area within two days, but I know it's because I want to put off returning to my base.

I can't avoid it anymore. Ryan doesn't move from his bedding when I enter the room. We don't greet each other. In the kitchen I dry the herbs I collected before setting the broth to heat. I'm grinding the herbs into their bottles when Ryan comes over. He stands just outside the kitchen, holding the book. I continue with my work, not looking at him.

"You don't have to put the sedative into my bowl tonight," Ryan says. "I mixed it in with the broth last night."

"How did you know which herbs to use?" I ask.

"We use them back at Fates. I took them after I was attacked by the stinger. We used to give them to sick Icarii. Collin had them slipped into our drinks the night before he kicked you out. He didn't want anyone to interfere."

I don't know why Ryan cares about making excuses to me now.

"We didn't know what he had planned," Ryan says. "When Andrea found out, she wanted us to sneak out and look for you and the others."

"I suppose you stopped her then too." My voice sounds snide to my own ears.

"I went with her," Ryan says. "We didn't bother trying the regular watering hole. We just went to Collin's rationing spot, and we . . . we found remains, in the water. We thought you all died there."

A strange feeling sparks in my stomach. It's warm, but it's also guilty. Andrea kept trying to help me. To help Felix and Gina. And now, because of me, she thinks she's lost Ryan.

As good as it feels to think Andrea cared that much, I can't handle the guilt. I crush the spark of warmth. At least I don't have to feel grateful toward Ryan. He just went along to protect Andrea, maybe out of concern for Gina. It had nothing to do with me.

But something he said is nagging at me.

"Rationing," I repeat. "I heard Collin use that word. I thought he just meant food rationing."

"Not food," Ryan says. "Icarii."

"So it's happened before? He sends people — *children* — out to be slaughtered?"

Ryan doesn't deny it.

"How many times has it happened?" My voice is rising.

"Three times. Before you it was always sick Icarii."

"And no one stops him."

"We never know until after it's happened. But you're right; no one's made an effort to stop him. Sometimes Andrea stands up to him, but that never lasts long since no one sides with her."

"You don't support her?"

"Collin shouldn't be leading us. Andrea would do a better job, but Fates would never accept her. Collin has too many allies. If Andrea thought she had any support from the rest of us she might really try to stop Collin. That would just end in her getting cast out or worse."

"So you don't stand up to him to protect her?" I twist the cap so hard onto a bottle that the glass whines. "That's a convenient excuse."

Ryan's quiet for a moment, then he says, "I got through more of the journal."

"And?"

I don't indicate that Ryan should sit down, so he keeps standing as he speaks. He tells me he's finished going through a section about stingers. He describes it much like he did to Addie the day after he was stung; indifferent to the creature that almost killed him. Like he is about most everything.

One of the last facts he lists is about what happens to a victim of the *skorpios*. Apparently, they start hallucinating in their final moments. Their skin bubbles and is scalding to the touch. The victim dies in the midst of all the bubbles popping.

This could have happened to Ryan. It started to happen to Ryan. I still remember the way the flesh around his leg bubbled. He probably has scars.

But all he says after this is, "There's a note in the margins around the section about the hallucinations. It says something about this being 'like the mist.' I don't know what it means yet."

When Ryan doesn't say anything else, I ask, "Is that all?"

"For now."

"Where was the map mentioned?"

Ryan hesitates. "Everywhere. Each entry has at least one note referring to the map. There's a map key too, although it's scattered. There are symbols that indicate each monster. I can explain them to you, if you show me the map."

I don't say anything to that, just serve up a bowl of broth, which I hand to Ryan. When he starts eating I ask, "How long will it take for you to finish going through the journal?"

"It's not a fast process. It would help if I had the map for reference. The journal was clearly written to be a companion to the map."

Which means Ryan could be here for weeks, and even then he might keep information from me until he gets the map. I'd rather work with what he's given me and sort out the rest on my own. I'm sure, with a careful eye, I can match up the symbols in the journal with the map. At least then I'll know what areas to avoid.

As for whatever other warnings might be in the journal, I'll just have to decide if it's worth the risk not knowing.

When I don't say anything else to Ryan, he returns to his bed, still eating. I realize I might be letting my guard down again, but I'm not as concerned about whether Ryan is out cold tonight or not. He knows he won't find the map, and if he was going to kill me he would have done so last night.

Sure, he might have changed his mind. Sure, he might have found something else in the journal he's not telling me about, but today I just don't care.

Except I must care a little, because I eat the unsullied food in my rucksack, just in case the broth really is drugged.

Ryan shakes me awake in the morning. I'm barely conscious as I draw my dagger, pricking his arm. He pulls back as he says, "I need to tell you something, so don't attack me."

As I shove myself into a sitting position, my hold on the dagger tightens.

"The journal," Ryan says now that he can see I'm listening. He's holding the book open in his lap. His hair is dishevelled, and his eyes are red. He looks tired but excited at the same time.

"You didn't sleep?"

"That doesn't matter." He holds up the journal. "It describes the exit."

I gape at him, but he's already turned back to the book, flipping through the pages. He shows me the entry, but the words mean nothing, and there's no sketch.

"It's not the actual exit," Ryan says, "but it talks about how to reach it. I need more time, to really figure out what it all means. Seeing the map would really help —"

"You need to sleep," I break in. "At this rate you'll pass out."

I try to take the journal from Ryan, but he doesn't let go. He says, "You have to take me with you."

"What?" I finally manage to get the book from his grasp.

"I'm keeping stuff from you about the entries. You have to know that. Without my translations, you'll get yourself killed. So you have to take me with you when you decide to leave."

"Just sleep right now. We'll talk about this later."

Ryan nods to himself, unsurprised, then pushes to his feet. He wobbles before stumbling back toward his bed. Once he's gone, I stare at the journal in my lap, at the page that apparently describes the way out of the labyrinth.

Ryan's right: without his help, all of this is meaningless to me.

Ryan's still asleep when I get back that night. I wake him, and we eat, this time neither of our bowls drugged. After that I hand him a blindfold.

"What's this for?" he asks.

"We leave tonight. Do you need help putting it on?"

I expect him to protest more about the blindfold, but instead he looks at me in blatant shock. "You're actually taking me with you?"

"Against my better judgement." I gesture to the blindfold again.

Ryan thinks on it a moment, then starts tying the cloth around his head. "What about bats?"

"I haven't encountered any lately." I toss Ryan's bow into his lap, making him jolt in surprise. "We should be fine."

"You expect me to shoot like this?" Ryan asks, running his hands over the bow.

"You won't be blindfolded all the way." I lay his quiver beside him, close enough for it to knock his leg so he knows it's there.

"You've fought bats?"

"Yes." I start strapping my equipment back into place. I stare at the Executioner's axe a few seconds longer before attaching it to my belt.

"How? You're alone. All three must go for you."

"You had the order wrong."

"What?"

I crouch in front of Ryan. I'm not sure if he's heard me approach, because he starts when I flick his forehead. "Here." I pinch his arm, making him wince. "Here." I squeeze his knee. "Then here."

Ryan doesn't speak as I push away to collect my own quiver and arrows. By the time I'm ready he's hoisted his own bow over his shoulder, next to his quiver. I pull him to his feet, then push him toward the door. Although I won't bind his hands this time, I still don't want him to see where we're going.

We make it up the stairs and outside after some minor difficulty. The night air is crisp and cool, like always, blowing stray wisps of my hair across my face. It's not enough to catch the attention of any creature, but I still push the hair back under my hood.

I push Ryan along. Neither of us speaks, and we both walk quietly and quickly. As I initially did on the way back to my base with him, I take multiple twists and turns to confuse him should he be trying to track our location. I decided our course earlier, and as predicted, it takes a while to cover the distance. Luckily I was able to map out a route not quite as long as the one we took the other day.

It's still dark out when we arrive at Fates.

We're not quite there yet. It's just down the next corridor, but I find myself hesitating. Not about returning Ryan. I have to bring him back. I don't want to give Fates more cause to hate me by leaving him somewhere dangerous. And I can't bring him with me — I'd rather risk the unknown in the labyrinth than what might happen traveling with him.

I hesitate because, although I scouted around here earlier, I haven't been this close to the door of Fates since I left.

I grip the bell for a count of three. Then I push Ryan around the corner.

There it is. Fates. As we get closer, I notice something I didn't before. Ancient Daedalic writing carved above the door. It's since chipped away, making it almost unreadable, but maybe Addie or Ryan can translate it.

I'm running over my escape route from here when I notice something. The door to Fates is open. I stop walking, grabbing Ryan's arm to make him stop as well. Then I'm pulling him back around the corner. He remains silent, no doubt thinking there's an enemy. Peeking around the corner, I watch the door, waiting for an Icarii to come out.

No one does, and I realize the open door spills no firelight. Why, then, is it open, if not to allow one of the Icarii to exit?

I panic. I don't know what's going on with Fates, but I know I don't want to be here anymore. Do I leave Ryan and run? That seems the best course of action, to do as I planned all along. Whatever's happened with Fates doesn't concern me.

As I start to edge away, Ryan catches hold of my hand. Glancing back, I find he's pulled down his blindfold. He's glaring.

"You were going to ditch me," he hisses.

I try to pull away, but he grips my hand even harder. If need be, I can easily stab him and make him let me go, but I wanted to finish this without bloodshed.

"At least you're not denying it," he says, stepping to the corner without dropping my hand. "I guess you can't when Fates is just . . . what's going on?"

His eyes have widened. He's seen the open door. His hold on me slackens, but before I can pull away, he does so himself, running silently but swiftly to Fates. This is my chance to get away, just as I planned.

Again, I hesitate. Ryan clearly thinks something's wrong, otherwise he wouldn't have run off like that. Could Fates really be in trouble? If it is, I shouldn't care. Fates didn't help me and Gina and Felix when Collin sent us to our deaths.

I shouldn't care, but I do, because Fates isn't just the people that abandoned me. It's a group of young Icarii who knew nothing of my situation, who sat through Cassie's classes as if the knowledge would mean something. There's Cassie herself, who was always kind, and Gus, who makes toys out of spare materials and loved Gina like an older brother. There's Andrea, who did more than I ever knew to help me. And then there's Elle.

I think of Elle and the chocolate she always wanted for her gruel and her horrible sewing and the way she hugged me to her all through my last night in Fates.

By the time I reach the door, Ryan's already inside. I'm fleetingly reminded of when we went in the back exit my first day of Fates, because ahead of me is darkness. Then I see Ryan with a lantern. He holds it aloft for a few seconds, then suddenly drops it. The lantern rolls, and the light goes out. In the silence that follows I hear Ryan scrambling for the lantern.

Light again. The same old Fates, except it's not. In the thin light I can see the table is nearly empty of supplies, because half of them are on the floor. Every box is broken, every sack open and spilling what's left of its contents.

My gaze goes from the mess to Ryan. He's left the lantern on the ground and is crouching a few steps ahead. I realize he's kneeling by someone prone on the floor.

It's Gus. He's been hit over the head, and there's dried blood in his hair. His eyes are wide and unblinking. As I start to move away, my foot brushes something. Looking down, I see the remains of a little wooden toy that must have been stepped on. A pain fills my chest when I realize it's a horse.

Ryan just kneels there by Gus, trembling. Then he's a rush of movement, launching farther into Fates, not even bothering to grab his lantern. I take it and follow him. I don't want to go any farther, but part of me knows I have to. The door to the boys' room is closed. The door to the girls' room is open. My heart skips a beat.

Ryan runs inside, and I follow. He disappears into the shadows of the room, knowing just where he's going. I'm warier, covering the lantern with my cloak to try and dull the light. I see Addie and Andrea, sleeping soundly, like the younger Icarii. I expect Ryan to be standing at the foot of Andrea's bed, but instead he's standing by another, unoccupied spot. It takes me a moment to remember who usually slept there. Cassie.

Dread washes over me as my gaze wanders to my empty bed. The spot next to mine is also empty.

Elle is gone.

Panic blossoms as I scan the room again. Elle isn't here. What happened? Did she run away? Is this part of Collin's rationing?

No. Collin would be subtler. What happened to Gus wasn't subtle. It also wasn't something a monster could do.

But Icarii could.

Ryan rushes past me, knocking my shoulder since I'm blocking the door. One of the Icarii nearby stirs, so I quickly follow Ryan, quietly shutting the door behind me. In the main room, Ryan pauses to look down at Gus, only for a moment, then he disappears down the corridor to the mess hall. Instead of following, I eye the front door. I want to escape this awful place and everything that's happened here, to me and now to the people I used to care about.

Instead, I kneel by Gus. Collecting the remains of his horse toy, I curl it into his cold hand.

"Gina never stopped missing you," I whisper. "But she found her mother, Gus. She's with her mother now."

I close the door behind me as I leave Fates. I tell myself not to look back. If I do, I might return and help Ryan scour Fates, looking for someone who probably isn't there. There wasn't any light coming from the mess hall.

There wasn't any light from the main room either, a part of me whispers, and Gus was there. Whose body might be lying in the shadows of the mess hall?

No. Elle isn't dead. But she might be in the labyrinth. I have to find her, and I have to get away from Fates.

When I hear the door to Fates open, I quicken my footsteps.

"Where are you going?"

I keep walking.

"Fates was just attacked, and you're leaving?" Ryan's voice is too loud for the labyrinth, especially at night. He must realize this because he goes quiet. Except he hasn't given up, because then I hear running footsteps coming toward me.

As soon as I turn around, Ryan's there. He draws up short, inches from knocking into me. "How can you leave now? No matter what Collin did to you, the rest of Fates isn't to blame! There are innocent people in there who might have been injured or . . . or . . . don't you care at all? How can you just leave them?"

Even if he's glaring at me, panting as he speaks, I feel like these words aren't entirely for me. I feel like Ryan doesn't even see me completely. Then again, he never has before.

"If I stay," I say, "the moment they wake up, they'll think I did this."

I start to turn, to walk away again. Ryan grabs my arm. "That's your excuse?"

We both know it's what would happen. I just look at him, first at his hand on my arm, then his actual face. There are tears in his eyes. I always knew Ryan was important to Cassie, but I never realized she was this important to him too.

I remember how Ryan never had any patience for my crying. He'd be cold or cruel, and it was always the opposite of what I needed. Am I being cold now by worrying about myself?

"I have to go," I say to Ryan. "Elle might still be nearby."

Ryan's eyes widen. He's so panicked, it hadn't occurred to him yet to look for Cassie outside. He says, "I'll help you look."

We search for half an hour, but we don't find any trace of them. It doesn't help that we have no idea which way they might have gone, let alone why they left. Ryan wants to keep looking, but I know I've stayed in Fates' territory too long. I'll keep looking for Elle but not here.

"I'm going," I tell Ryan. "You should head back to Fates, and get someone to search with you."

"So you can handle the labyrinth alone at night, and I can't?"

It isn't so much Ryan's abilities I doubt but his present state of mind. Cassie's disappearance, the attack on Fates, and Gus's death have really shaken him. I'm shaken too, but I have more to lose than he does if I don't keep it together. I can't let Collin catch me.

When I turn to go, Ryan says, "You're giving up on Elle?"

"No. I'm going to keep looking, deeper in the labyrinth if I have to. But she's not here, and it's dangerous for me to stay."

"I'm coming with you."

I stare at him, surprised.

"Elle and Cassie might be together," Ryan says. "If they're deeper in the labyrinth, you're better equipped to find them than anyone at Fates. You have a map. Let me come."

"I'm not showing you the map."

"I don't care about that anymore!" Ryan takes a shaky breath and then says, "Help me find Cassie, and I'll translate the whole journal. You don't have to take me with you when you go for the exit."

He'd give up his chance to escape the labyrinth for Cassie?

"What about Andrea and the others?" I ask. "Are you really OK to just leave them behind?"

"It's not like you'll wait around for me if I try to talk to them. You'd probably take the chance to ditch me again."

No point in denying that.

"So?" Ryan asks. "Do we have a deal?"

I hesitate before nodding. Ryan's quiet for a long time. Then I hear him whisper, "Thank you."

We reach my base with the dawn and sleep for a few hours, just enough for us to get rested. It's a long journey, and I want to clear a certain area before nightfall. Just beyond digger territory is a shortcut I like to take to get to Kleos' territory, but at night it's rife with bats. If we leave now, by my calculations we'll have an hour or so of extra time to clear the area, in case there are complications.

I managed to convince Ryan, before we went to bed, to leave me in charge of a search route. Rather, I told him he could follow my search plan or go back to Fates. More than half of me expected him to go.

I prepare my rucksack and an old one for Ryan to use, letting him sleep longer. When I do wake him and push a bowl of broth into his hands, he eats without complaint. He does so quickly too, although I'm sure he's not hungry. It's hard to be after last night, but at least he understands the importance of keeping up his energy.

Of course he understands that. He's been in the labyrinth four years longer than I have. Even if I feel like I'm the one who's better prepared to survive out of the two of us now, he's still technically my senior Icarii.

The sky is just shifting out of early morning when we leave my base. We walk in silence for a while. I veer off course — not that Ryan would realize I'm doing this. I lead him to an open area, marred with black at the center. As I turn to him, I see Ryan tense.

Ryan reaches for his bow. "Are you going to knock me out again? Get rid of me?"

I shake my head before approaching the center of the clearing. I gesture to the pile of wooden toys and dried flowers. Hesitant at first, Ryan approaches it, clearly puzzled.

"This is Gina's grave." I'm surprised at how easy it is to say. Surprised at how hard.

Ryan's quiet for a very long time, staring at the spot until his eyes go unfocused. "You burned her body."

"Not me," I say.

"Who?"

"The woman who saved me," I say, and it's the first time I've said this aloud: "The Executioner."

Before we leave Gina's clearing, Ryan places one of his old arrows on her grave. He does it when he thinks I'm not looking. We start out in earnest then. At first Ryan is as silent as before. Eventually he says, "The Executioner is a legend."

"She was real to me."

"Was," Ryan repeats. "She's dead?"

I nod and find myself clutching the bell at my throat.

"Did she give that to you?"

I glance back at Ryan. He gestures to the bell. I hold it a moment longer before letting it go. I nod again.

"So she's the one who taught you how to survive," Ryan says.

A final nod.

"That was her base," I say. "After she saved Gina and me from the screechers, she took us back there. She taught me how to cook and make medicine and how to hunt and how to fight monsters and how to navigate the labyrinth. It's thanks to her that I'm alive."

"Did she teach you how to gut a rabbit?"

I glance at Ryan when he says this. "I wasn't going to kill you," I say. "Even before I found out you could translate the journal. I was going to bring you back alive. I wouldn't kill another human."

"No? I guess some of the softness of the old you is still left."

His jaw is clenched. Even for Ryan, I didn't expect this reply. "You'd kill someone else?"

"When we find Cassie," Ryan says, "if someone's hurt her, I'll do it in a heartbeat."

We don't talk again after that. Partly because we enter a less-deserted section of the labyrinth, but mostly because we're both consumed by our own thoughts. Of course Ryan wants revenge. I want revenge on Fates, but if given the chance, I don't think I could kill any of them.

I flash back to the moment I was hiding, spying on their planned ambush, watching Collin's back. I remember how it felt, fantasizing about cutting him down.

I clutch the bell again.

"Why doesn't it make any noise?" Ryan asks. His voice is much quieter than before.

"I don't know. She never told me. She couldn't tell me. She couldn't speak."

"I guess you two made a perfect pair."

I scowl at him.

"I thought we could have made a good match," Ryan suddenly says.

"What do you mean?"

"You were quiet," Ryan says. "Clumsy but quiet. When you made it over the wall, I thought, with training, maybe you could join our scavenging group. "

This admission surprises me. Ryan certainly never acted like he wanted to recruit me for his group. Quite the opposite. "You could have picked Kyle or Felix if it was a new teammate you wanted."

Ryan makes a face. "Kyle's not quiet. He can be when he needs to, but it's not ingrained in him. Training him was frustrating enough. Felix is . . . *was* too soft."

"Felix was stronger than me back then." He would be now, if he was still here.

"It was never about immediate strength," Ryan says. "It was about potential."

I'm unsure of what to say next, so I go for a very awkward, "Thanks for considering me, I guess."

For whatever reason, this makes Ryan frown at me. Does he think I'm being sarcastic? Am I being sarcastic? I was never one for sarcasm, but maybe that part of me has changed too. Clara was always the sarcastic one, especially when she was with Tanner.

Clara.

My chest feels like something heavy's pressing on it. The pressure starts to lift as I methodically go over gutting instructions in my mind. I picture the rabbit and my fingers in its stomach. I let the squelching sound echo in my ears as the entrails slip free. What used to disgust me has become a calming salve.

Finally, we turn the corner that leads to digger territory. When Ryan notices that the floor gives way to dirt, he pauses.

"Walk lightly," I whisper. "Diggers."

When I continue, Ryan doesn't move. His eyes are wide on the dirt floor. I start to ask him what's wrong, but he speaks over me: "I can't go this way."

"Why?"

"I just can't." Abruptly, Ryan turns around. "There has to be another way. There is one, isn't there?"

"There is," I say, following after Ryan as he retraces our steps. "Hold on. We need to go this way, otherwise we'll have to deal with bats later."

"We've both dealt with them before."

I speed up to get ahead, then stop directly in front of him, causing him to stop as well. "We can avoid the diggers, but bats will be harder. We both know this is the more secure route. You've faced diggers before, so what's the problem?"

"Just leave it," Ryan snaps. "I'll handle the bats if you don't want to."

Ryan starts to walk around me, but I move to block him again. When he tries to walk around my other side, I step in front of him that way too. He glares and starts walking straight at me. I glare back, planning to hold my ground, even if we knock into each other. At the last moment, however, I instinctively back up. My heel catches in the jagged floor, and I end up losing my balance. I grab a handful of Ryan's tunic to keep from falling down, and at the same time, he snags an arm around my waist to keep me up.

In the middle of finding my footing I realize how close we are. Ryan and I have been in several situations now where we're this close or closer. But instead of getting used to it, I find myself even more unnerved. Especially when the sun highlights all the different shades in his hair, from dark brown, to chestnut, to strands that seem almost gold. His pupils have grown impossibly wide, making the pale green rims around them even more vivid. I can feel the heat coming from his body, his breath against my cheek, his arm against my waist.

I'm flustered, but even if he's matured a bit more this is still *Ryan*. Just as I'm about to push him away, he scowls and lets me go. I find my footing just in time, and as I do, he walks around me, indifferent as ever.

As my senses return to normal, I find myself tensing. We're not alone. There's something coming. From underground? No. It's not a digger. But I don't know what it is. Confusion mingles with sudden panic. I should be able to identify the movements, the tremors and the sounds of every monster in this part of the labyrinth. Unless . . . what if it's the screecher-eater?

Suddenly Ryan spins around. He grabs my arm as he passes me, pulling me after him and forcing me to match his speed. There are no turns, so we have to go straight through digger territory. The moment our feet slam against the dirt I try to slow down. Running this fast, with this much force, we're sure to attract diggers of all sizes.

Ryan won't let me slow; if anything, he increases our pace, keeping a firm hold on my arm as he does so. A second later, I see why. The skittering sound I heard intensifies to a sharp scraping, and suddenly something crashes around the corner behind us. I glance back at a monster I've never seen myself. The sight of it, for the first time, throws my heart straight into my throat. It looks just like it did in the journal but now in color. The sun glints off its blackish-red shell.

Skorpios. Stinger.

It's no surprise Ryan's in such a hurry to escape the monster. I run with him, trying to focus on locating diggers and keeping an eye on the stinger at the same time. It's clacking its pincers together and making a horrible hissing sound that echoes down the corridor. It scuttles down the hall after us, pincers so large they scrape against the walls as it wobbles back and forth in its clumsy hurry. It's fast. Fast enough to catch us.

We turn a corner. Seconds later, the stinger slams into the wall behind us, leaving a dent and making the floor shake. The shaking continues as it regains its balance and comes after us. I'm panting. Ryan's panting. The shaking gets more intense. The stinger is catching up.

It clicks, almost too late. *The shaking and the stinger aren't connected!*

I pull back sharply, trying to get Ryan to stop. Instead he releases my arm. At the last moment, I catch his hand, yanking him back toward me. I stop him, if only for an instant. Before he can start running again or pull away, a huge tremor shakes the hall. I don't brace myself in time, and Ryan and I lose our balance. Even the stinger is sent off course, banging into the wall.

As we push ourselves up, another tremor, even more intense, shakes the hall. Ryan's eyes are wide with horror. He knows what's coming, and he's terrified — so terrified it takes me a moment to push him into action. I think I'll have to drag him to the wall, but eventually he gets himself together, at least enough to move. The ground is shaking so badly, so constantly, that we basically have to crawl to the side of the hallway. Once there, I use the chipped bricks in the wall to pull myself to my feet, screaming at Ryan to do the same. I don't know if he can hear me over the earthquake, but he sees what I'm doing and copies me, just as I copied the Executioner the first — and last — time I encountered this monster.

The ground spikes up a few feet from us as the adult digger surfaces, more quickly than it did the first time I saw it. I go flat against the wall, but Ryan just stares. I reach over and press my hand against his chest, pushing him back against the wall. Under my palm I can feel the rapid beat of his heart, the way he's trembling. I want to tell him not to look, but there's no way he'd hear me now.

The adult digger surges past us, coating us in a shower of dirt that makes us cough. As the grit clears from my eyes, I see the digger go straight for the stinger. I expect it to be the same as the time the adult digger ate the younger one's body, but to my surprise, the stinger scuttles up the labyrinth wall, out of the way of those gaping jaws. The digger's mouth stays open, even as it slams the side of its head into the wall the stinger climbed on, causing the wall to buckle inward, almost caving into the corridor behind it. The stinger isn't hit but is dislodged. It falls onto the digger's back and scrambles for purchase as it jabs its tail in every direction. It hits the digger twice before the creature starts thrashing. The stinger falls sideways between the digger's body and the wall. The digger, too large to back up or turn and swallow the stinger, dives back underground.

As the end of its tail disappears from view, I can hear our frantic breaths. A moment after the earth falls back in jagged pieces and the tremors quiet, the stinger collects itself. Rising, it uncoils its tail and charges right at us, pincers snapping.

Even as I start swinging my spiked ball, I feel a sweat breaking out at the back of my neck. I've never fought a stinger before. The Executioner gave me no hints. If we get stung, I don't have the equipment to save us, nor the experience. The desire to grasp at my bell is overwhelming.

A sudden tremor rockets the ground. Ryan and I drop our weapons and go sprawling. Before I can process anything more than this, the ground below the stinger explodes, raining more dirt, and the adult digger shoots straight up, jaws wide and gnashing. The stinger disappears into the digger's mouth as the monster stretches skyward. For a split, eerie second, it's so tall and rigid in the air it reminds me of the towers back in the city of Daedalum. Then the digger starts to sink. I'm frozen as it passes by right in front of us, back into the ground. After it disappears, the ground falls back into place. Silence returns to the hall too soon.

Instead of pushing himself up, Ryan falls on his back. I panic, thinking he's collapsed, but his eyes are wide open and he's staring skyward. I start giggling. The giggles rise like bubbles in my throat and pop the moment they reach my lips. Ryan cuts his gaze toward me, and for a moment, I think he's going to glare. Then he too starts laughing. Eventually tears are streaming down his face, and I don't know if it's because he's laughing so hard or because of the relief or because last night his life was turned upside down.

We encounter a junior digger on our way out. I take care of it. Apart from that, we don't have any more problems. We even manage to clear the bat area before nightfall. Unfortunately, we don't find any signs of Elle or Cassie. Maybe that means they made it past the really dangerous areas — if they came this way. Ryan's on edge from our fruitless search, but I don't try to reassure him. It's hard enough reassuring myself.

The sun's descending behind the labyrinth walls when we reach the mossy spot I use for camping between my bases.

"We'll spend the night here," I tell Ryan. "I'll patrol the area and make sure nothing's around. You get some rest."

"Never thought I'd hear that from you." Ryan frowns, but I can tell it doesn't have to do with his statement. "How often do you camp outside?"

Is he worried about spending the night in the labyrinth? "Not that much, but I've camped here before. It's safer than anywhere else, and we can't risk going deeper this late. We'll take turns on watch."

"I'm not a coward."

"I didn't say you were."

"I've just . . . I've never been in this deep before."

I felt the same way my first few times traveling this far, but I'm sure Ryan won't appreciate my sympathy, so I keep my mouth shut.

Since Ryan's here to watch our stuff, I leave my rucksack while I'm scouting. The area seems fairly clear. No stray diggers, no screechers, no bats, or bronze beaks — not that I've encountered bronze beaks very often. Only twice, and I've only had to fight one once. It ended in a sort of stalemate since its hide was too thick for my weapons to pierce, and I was too quick for it to catch. Since then, I've been carrying my bronze-beak dagger into the labyrinth, since that seems capable of piercing everything and might be the one thing that can pierce the bird creatures themselves.

I start back to the mossy area, taking a different route. The next corridor seems empty too, but when I round the corner something catches my attention. It's not a monster but a wooden object, discarded on the ground. It's bizarrely familiar, and upon closer inspection, I realize why. It bears the symbol of a bucking horse.

Kleos.

I glance around. There aren't any bodies, nor blood, but the walls in this area seem a little dented. One wall has a hole in it, the kind that can't be made by human weapons. The hole doesn't go all the way through the wall, and at its center is a hardened black spot. I'd bet on it being stinger poison.

I return to the shield. We're too far from Kleos' territory for this to make sense. They've got plenty of game and resources in their area, and they aren't interested in expanding — at least, not to my knowledge. The shield's in relatively good condition too, despite a dent near the middle. It's been properly maintained.

Fates was attacked, but not by monsters, which leaves two possible culprits: Kleos and Harmonia. And here's a piece of Kleos, where it shouldn't be, on the road to Fates.

But why would they do it?

Leaving the shield, I head back to the mossy area, increasing my pace. If Kleos is nearby and hostile, I don't know what they'll do if they find Ryan.

When I reach the mossy area, I pull up short. Ryan's sitting by the water's edge with his back to me, and he isn't wearing a shirt. Although it's gotten dark, by the moonlight I can still see the muscles tense in his back as I approach.

"It's me," I say, and he relaxes slightly. He pulls a dry tunic from his bag.

"After what happened, there was a lot of dirt on my clothes and stuff."

As Ryan speaks, he pulls the tunic over his head. I catch myself watching the muscles working in his back and immediately glance away.

"Yeah," I say. "My clothes and stuff are dirty too."

Stupid. That was a stupid way to phrase it, exactly as he did. Maybe I should go back to not talking.

"I'll wait in the hall," Ryan says.

"Why?"

Ryan immediately looks over his shoulder at me. "What do you mean why? Do you want me around while you clean up?"

My face heats. "No! Never!"

"Never?" Ryan scoffs, pushing himself up. "A 'no' was enough."

I'm flustered. "Just leave already!"

"I am!"

"Don't look!"

"*Never* would." Ryan disappears through the entrance. I bristle, annoyed that he got the last word like that, then annoyed with myself for being annoyed.

I hesitate to remove my weapons belt, let alone any of my actual clothing. I tell myself I'm being ridiculous and wasting time we could be using for rest, and then finally I remove my tunic.

Dirt and grit cling to my clothes and skin. It's even coating my chest-band in a thin layer, but no way am I taking that off. My face heats at the mere idea of stripping down entirely when Ryan's only in the next hall. No, it's not just Ryan. If it were anyone in the next hall, I'd still be this reluctant and this embarrassed.

I lay my tunic out to dry next to Ryan's. His is so much longer than mine, larger to fit his frame. Still, it's not as if the width of the two are that different. He's still rather thin, despite his broadening shoulders, but as my chest and hips continue to fill out I've found myself switching to a slightly wider tunic than the one the Executioner originally gave me.

As I wash my hair, I think about the girls back at Fates who are around my age. They're all thin, and some of them, like Addie, are especially underdeveloped for their age. Although I lost weight during my time at Fates, I put it back on after staying with the Executioner, and since then I've been filling out. I guess it has to do with our different diets. While I eat my fill almost every day, knowing I need to keep up my energy and growth, the people at Fates hardly ever get enough, let alone the proper nutrients. I can't imagine their simple gruel gives people our age what they need to grow properly.

The girls from Harmonia, on the other hand, and the boys from Kleos are all fairly strong. Those who aren't as large as the others, like Silas, seem to be built with smaller frames. The only factors inhibiting the growth of those Icarii are their genes.

I wonder, if Ryan were a member of Kleos, would he be taller by now?

The thought of Kleos reminds me of the shield. I shove to my feet, leaving my hair unbraided as I hurry to the hallway. Even calling out for Ryan might be too dangerous if they're nearby. It's not that I think Kleos would definitely harm us; it's that there's always the potential for that, the risk. I've never been a risk taker. That's the one trait I brought into the labyrinth that works for me.

I find Ryan leaning against the wall outside the mossy area. Before we left the Executioner's base I gave him a few of my arrows to mix with his own. He's rolling one of them between his fingers, his gaze intent on the tip. He's turned slightly away from the entrance to the mossy area.

"Ryan." My voice is quiet as my hand closes over his shoulder. He's unsurprised, gaze flitting from the arrow to me. "You need to come back in —"

He drops the arrow, and it clatters off the ground. "Are you an *idiot*?"

I'm instantly confused, but then I notice the way his eyes have widened and strayed from my face. Peeking down at myself, I feel my face flame. In my hurry to drag Ryan away from the possibility of a Kleos encounter, I forgot to put on my clean tunic. I'm fleetingly grateful I left on the band, which covers some of my chest, at least. Still, I immediately release Ryan and cross my arms over myself. When I look up he's already turned away. He's covering his face with his hand.

"I forgot," I stammer.

"How can you forget? You're such an idiot." His voice is lower when he speaks, huskier. The change in tone and pitch surprises me and makes me blush harder.

"We can't stay out here," I say, trying to force back the odd feelings assaulting me, which I choose to label entirely as embarrassment. "They might find us."

"Whatever. Just go and put something on."

"Fine," I say, but I don't move. I'm oddly insulted. If I was someone else, would he be so quick to tell me to go away? I can't believe the thought, and I can't believe myself when I say, "At the dinner you stared at me. Is there something wrong with me now?"

I cover my mouth after I say it, because it's too forward, especially for me, and probably conveys something I don't mean. I don't want him to look at me. I want to go and put my tunic back on and disappear inside the material so I never have to face Ryan again.

At my words, Ryan actually looks at me again, completely dumbfounded. He's angry but still flustered, I realize. "Would you stop bringing up that night?"

"Why? It happened to me, not you."

"It happened to all of us," Ryan snaps. "We all have to live with letting Collin get away with that and Jay . . . damn it, would you just go and get dressed?"

Although he'd been careful to only look me in the eyes, his own eyes wandered for a moment. Now he's covering his face with both of his hands, although he's still facing me. He says, "What's wrong with you?"

Apparently a lot, if even an adolescent boy is this quick to get rid of me. Realizing how shallow I'm being, on top of ridiculous, I spin around and head back into the clearing. I promptly fall to my knees next to my bag, digging through it for my spare clothes.

Tanner had a friend, Martin, who was a year older than us. I was fourteen when Martin started talking to me. Even though I was practically mute around him, as with all other boys, he still made an effort to ease me out of my shell. Clara was so happy for me. I remember her saying Martin and I looked "cute together." That was the first hint I had about Martin's interest in me, and the interest I should have in him. He wasn't bad looking and was genuinely sweet. After Clara brought the possibility of romance to mind, I developed a crush on him.

We started dating, in a way. It was never explicitly official, and we never went on any real dates, except once on the shopping floor. Clara was the one who, after my retelling of Martin encounters, determined we'd become a couple. The others who found out about it were surprised. No one expected Clara's quiet friend to get a boyfriend when Clara — beautiful, brave, charismatic Clara — was still single.

I let Martin kiss me. It wasn't romantic. It was nerve-wracking. He asked if he could kiss me in the elevator on our way home from the shopping center when we were alone. He asked me, and I was instantly so anxious I wanted to throw up. I could barely make myself nod, because I felt entirely frozen. He kissed me, and it was dry, and I don't remember responding in any way. It was like sandpaper, and when it was over I felt as if I'd been cut, but there was no blood and no scar.

Later that week Martin unofficially dumped me. It was all unofficial, even that kiss. A week after that he tried making a move on Clara, who rebuffed him immediately and publicly revealed his underhanded nature to our whole group of friends. Martin was slime, she declared, because he'd been using me to get to her. And if anyone did that again, she'd do more than publicly expose them.

Clara was furious with Martin, and although I kept it hidden deep down at the time, I was furious with Clara. Even if Martin had told her he'd only used me to get to her, did she really need to tell everyone else? She probably thought she was standing up for me, but it was a public declaration about my character as much as it was about Martin's. I was officially Clara's undesirable best friend, useful for bridging the gap between admirers and the one they all admired, but nothing more than that.

It seems so trivial, thinking about it now, when I'm here. I was a stupid, naive girl back then. I still am, evidently, if I'm letting the current situation get to me. Martin was never chosen to become an Icarii, and he never will now that he's over sixteen. He's probably already turned eighteen. He probably has a steady girlfriend, who isn't as pretty and perfect as Clara. He probably doesn't remember what happened between us, and if he does, he probably doesn't care.

I don't care either, not really, not anymore. But I care about what just happened with Ryan and how I acted. I want to forget it. I want to go back to being what I was like when I traveled alone. Focused and indifferent and silent.

I want to be like the Executioner.

I'm long dressed by the time Ryan re-enters the mossy area. I don't look at him, and he doesn't look at me. He sits by the water, as I do, but as far from me as possible.

"Who are 'they?'" Ryan asks.

"A group of male Icarii. They call themselves Kleos. They've never come into this part of the labyrinth before, but I found one of their shields."

"Kleos," Ryan repeats.

"They say it means 'heroes' in Ancient Daedalic."

"Idiots. The *word* 'hero' comes from the Ancient Daedalic word for protector." Ryan doesn't seem surprised by any of this.

"You knew about Kleos, didn't you?" I ask.

"A scavenger has to know what's in the labyrinth."

I remember a conversation I overheard at Fates, when Collin informed his inner circle they'd try scavenging deeper in the labyrinth. They discussed the risk of 'the others.' Ryan wasn't there for that conversation, but if he knows about Kleos and Harmonia, I'm betting most of Fates does. The scavengers and the older Icarii, anyway. I guess Collin didn't tell me because, as Clara, he didn't see a point in me knowing about anything in the world outside Fates.

I pull my fingers through my hair, working out stray knots in place of my irritation. My hair's still extremely damp. I should have waited until morning to wash it. At this rate, I might catch a cold. Back in Daedalum, a cold isn't a big deal, but I'm afraid in the labyrinth it might develop into something worse.

"You've been in contact with them," Ryan says. "Kleos."

His voice drips with disdain as he says the word.

"Their camp is near one of my bases. I run into them regularly."

"Do they give you any trouble?"

"They haven't tried to kill me yet. Mostly they're a bother, usually avoidable. Their leader's annoying. Really annoying."

"That's not what I meant by trouble."

I glance sidelong at Ryan. He's watching me, and from this distance his eyes look black. "What did you mean?"

Ryan looks away. He rolls his shoulders, and I'm not sure if he's shrugging or stretching. "You *are* a girl."

My skin crawls at what he's suggesting. "Not all guys are like that. Kleos is annoying, but they're not Fates."

"What's *that* supposed to mean?"

I didn't mean to say *that* at all. It just slipped out.

"So what?" Ryan demands. "Is every guy from Fates a pig, and every other guy's all right?"

"No," I say. "It's just that . . . it's . . ."

"What?"

When I don't reply right away, Ryan says, "So now you can't speak again? Convenient."

"You shouldn't have asked me something like that," I say, which doesn't come out right either. I should just stitch my lips shut. I've got some needles and thread in my bag for wounds and everything.

"Fine." Ryan's voice is sharp. "I won't ask again."

We're both silent. When I risk a glance at Ryan, he's glaring at the pond. I say, "I can take first watch if you want to sleep."

"First?" Ryan asks. "I'm surprised you'd let me take watch at all. I'm from Fates. What if I do something?"

My embarrassment suddenly gives way to anger. "You don't have any right to be this . . . this childish! A few nights ago you searched me while I was sleeping!"

"You hid the map from me!"

"I didn't trust you!"

"Because I'm from Fates!"

"Yes," I snap. "Because you're from Fates. Happy?"

"Tired." Ryan pushes to his feet, going immediately to his rucksack. As he passes me, he says: "Your hair looks bad when it's down."

I hate that the first thing I do is grab for my hair. "Childish."

"Not that your hair looks good braided either."

"I don't know why I expected a fifteen-year-old to be mature."

Ryan sets out his blanket on the other side of the clearing. "I'm sixteen now, same as you."

"I'm *seventeen* now."

"Whatever." Ryan curls into his blanket. "Don't talk to me; I'm going to sleep."

You're the one who kept talking, I think, managing to keep my mouth shut this time. Agitation simmers under my skin, bringing with it a heat so intense I'm sure if I was wearing my wet clothes they'd be long dried. Moving to sit with my back against the wall, I glower at Ryan's distant form. He's turned away from me, perfectly still. I always thought he was mean, but I never realized how truly frustrating he could be. It's a different sort of frustrating than Gammon, though. Still, I'd love the chance to push Ryan into a body of water. My gaze flits to the pond. Maybe in the morning.

Hours have passed. I spent some time checking my arrows. Now I'm sharpening my short sword to perfection, going as slowly as possible to kill time. Guarding is so boring, but with Kleos potentially nearby, I don't want to risk both of us being out cold.

Ryan's asleep. Has been for a while. He started shivering a little while ago, but I'm not giving him my blanket, because I'm shivering too. My still-damp hair, lying against my neck, makes it feels as if someone's dumped a bucket of ice cubes down the back of my shirt. Clara did that to Tanner once, when we graduated to level three. It was at someone's birthday party. No wonder so many of our classmates whispered about Clara as much as they did, when Clara would steal the limelight even at another person's party.

I try to shut down the memory, but I don't manage to banish it until I hear whimpering. I'm instantly alert but realize almost immediately that the sound's coming from Ryan.

Laying aside my short sword, I pull my blanket around my shoulders and push to my feet. He's quieted by the time I reach him. Since falling asleep he hasn't moved at all, so I have to step around him to see his face. His brows are knit together, and he's frowning. As I crouch to get a better look, he starts whimpering again. Suspicious, I gently touch his cheek. My fingers come away damp.

I shake his shoulder. He needs his sleep, especially to finish the trek tomorrow, but I keep shaking him. I even say, "Ryan."

He wakes up. When his eyes land on me, I see they're bloodshot. His voice is groggy. "What are you doing?"

"Are you OK?"

"I'd be better if I was sleeping. What's your problem?"

"You were crying."

He touches his cheek, then starts rubbing at his eyes.

"Damn it," he says. "*Damn it.* I didn't even do this when she died."

At first I'm puzzled. We don't know if Cassie's dead or not. Then I remember how long Ryan's been in the labyrinth. "She" could be anyone. An old scavenger, even a girl from his Fallen Day.

"Did you have a dream?" I ask.

"What's it to you?" His voice breaks as he says it, taking away the venom. He presses both hands to his eyes and curses.

I sit next to him. The edge of my blanket laps over the edge of his. "When I first entered the labyrinth, my friend died."

"Oh, so now *you're* telling *me* survivor stories?"

I ignore him. "We'd been best friends since we were little, and she was ripped apart right in front of me. I gave her a present when we became Icarii. A hair clip. It fell when the screechers caught her. I wonder, sometimes, if it's still there."

Ryan's quiet a moment. Then he rolls on his back so he can stare up at the sky. "Cassie was the first Icarii I ever saved. Her first night in the labyrinth, after we brought her back to Fates, I took her out to see the sunrise. I had this speech planned, sort of, to tell her about how every sunrise was an accomplishment, so she could understand what it really meant that she'd made it through her first night. I didn't get to say any of that. When the sun came up, she gasped and said, 'It's beautiful.' She was so in awe of the sunrise, and I was so in awe of her, neither of us said anything. When it was over I just took her back inside, and I told myself that she would be the one I'd protect, no matter what."

When Ryan's done, I don't know what to say. I didn't realize there was a sweet side to him. He's got a faraway look in his eyes now, which makes me feel oddly lonely.

"I'm glad I didn't give the speech," Ryan says. "I would have butchered it. I was taking it from Sybil. She took me out after my first night in the labyrinth, just like that, to see the sunrise, so I'd understand. Sybil did that with everyone. It was a ritual. I was the only Icarii to make it back to Fates that year, so it was just Sybil and me, watching the sunrise. She told me she'd do everything in her power to make sure I never missed a sunrise. Then she said whether I wanted to sleep through it or not was up to me. She just wanted me to have the choice."

Ryan falls silent. He's still shivering. So am I. I edge closer to him. If he notices, he doesn't let on.

"Sybil used to go farther into the labyrinth than anyone," Ryan says. "It's why Fates knows as much of it as we do. It's how we know what digger territory looks like, even though most of us have never seen it. Sybil was killed in their territory by an adult digger a week before my first Fallen Day as a member of Fates.

"I told myself I'd kill the digger. I'd just turned twelve. The Fallen Day after Sybil's death was when Andrea joined us. She was older, so she advanced more quickly through training until it got to the point where we were training together. She looked out for me. She said I reminded her of her brother if he'd known how to shut up. I started looking out for her too. Eventually I told her about my dream to kill an adult digger. She said she'd help me. Neither of us had seen a digger before.

"One day our group strayed into digger territory. We were attacked by a digger. It wounded our group leader before I killed it, with Andrea's help. I was so excited, but then the tremors started. We thought it was an earthquake. Somehow, Andrea and I found enough sense to get out of the way before it appeared. We thought we'd killed an adult, but it had been a newborn. The real digger appeared and swallowed the infant and our group leader both. It took Andrea days to recover. It took me way longer. Even though a boy had been killed right in front of me, I didn't care about him. I only cared because after that I knew what it looked like when Sybil died."

I don't know what to say, so I don't say anything. I'm full of sympathy for Ryan, but if I try to express that he'd probably think I was pitying him and get angry. Still, I wish there was something I could do.

Hesitantly, I ease myself down next to him. His gaze darts to me, slightly startled, as if he forgot I was here.

"What are you doing?" he asks.

"You're cold," I say, looping half of my blanket over him.

"Don't you have to guard? You'll fall asleep if you lie down."

"I won't fall asleep," I say. In truth, I'm probably too cold to fall asleep. Despite my exhaustion, if I focus on the chill rolling over me, I can stay alert.

Abruptly, Ryan sits up. I think he's going to move away from me, which is even more insulting than him telling me to leave him alone. Instead, he pulls off his blanket, so that mine is against him. My cheeks heat when I realize this leaves us directly under the same blanket, but I force myself to push away the stupid thought. Ryan spreads his blanket over both of us before lying down again. He shifts around more than necessary. I think he's trying to get as far away from me as possible while still staying under the two blankets. Even as he shifts away, I feel the warmth radiating off him.

The next morning I wake Ryan up, we eat, and we leave. I tell him we'll reach my base before nightfall. It's just within Kleos' territory, so we can keep searching from there. Apart from that, our walk is silent until Ryan asks, "Is that it?"

Glancing back, I find he's stopped beside the Kleos shield. I didn't even notice we were passing it. I nod and continue on. After a moment, I hear Ryan follow. A moment more and he asks, "Why don't you want to run into them?"

"I told you. They're annoying."

"No. You were in a panic. You didn't want them to find us. Why?"

I increase our pace. He matches it easily. His legs are longer than mine now.

"If we're doing this together," Ryan says, "I need to know what's going on."

"I didn't have to take you with me."

"And I'm supposed to be content with that?"

He is supposed to be, yes, so I don't reply. I walk faster. Ryan stops walking.

"What are you doing?" I ask, turning to him.

"I'm not going into the labyrinth blind when the person with me knows what's ahead."

I did that with the Executioner all the time. "You're being —"

"Childish?"

I clamp my mouth shut, flashing back to last night. I'm suddenly afraid he'll bring it up. "I don't know why Kleos was out here, and I don't want to chance an encounter until I do. I want to avoid them. Call it instinct."

"Instinct? Since when have you had that?"

"You're such a brat." I turn back around. Ryan picks up his pace and passes me in seconds, only to block my way. I try to step around him. He moves with me.

"Annoying, isn't it?"

"We need to get to my base. Bother me about this there."

"What if we run into Kleos before that?"

I should just tell him. But all I have are suspicions, and if they're wrong, I don't want to upset him over nothing.

"Do you not want them to know I'm with you?"

"What?"

"You did say they're a group of guys," Ryan says. "At least one of them must have caught your interest. You *are* a girl."

So one moment he's asking if the guys are giving me problems, and the next he thinks I'm with one of them? "Don't be ridiculous. That's not it at all."

"It makes the most sense. Maybe it's the leader? You did mention him specifically. He must be an impressive guy."

"He's not. But right now he's much more impressive than you."

"Then again," Ryan continues, "maybe you've got more than one of them."

I shove him, both hands flat against his chest. He takes a half step back, but his impassive expression doesn't flicker.

"It must be nice," Ryan says. "You're self-sufficient, you've got all these bases and your own map, and you've got some guys for when you get bored with the monsters."

He's goading me, and it's working. I let it work. If he's going to be like this, he deserves it. "I think Kleos might be involved with the attack on Fates."

Ryan's expressionless mask breaks. *"What?"*

"They never stray this far from their territory," I say. "If they do, it's not back toward Daedalum; it's deeper into the labyrinth. And they know about Fates. They look down on it. I'm not sure if they'd attack to loot or if they have some kind of vendetta, but they could have done it. They have the numbers."

"You said they were just annoying. You said they weren't that bad."

"They're not. At least, I didn't think they were. But humans attacked Fates, and the shield's there, so —"

"That could mean anything! Why would you jump to such a stupid conclusion?"

"I haven't," I snap. "I know I could be wrong, that's why I didn't want to tell you until I was sure."

"How could you ever be sure?" Ryan's shaking. "Go on. Tell me your plan. Tell me how you'd prove something so stupid."

"Tailing them. Checking out their base. They reveal things when they think I'm not there, so I thought they might say —"

"Might. You don't know anything. You don't know *anything*!"

Ryan immediately falls silent, his chest rising and falling rapidly. I don't know how he lost his breath this quickly, but I understand the pain in his eyes, and it's unbearable.

"Do you think," he asks quietly, "it really could have been them?"

"I don't know." I touch his arm lightly. I don't think it registers. "We've got to keep moving."

After a moment, Ryan presses his lips together and nods. He turns away from me, but when we start walking, he quickly falls to his place at the back.

I shouldn't have told him. I should have put up with his teasing. The moment I decided to tell him, I knew I'd regret it, but another part of me knew I had to tell him. That part of me said I had to get used to hurting people like this, because now that I've learned how to take the harsh truths of the labyrinth, I need to learn how to deliver them.

Later in the afternoon we hear screechers in the distance. They're off our main route, but just in case I lead us a bit farther from the spot. I don't have any reason to fight screechers right now, and after the journey, I want to save my energy for an emergency.

Finally, we reach my base. Once we're inside with the doors locked behind us, I feel a small weight lift off my shoulders. We made it, and we didn't run into Kleos.

Ryan looks around the room, silent. He's been withdrawn ever since our conversation earlier. Then he says, "Does Kleos accept new members?"

"That's not a good idea."

"If they think I'm one of them I can find out if they were involved. They don't have to know where I'm from. I can tell them I'm a new Icarii and that I've managed to survive since Fallen Day and wandered through here. It won't be hard."

"It's going to be more than hard if they find out why you're there. It's too risky. We're better off tailing Kleos members to get information. If they've taken Elle and Cassie, they're bound to talk about it —"

"You can't know that," Ryan snaps. "Besides, that would take too long. Anything could happen to Cassie by then."

He falls abruptly silent, and I'm sure he didn't mean to say the last part out loud. But it doesn't matter. I know he's doing this — willing to risk so much — for Cassie. It's not my place to stop him. Besides, he might find out something about Elle.

Still, the silence stretches between us, and I try to ignore the pain in my chest. I'm sure it's because of Ryan's determination to save Cassie; there's no one in the labyrinth who would be that determined to save me. Not anymore.

I say, "I'll help you under one condition. If we manage to get you into Kleos, then after they've accepted you, you have to meet me somewhere."

"You want me to check in with you?"

"I want to know what's going on."

Ryan studies me, a strange look on his face, so I add, "You still have to translate the rest of the journal."

"Right," he says, and he almost sounds annoyed. Then he says, "Fine. I'll check in with you."

"Then I'll get you into Kleos."

The next day I show Ryan one of my spots for running along the top of the wall. Even though he tries not to let on, I can tell my tactic has impressed him. It takes us a little over an hour of patrolling to find a pair from Kleos meandering through one of their preferred hunting areas. As quickly and quietly as possible, Ryan and I pass them to the nearest drop spot.

"Down the end of the hall," I say. "Two lefts and you'll meet them."

Ryan nods. He's scowling.

"What's wrong?"

"They were carrying spears."

"They probably won't attack you."

"If they do, I'll just shoot them," Ryan says, far too dismissively. He's still frowning.

"Is there a problem?"

"Am I going to have to switch to a spear?"

"While you're there, yes. All Kleos members use spears."

"But I hate spears."

I unsheathe my short sword and with the flat of it, whack Ryan's leg. He gives me an irritated look, which I return. "End of the hall, two lefts, and probably an extra hall by now."

Ryan glares at me a moment longer before taking off. I start to follow him — at a distance. I don't want the Kleos members spotting me and getting scared off before they make contact with Ryan. At the same time, if something goes wrong in the meeting, I want to be there to back him up.

The Kleos pair haven't moved too far beyond their original spot. They're taking their time, talking quietly. One of them is carrying a bag over his shoulder, which is dripping blood. It's no wonder they're taking their time if they've already caught something.

Their reactions are slow when they see Ryan. I'm not surprised, as they're relatively young Kleos members, likely without the experience of Gammon or Jack. Still, this pair has been trained well enough to know to draw on a stranger. Ryan's kept his bow over his shoulder, but I know he could draw and shoot both of them before they get close enough to wound him.

One of the boys shouts at Ryan, but the other shushes him, reminding him they're still in the labyrinth. They approach Ryan slowly and speak more quietly, so I have to strain to make out what they say. They ask him how he got here, who he's with — the usual. Ryan's aloof as ever, but that's not to say he doesn't play the part. The Kleos pair are still wary by the end of it, but they offer to take him back to their base, provided he gives up his weapons.

Despite the gravity of this encounter, I find myself grinning a little. The pain on Ryan's face as he hands over his bow is palpable.

I follow Ryan and the Kleos pair for a while. They don't attack after disarming him, which is always a good sign.

Eventually they turn down a hall where I can't follow due to a break in the walls. They're close enough to Kleos' base now that I feel like Ryan will make it.

Still, as I turn away, I can't help a spark of worry.

It's hard trying to carry on as normal when I have no idea how Ryan's doing at Kleos. I hate the waiting. It reminds me of my time in Fates — waiting for Cassie to give me more sewing, waiting for Addie to tell me about the labyrinth, waiting for Collin to come back and comfort me.

I wonder if Collin's convinced the others that the attack on Fates was my fault. Maybe he's already sent people after me. Fates has never ventured this far into the labyrinth before, so I know I shouldn't be concerned, but I can't help my unease.

To distract myself, I go hunting. I come across a boar sooner than expected. We surprise each other, and the animal recovers first. It plows away, and I give chase. I could catch up and kill it quickly, but as I've learned to do, I focus on herding it closer to my base, so I won't have to drag it as far.

The boar is being uncooperative. It leads me to a dead end, which is frustrating. I either kill it here or risk it doubling back, farther from my base. Gritting my teeth, I swing my bow free and notch an arrow.

There's a hiss, and an arrow embeds in the boar's hide. The boar squeals. Another arrow hits it in the head. The animal collapses.

I whip around and find myself face to face, arrow to arrow, with Gammon. Silas is skulking behind him, and Jack is leaning against the wall.

"It's been a while since I used one of these," Gammon says, nodding to the bow. "But as you can see, I'm a man of many talents."

I don't say anything. I'm waiting for a sign — a flinch, a movement — something to let me know he's going to shoot. If he plans to take me down, I'll take him down at the same time.

"I do, however, have one glaring weakness," Gammon continues, as long-winded as ever, despite being poised to attack. "Hubris, to put it bluntly. Now, I've always believed pride can be a strength as much as it can be a weakness. Like everything, it depends on balance, and I'll admit to tipping the scales now and again. See, I hate being toyed with, made a fool of. Then again, who doesn't? But, as I've got to allow myself this one weakness, I've got to indulge that weakness. I've got to sate it, you could say. With this, I think I'll be sated, and we can call it even."

I guess Gammon isn't over the watering hole incident.

"You cut it down a bit," Jack breaks in, running his knuckles over his arm guards as if testing them. "You took out the bit about it not being personal."

"On re-evaluation," Gammon says, "it's very personal. Should I have added something else?"

"Nah," Jack says. "Much as I like your voice, chief, I like your actions better."

Silas shoots Jack an exasperated look, then jumps when Gammon laughs. His laughter makes his arms shake a bit. The arrowhead bobs. I tense so much my muscles throb.

"What do you want?" I demand.

"She's talkative today," Jack says.

"You're hunting in our territory," Gammon says. "We want our due. And we'll take it. Jack?"

At the prompt, Jack moves forward. My gaze skips between him and Gammon as he approaches. He's not looking at me, eyes fixed instead on the boar.

"Now, now," Gammon says to me. "He's just collecting tomorrow's dinner. Speaking of meals, we're having a feast tonight. Care to come? You'll be our guest of honor."

I glare at Gammon, not moving a muscle.

"I think that's a no," Silas says. "Typically, when she doesn't say anything, it's a no."

"Typically," Jack calls from behind me, and I have to stifle the urge to aim at him, "she doesn't say anything."

"That's too bad," Gammon says to me. "They'll be disappointed. Our new recruits were looking forward to seeing you. So that we could find you sooner, one of our recruits lent me this, to speed up our hunting." Gammon nods to the bow as he speaks. "Then again, maybe 'lent' isn't the right word."

I didn't notice before, but now I do. Gammon has Ryan's bow.

"Good news, boys," Gammon says, "I think our little Fey Bell has changed her mind about joining us for dinner. Or should I call you Clara?"

I freeze. "Where did you hear that?"

"She's *really* talkative today," Jack says.

"From our new recruit," Gammon explains. "In fact, he shared several interesting facts about our little Fey Bell. I, for one, never would have guessed that you're a Fates alumni."

"Ex-Fates, more accurately," Silas breaks in, "as she was kicked out, instead of leaving or 'graduating' in any sense."

I can't move, and yet I'm shaking all over. I can't believe Ryan's actually told them all this. Why would he tell them?

"What did you do to him?" I ask, wishing my voice didn't sound so choked.

"What did we do?" Gammon repeats. "We made him comfortable, and he in turn was very forthcoming. We're very hospitable at Kleos. You'd know that if you'd ever accepted my invitations. But we won't dwell on the past. There's no need, not now that you're joining us for dinner, right, Clara? Oh, but that isn't your real name, is it?"

No. Kleos can't know this. Gammon can't know this. I've come to terms with it and moved on, so it can't come up like this again.

"What *is* your name, Fey Bell?" Gammon asks.

I don't say anything, as much out of rebellion as inability. I wished the other day that my lips were stitched together. I think, now, they are.

Gammon sighs. "Maybe another time. Let's head back. Why not give me your weapons, Clara? You'll get tired carrying all of those."

Clara. *Don't call me that.* The words are on the tip of my tongue, but I can't say them. If I do, he'll know how much it gets to me, if he doesn't know already. I have to hold back. I have to endure.

My arms sting from being clenched so long, but I manage to lower my bow. Silas comes to take it from me, then reaches for my quiver. I shove him away roughly.

Silas trips a bit and glances back at Gammon, but Gammon only grins. We'll see if he's that amused when it's him I'm pushing into a temple lion's den.

I take off the quiver myself and hand it to Silas, followed by my short sword. I understand Ryan's pain when I pass over my spiked ball and chain.

"And the axe," Gammon says. When I don't move, he presses: "The axe, Clara."

Everything in me is screaming to throw the axe at him instead. But he still has his arrow notched. And I still don't know what's going on with Ryan. Even if not for the bow, I'm cornered, and it's three on one. My odds aren't good no matter what.

Giving Silas the axe is a different kind of pain than the chain. It's not my preferred weapon, not by far. When I hold the hilt of my spiked ball and chain, it's like an extension of my arm. The axe is like holding someone's hand. A scarred, rough, warm hand.

"Now your daggers," Gammon says. "We know you have them. In your boots, perhaps?"

I glare at him and keep glaring as I remove those very daggers. I want to cut Gammon's smirk right off his face.

Silas is bogged down with weapons by the time Gammon's ready to leave. Silas transfers them to his rucksack, and I have to bite my tongue on a curse when the spiked ball's long chain tangles and the short sword and axe scrape off each other. If he dents so much as the hilt on any one of my weapons . . .

Jack takes the rucksack from Silas, easily supporting this weight as well as half the weight of the boar, which has been tied to Jack's spear. He and Silas carry the boar between them while Gammon swings Ryan's bow over his shoulder. He waves back the way we came.

"After you, Clara."

Kleos' entrance is a fortified steel door at the center of a hall like any other in the labyrinth. From creeping atop the walls near here, I know there are small smokestacks jutting from the top of Kleos' roof. Inside, I see at least one of those stacks leads to a fireplace at the far end of the main room. To my left are large tankards, presumably for water, though I imagine it must take several dozen trips to fill them up completely. Kleos has the same packed dirt floor and wooden supports as Fates, but it's all in better condition. The layout is different too from what I can see. Admittedly, what I can see isn't much as the room's blocked with Kleos members.

They're all dressed in their usual tunics and trousers, much like the scavengers' clothing at Fates. Some of the Kleos members do have pieces of armor, though. A dented chest-plate here, a rusted gauntlet there. No one has a full set.

Kleos falls silent as we enter, the members' slack-jawed attention on me rather than the boar Jack and Silas carry in. I work at maintaining my cold expression until Gammon's hand clamps on to my left shoulder, making me jump. I hate that Gammon knows he's surprised me.

"Take a seat," Gammon says. "Get comfortable."

"Where is he?" I hiss.

"All in good time," Gammon says. The Kleos crowd parts to allow Gammon to lead me down the table. It's much longer than the one at Fates but has the same benches on either side. There's a chair at the far end, its back to the fireplace. Gammon's chair, I'm sure.

As expected, he directs me to the end of the bench, to the right of the chair. "How's that? Nice by the fire, hmm?"

I glare at him.

He pats my shoulder. "Let the others know if you get thirsty. I'll be back in a moment."

I grab Gammon's wrist before he can leave. When I squeeze as tight as I can, he smirks. "Between your grunts and Harmonia you have enough playmates. I'm not interested in joining the game."

"But I'm not being a proper host if there aren't any games." When I don't respond to this, Gammon sighs. "I believe I've never lived down my first impression with you. Won't you change your mind about me? I really am trying to make you feel at home."

"There's no such thing," I snap, immediately adding, "in the labyrinth."

"Your six months is showing. Just sit and relax. Nobody's going to do anything to you while I'm gone. To be honest, I'm more worried about what you might do to them. Although you're cute when you're like this. I didn't realize you were so clingy."

Immediately, I release him.

"Relax," Gammon says again, and his voice almost sounds genuine. "I'm not as bitter over your previous . . . rebuffs, shall we say? Yes, I'm not as bitter over your past rebuffs as you might think. Quite a bit has happened to both of us since you left. We'll catch up in just a moment, I promise."

I don't care for Gammon's promises, but I don't say anything, letting him leave this time. Gammon slips down the hall to the right of the fireplace. The room is almost completely silent now that he's gone. The Kleos boys are still staring at me. Jack returns from the hall to the left of the fireplace, wiping his hands off on his pants. He spots me immediately and comes over, unperturbed by the tension in the room.

"Water?" he asks. I shake my head and he shrugs. "All right. Just figured you'd be thirsty with all this talking you've been doing. Do you have some kind of throat disease?"

Behind me, someone laughs. It's a surprisingly familiar sound that makes a shiver run down my spine. "That's a new one! I always thought it was just shyness."

"Shyness?" Jack scoffs. "A girl who can drive an axe through a screecher's skull without breaking pace isn't shy."

"That just means she isn't shy with the screechers anymore. I, for one, am glad to hear it."

I turn, then, and he's standing right behind me. He seems even taller, even broader, but that could be his new tunic, which stretches taut over the muscles in his chest. His hair is cut shorter, but in contrast, stubble has started growing on his chin. His grin is so familiar it hurts.

"Hey," Theo says. "Welcome to Kleos."

I wish I'd accepted the water now. My mouth — my whole throat — is as dry as paper.

"Jack," an irate voice calls from the left hall. It's surprisingly distracting, because it's not only female but familiar.

A girl with long curly hair tied in a loose ponytail appears at the mouth of the hall. She throws a bloody spear at Jack's feet. "Unless you want a mouthful of splinters, take your skewer out next time."

"That's my favorite skewer. Be gentle, please . . ." Jack trails off when he realizes the girl isn't looking at him anymore but at me. Her eyes are wide with shock. She takes a stumbling step back.

Cassie's voice is just above a whisper: "What are *you* doing here?"

I shove to my feet. Everyone, apart from Jack, reaches for what weapons they have on hand. I don't know who I'm speaking to, but I know I'm desperate when I ask, "Is Elle here?"

I feel a hand on my shoulder again. This one is gentle, tentative. Theo. "We've got a lot to tell you. For now, just sit back, and when Gammon's done —"

Before I know what I'm doing I've smacked Theo's hand away. "Don't touch me!"

For a moment, Theo looks hurt. Then he backs up, avoiding my eyes. "Got it. Sorry."

My chest throbs. Theo saved me on my first night. He was always kind to me. I feel bad for hurting him, but I can't forget what happened in Fates. It might have been Jay that I ended up stabbing, but as Ryan pointed out before, Theo was going to volunteer. I can't trust him. I can't trust anyone in Kleos.

"Where's Elle?" I repeat. My voice starts to go shrill. "Is she . . . is . . ."

"She's alive," Theo says quickly. "At least, last we heard. Look, we really have to explain what happened. And we will. Soon."

Soon? "I need to know now!" I'm starting to panic. I'm trapped in this tiny place, and there are too many people here and none of them are Elle. My gaze skips back to Cassie. "Where's Ryan?"

Cassie edges behind Jack and says, "Make her leave."

"Might be a bit tricky, seeing as I'm unarmed. Now, if you hadn't thrown my *skewer* on the ground but handed it to me like a civilized —"

Cassie's nails dig roughly into Jack's shoulders. "Do something."

Jack sighs and lazily reaches for his spear. The moment he moves, I slide a hidden dagger out of my sleeve. It catches the firelight, and everyone goes still.

Theo's tone is cautious when he speaks, making an attempt to calm me, almost like he did my first night in the labyrinth. But his tone doesn't matter, because what he says is: "Clara."

I stiffen.

Theo curses. "I'm sorry. I just got used to it, and . . . I'm so sorry."

My eyes are stinging. I'm going to cry. After all this time, after all *this*, I'm going to cry now?

Of course this is when Gammon returns. He's not alone. For a split second, my heart leaps, thinking it's Ryan. But this boy has shorter hair. And it's red.

Kyle glares openly at me, his hatred so raw it burns. Then he averts his gaze, heading for the left hall. Gammon sighs and takes the chair at the end of the table.

"Want me to talk to him?" Theo asks, gaze lingering on the left hall.

"It would be a wasted effort," Gammon says. "He's relatively calm at least and has promised not to take his spear to dinner."

"Yeah," Jack says. "But what about his daggers?"

Gammon cracks a grin, but it's weak. "Speaking of which . . ." His expression shifts to disappointment as he turns to me. "You didn't need to bring your own cutlery. Put that away, Clara."

I throw the dagger at Gammon. Cassie shrieks, and the room erupts. Half of Kleos moves toward me. Jack snatches up his spear. But all that matters is the sweet shock on Gammon's face. It takes him a moment to realize the dagger's not in him but in the wall behind him.

It takes me a moment to realize someone else has entered the room.

"What are you *doing*?" Ryan demands from the left hall, staring at me in shock. I can only stare back.

Seeing Ryan, Cassie immediately releases Jack and runs to him. She latches on to Ryan's arm, trying to tug him back down the hall. "It's OK. They'll get rid of her. C'mon."

Ryan pulls away from Cassie. He glares at me as he snaps, "Back off!"

I'm shocked until I hear Theo right behind me. "I'm just trying to defuse the situation."

"Do you need your sword for that?" Ryan demands.

I glance back just in time to see Theo sheathing a short sword. Theo looks at me, something in his expression begging. "I promise I'd never —"

Ryan appears beside me and shoves Theo. Startled, Theo stumbles back a step.

"Ryan!" Cassie's voice is shrill. "Stop it! She tried to *kill* you!"

Ryan's fury clears, and he returns to Cassie, not looking at me. He stands close to her, hands on her shaking shoulders, trying to comfort her. He speaks to her in a quiet voice, "It's all right, Cassie. I'm all right. It's not like you think. I'll tell you what happened, OK?"

Ryan and Cassie must have reunited this morning, yet since then Ryan hasn't thought to tell her what happened to him with me? What have they been talking about?

It bothers me, although it shouldn't. I'm still in Kleos. And I just threw a dagger at their leader.

"If it's any consolation, Cassie," Gammon says, pulling my dagger from the wall, "trying to kill people is how our Fey Bell's been showing affection as of late. Now that we've gotten all that out of the way, who's hungry?"

Cassie's voice still trembles as she says, "Dinner's not ready yet."

"Kyle offered to give you a hand. Why not check on him?"

Cassie eagerly takes the escape. With a skittish glance at me, she whispers something to Ryan, takes his hand, and tugs him down the hall. Ryan looks back at me, and I think he hesitates, but then he follows Cassie.

Gammon addresses the room. "Come now. This is supposed to be a celebration, and we've got a lot of catching up to do. Sit down."

Hesitantly, the boys do so. Half of them are carrying weapons, which, instead of putting away, they lean in between each other at the benches.

"Your reputation precedes you," Gammon says, catching me eyeing the weapons. "They usually put those away before dinner."

I scowl at him.

Out of the corner of my eye, I see Theo move to sit beside me. He hesitates when I tense, then goes around to the other side of the table. He sits next to Jack, who's directly across from me on Gammon's left. To my left there are at least three free spaces until the first Kleos member. That's fine with me.

As several water pitchers are passed down the table, Gammon waves to Theo. "You've met one of our new recruits already, haven't you, Fey Bell?"

I glare at Gammon, and when the pitcher reaches the Kleos member closest to me, I glare at him. He grimaces and passes the pitcher back the way it came.

"As we, the hosts, are making an effort," Gammon says, "you, as the guest, might do a little as well. And by effort, I of course mean politeness, as opposed to dagger throwing."

For a quick, rash moment, I wish I really had thrown the dagger at his head.

Gammon turns his attention to Theo. "Did she glare this much at Fates?"

"No," Theo says, then in a quieter tone: "But we gave her good reason to . . ."

He's looking at me. I don't meet his gaze. He drew a sword on me a few minutes ago.

"This isn't catching up," I say to Gammon. "This is small talk."

"If Silas were here," Jack says, "he'd point out the two are basically the same. But he's too busy snagging the fatty piece of meat for himself, so I think you owe the lady some answers, Gammon."

"I suppose so." Gammon glances at Theo. "Shall you start, or shall I?"

"I will." Theo looks at me again. "Fates knows about Kleos. The older members, anyway. Collin's done his best to keep us away from Kleos; he doesn't want anyone threatening his power. You . . . you know what he's like."

I don't say anything, because I do know.

"After what happened to you and Felix and Gina, Kyle and I couldn't stand it at Fates anymore. We told Collin we were trying new scavenger routes, but we were really trying to find Kleos. Finally we did, and Gammon agreed to let us join. But then you took Ryan. We all thought you were dead . . ." Theo seems about to say something else, but he pauses. Then he continues. "We stuck around Fates to find out what would happen. When Collin wouldn't make the exchange, we went to Gammon and asked him to help us find you and Ryan. I couldn't believe it when he said he already knew you. We decided to make the move to Kleos right away. But we couldn't leave Cassie. She was falling apart. So I told her what we had planned, that Kleos would help us get Ryan back, and she agreed to come.

"You must know how dangerous the route is from Fates to Kleos; we needed help to get there, especially since Cassie was coming. Aside from her Fallen Day, she'd never been farther from Fates than the watering hole —" Theo cuts himself off quickly with a glance at me, as if concerned. I fight to keep a neutral expression, and eventually he continues. "We asked Cassie to drug dinner the night we left, so the others wouldn't wake up, and when Kleos came we left."

"What about Elle?" I ask immediately. My voice breaks. "Gus?"

Theo's gaze becomes hooded. Before he can say anything, Gammon takes up the retelling. "We didn't know until it was too late, but we were tailed by Harmonia. We ran into them on the way back to our base. It looked like they'd raided Fates, and they had the girl, Elle, with them."

"We tried to save her," Theo breaks in, "but it all happened so fast, and Elle . . . I don't think Elle knew what was going on. She must have followed them, or maybe they decided to recruit her, or —"

"We can't know," Gammon says, giving Theo an almost pitying look. "Harmonia has always been dangerous, but for them to go this far . . . their leader must have gone insane."

"Like Collin," Theo says bitterly.

"You know about Gus?" I ask Theo.

Again, Gammon answers for him. "Ryan told us. Gus must have awoken when Harmonia broke in. My condolences for your friend."

A lump forms in my throat. I always liked Gus, but I never considered him a friend. I never considered any of the kind people from Fates my friends, because back then I thought it was too presumptuous. But now I know, Gus was trying to be a friend to me all that time. Just like Andrea and Cassie and Felix.

But Andrea is back at Fates. Cassie hates me for what I did to Ryan. And Felix . . .

My hand goes to the bell. I squeeze it like it's the lump in my throat, like I can squeeze it apart.

"Are you sure it was Harmonia?" I ask. Although I don't like the leader of Harmonia, I still can't imagine they'd do this.

"We saw them," Theo says. "They were carrying supplies from Fates."

"It was night, wasn't it?" I demand. "Maybe you saw wrong."

"We aren't the enemy here," Gammon interrupts. "Not unless you've made an alliance to which we aren't privy?"

"I'm not with Harmonia," I say, adding mentally, *I'm not with you either.*

"But you've had run-ins with them," Gammon says. "I know attacking other Icarii groups is senseless, but can't you see how Harmonia might be capable of this?"

"You both attack each other all the time."

"Technically," Jack breaks in, taking his time in filling his cup, "we have a truce."

"A shaky truce, admittedly," Gammon says, accepting the pitcher from Jack. He fills his cup, then mine, without asking. "After our fight in the labyrinth, I wonder if we have a truce at all."

"I've offered to go and check," Jack says.

"As much as I appreciate that," Gammon says doubtfully, "we have more appropriate emissaries available."

Jack shrugs and says to Theo, "A guy gets ambushed and accidentally concusses his attacker — who happens to be the second-in-command of Harmonia — and he never lives it down. What a world."

"It's a lot to take in," Gammon says to me, and I get a sense of *déjà vu*. Did someone say that to me back at Fates, when I first arrived at the labyrinth? If so, I can't remember who. "Think on it through dinner. You can let us know later if you'll be staying with us."

I thought he might bring up my staying the night. "Am I supposed to believe I have a choice?"

"Of course you do!" Theo says before Gammon can reply. "This isn't like Fates. You're free to do what you want. Nobody's going to force you to do anything, not here."

I nod at Gammon. "He made me come here."

Theo gives Gammon a sharp look.

"She wouldn't have come otherwise," Gammon says, then to me, "From here on out, you're free to do as you please. If you wish to leave this very moment, we won't stop you. I do, however, implore you to stay, if for nothing more than because we took your kill, and we owe you a meal."

He's got a point there. "Fine," I say, "but only if you give me my weapons back."

Even though the rest of Kleos are pretending to talk among themselves, when I say this, I see several of them reach for their spears. Gammon simply smiles and nods at Jack, who pushes back from the table. He disappears down the left hall, only to reappear a minute later with the rucksack of weaponry. He dumps it on the floor beside me and returns to his seat.

As I bend to open it, Gammon says, "I would appreciate it if you don't arm yourself at the table. This is meant to be a feast of peace, not war."

I push back the flap of my bag. My chain has tangled thoroughly in every hilt available. It's going to take a while to unwind. For now, I free the axe, return it to my belt, and sit back on the bench.

Gammon sighs, unsurprised. "I suppose this is what I like about you, Fey Bell."

"You're the only one who likes that about her," Jack says.

After this, Gammon starts talking to Jack and Theo about one of their hunting routes, as apparently the two were out hunting today and came across a pair of deer, which they'll continue tracking tomorrow. Although Theo engages in the conversation, he keeps stealing glances at me, which I don't return. I soon decide to take the chance to untangle my chain, not caring about the awful scraping sounds my weapons make. Every time a Kleos member looks over I glare until they stop looking over entirely.

Eventually, Silas and two young men appear from the left hall, carrying a pile of roasted hares on a platter. Kyle, Cassie, and Ryan are nowhere to be seen. Jack scoots down to make room for Silas. This puts Theo even farther away from me, and I'm not sure if I'm glad or not.

The hares are carved up, and pieces are passed around, at which point everyone starts eating. Eventually, I need a drink. When I tip the cup to my lips, however, the liquid within burns my mouth. I immediately spit it back into the cup, gagging.

Jack laughs, and Gammon smirks at my expression. Silas says, "It's a special drink, which takes around two to three weeks to make at a time. It uses the vines found —"

"It's disgusting," I say, pushing the cup away.

Theo rises and says, "I'll get you some water."

"I can get it myself." I give Gammon a pointed look.

He gestures down the table. "In the barrel by the door."

I push to my feet and stride back through the room, not missing the way each Kleos member goes rigid as I pass behind them. I catch a few glancing at my axe.

There are several barrels by the door. Extra cups are stacked on top of one of the barrels, which has a tap in its side. Uncertain, I take one of the cups and reach for the tap.

"Not that one," Theo says, coming over to me. "That's the same stuff you had before. This one, here, is the water."

I wait for Theo to move out of the way. When he realizes that's what I want, he steps back. I fill up my cup, wondering why he's waiting for me. Did Gammon send him down here, afraid I'd escape when given the chance?

"Hey," Theo says quietly, when I'm finished at the barrel. "Can we talk for a minute? Outside. Would you mind?"

My hand tightens around my cup so hard it shakes. Water sloshes at the rim, threatening to spill over.

"Stupid question," Theo says. "Of course you'd mind. Look, it won't take long, and you can leave whenever you want. I just think we need to talk about . . . OK, how about this: I'm unarmed, and you can keep that axe at my throat?"

When I don't say anything Theo rubs the back of his neck. "Bad joke. But really, I don't have anything on me. And we can leave the door open if you want."

As if that would make me feel better. After a moment I put down my cup and head for the door. Theo follows.

It's gotten dark outside. I'm not surprised; the sun was setting when we arrived at Kleos. Theo comes out behind me, keeping a careful distance. He leaves the door open but I say, "You can close it."

Theo seems to take this as a good sign, smiling a little, if uncertainly. He closes the door. He doesn't get that, this way, if we wind up in a fight, it'll take Kleos longer to rescue him.

Even thinking about it, the idea of hurting Theo, causes a knot to form in my stomach. I know it's all sentimentality, but I can't help it. I start to reach for my bell.

My hand clenches. Falls to my side. This too is sentimentality.

"Your new nickname," Theo says, "it's fitting. I was kinda confused, when I first heard it, because of the bell part. Still, it sounded fitting, somehow. Anyway, I get it now. So, what's up with the bell? I'm either deaf, or it's not working."

"It's working," I murmur.

"Sorry, what was that?"

"What do you want?"

"I want to talk about what happened the night before you left. I didn't know Collin was planning to send you guys to the watering hole."

"So?"

"What I mean," Theo says, "is if I'd known, I would have stopped it. Even if it meant leaving Fates. I wouldn't have let that happen to you. None of you deserved it."

"No?" I echo. "Did I deserve everything else Collin did?"

"Of course not!"

"Then why were you going to volunteer?" My voice breaks, and I hate myself for it. Not only is my voice broken, but it's weak and shrill. It's the voice of the girl who was trampled in Fates, not of the girl who fought a hundred-headed monster.

"I was trying to help," Theo says. "I thought if I played along, I could get you out of it somehow. Everyone knew what Collin was planning at that point, and I thought if I volunteered, I could keep you safe. I was never going to do anything to you. I'd never . . . I'm sorry. I was being a coward. I should have just stood up to him, like Andrea. Even after you and Jay left, I could have gone after you, but I was afraid of what Collin would do. Everyone was afraid of what he would do."

"Jay wasn't afraid," I say. "Addie wasn't afraid."

"Addie wasn't always that way. The labyrinth's changed her, like it changes everyone."

"Is that an excuse?"

"No," Theo says. "I'm sorry if it sounds like I'm making excuses. I'm not. Or maybe I am. I don't know. I just want you to understand I'd never hurt you." Theo's tone becomes harder, frustrated. "I didn't save you on Fallen Day just so Collin could do what he did. That's not what Fates stands for — not what it stood for."

Theo must be talking about Sybil. I don't say anything, and after a moment, Theo continues, "I really thought you were dead, all this time. After what we saw at the watering hole . . ."

"What do you mean?"

"Ryan didn't tell you? We went after you, Ryan, Andrea, and I. But it was too late."

I stare at Theo, surprised but probably not for the reason he thinks. Ryan told me he and Andrea did that. He didn't mention Theo at all.

I realize, then, that Theo is staring at me too. "It's crazy how much you've changed."

"The labyrinth changes people, right?"

I know I shouldn't have said it the moment it's out. Theo deflates. "I guess so. I just meant that you seem more confident. Older. I almost wouldn't have recognized you if not for the braids."

"You look older too," I say, and again I find myself regretting my words. This time, it's a different regret, and I get a different response. He grins.

"Do I look like an old man yet?"

"You're not that old."

"I am, though," he says, sobering again. "For being here. I've got a year and a half until Sybil's record. Less than that."

Unsure of what to say, I reach for my bell again and again stifle it, instead choosing to squeeze the hilt of my axe.

"Whoa," Theo exclaims. "What did I say?"

"What?"

"The axe. If you're going to hit me with it at least tell me what I did wrong. But please don't hit me with it."

"I'm not . . ." I release the hilt. "It's just a nervous habit."

"Hitting people with axes is a nervous habit? You really have changed."

Glancing up, I find Theo grinning. I don't return it. "You drew on me in there."

Theo's grin disappears. "I wasn't drawing on you. I just had to let them think that. Gammon's way better than Collin, but I still don't trust any of them entirely. If they'd attacked you, I was going to back you up."

"Oh." I can't think of anything else to say. I feel suddenly, stupidly, embarrassed. I thought the worst of Theo just because Ryan did. I shouldn't trust Ryan so instinctively.

Then again, I can't trust Theo either.

"You're talking more," Theo says suddenly. "I like it."

I feel my face heat, and I'm instantly glad it's so dark out. "I don't see why everyone has to make a big deal out of it."

"It's because you have such a pretty voice," Theo says. "No one can understand why you don't use it more."

I know Theo's only joking around, but I feel myself blush again. I fight the urge to slap my cheeks. I need to pull it together.

"How did you do it?" Theo asks. "I don't mean I had no faith in you, but you left Fates without weapons or knowledge about how to survive in the labyrinth, so how did you make it this far?"

"You don't know?" I ask, surprised. I figured Ryan would have told them, along with the other information.

Theo is equally surprised. "How would I know?"

Suspicious, I ask, "Who told Gammon about my time at Fates?"

"Oh. That. Um . . . sorry. It's just, between exchanging stories and stuff, Kyle and I ended up forking over some sort of delicate details. That drink of theirs didn't help matters. If you ever start liking the taste, don't have too much in one sitting. It makes people kinda dumb and definitely loose-lipped. So, yeah, sorry. What did he say to you, exactly?"

"It doesn't matter." I don't want to dredge it up any more than necessary.

"I ruined it, didn't I?"

"Ruined what?"

Theo gestures between us. "This. Our reunion. Or whatever it is. My attempt to make things up to you."

"You don't have to," I say, not so much because I think I've forgiven him, but because agreeing to him owing me a favor means I think I'll stick around. I could be gone again in a couple of days. We could never see each other after that.

I don't know why, but the thought upsets my stomach. Then again, so does thinking we'll stay together.

"I'll definitely make an effort to make things up to you," Theo says as if it's decided. "So, uh, not to ruin things even more, but I want to know. Gammon and the guys didn't use force to get you here, did they?"

"Not exactly," I say, "but Gammon did have an arrow pointed at me."

"He *what?*"

"To be fair, I had an arrow pointed at him too." I don't want to be generous with Gammon, but at the same time, I don't want it to seem like I was so taken by surprise I couldn't defend myself. *When did that become an issue for me?*

"You had an arrow pointed at him? Right, I forgot. You can shoot now. You took out all those screechers, didn't you? Back when you took . . . um, back when you ran into Andrea and the others."

He was going to say, "back when you took Ryan." I stare at my boots, suddenly feeling very guilty.

"I knew you wouldn't hurt him," Theo says. "I was stunned you'd managed to get the better of three of our scavengers, let alone take out a flock of screechers, but I knew you'd never hurt Ryan."

I think about all the times I drugged Ryan and tied him up and punched him and knocked him out. But the punching was his fault.

"I've gotta admit," Theo says, "I'm curious how you two went from kidnapper and kidnappee to . . . well, to him defending you back there."

"Necessity."

Theo laughs. "That explains a lot."

"I was going to return him to Fates," I say. "That's when we found out what happened. He wanted to find Cassie. I want to find Elle. We ended up going in the same direction."

Theo nods, seeming content with this. Then he gets serious again. "These Harmonia people — you've encountered them, right? What reason do you think they'd have to attack Fates? Silas thought it might have something to do with finding new recruits, but if that's true I don't see why they'd just take one girl and Elle of all people. She's not physically strong, and from what I've heard, that's what Harmonia's looking for."

"I don't know," I say. Theo's making valid points. Why would Harmonia only take Elle? They don't know her. The reward isn't worth the risk.

"It doesn't make sense," Theo says, echoing my thoughts. "I just hope Kleos comes up with something soon. I'm worried about Elle, and I'm worried Harmonia's planning another strike on Fates."

Although I couldn't care less about what happens to Collin's side of Fates, I don't want the rest of them to get hurt. And I certainly don't want anything to happen to Elle.

"Kleos wants to do something?"

"Of course," Theo says, surprised. "When we told them Ryan was taken, they agreed to help. Why wouldn't they do the same for Elle?"

Because I never pegged Gammon, or any of Kleos, as that generous.

"We should get back," Theo says. "Dinner's probably cold by now. My fault. I should have waited, I know, but I wanted to get everything out in the open."

"No," I say. "I'm glad you did."

Theo smiles but only for a moment. "What are you going to do?"

"What do you mean?"

"Will you leave after dinner?" Theo asks. "I know Gammon will let you stay the night if you decide to do that. Cassie has her own room. It's tiny, but you could bunk with her. And in the morning we could discuss what to do about Harmonia. But I'd understand if you want to get out after this, considering how they brought you here."

"I might stay," I say, which clearly pleases Theo.

Theo reaches for the door, but before he can open it I say, "What's wrong with Kyle?"

"It's nothing," Theo says, then: "Well, it's something. But we're working on it."

"Tell me."

"It's just . . . and don't worry about it too much, because I'll get through to him eventually — he blames you for Felix's death."

Theo is right about the meal being cold. I don't care. Meat is meat. I'll eat what I'm given, even when I don't have an appetite. I've learned by now to eat my fill whenever possible. Food isn't just about hunger anymore; it's about building up my store of energy.

As expected, Gammon is disgustingly pleased by my decision to stay. He declares that we'll discuss the Harmonia issue in the morning. After the plates are cleared away, Theo shows me to Cassie's room. It's not really a room but a small amount of floor space in a storage closet. A pile of blankets are shoved in the corner.

"It's not exactly a deluxe suite," Theo says, "but it's better than bunking with all these guys. I thought Fates was a tight fit, but this place? There isn't even room to roll over."

There won't be room for that in here either. I can't say I relish the thought of spending the night in close quarters with a girl who thinks I've gone crazy. But I don't say any of this to Theo, just drag my bag of weapons into the closet. After he explained himself outside, I'm starting to feel more comfortable around him again, which, in a way, is making me uncomfortable. I'm wary of letting my trust return so easily.

"Can you really use all of those?" Theo asks, gesturing to my bag. When I nod, he says, "Which is your favorite?"

Surprised, I gesture to the chain and spiked ball on my belt.

"Really? That's too bad. I was hoping you'd join my team." Theo pats the hilt of his short sword.

"Don't you use a club?"

"Sometimes, but I left that back at Fates in the rush. I prefer swords, anyway. Andrea and I would take turns on club duty when we scavenged together. Hey, you're lucky I was the one with the club on your Fallen Day. My reflexes are much quicker than Andrea's."

"No, they're not." Ryan's irritated voice comes from just behind Theo. Theo turns, revealing Ryan and Cassie in the hall behind him.

"What's going on?" Cassie demands. "Why is she in my room?"

"She's staying the night," Theo says.

Cassie starts to shake again, and for a moment, it looks like she's going to cry. Then she says, "I'll just sleep in the kitchen."

"Don't be silly, Cass. She's not going to do anything."

"How can you say that when she has *that*?" Cassie jabs a finger at my bag of weapons. "She's crazy and dangerous!"

I'm not sure if Cassie is wrong, but I'd never hurt her, even if her reaction is hurting me. I guess I deserve it for taking Ryan from her, but now they've reunited, and he should have explained everything.

"I'll go somewhere else," I say, picking up my bag again.

Theo starts to speak, probably concerned that I'll leave Kleos, but Ryan beats him to it, speaking to Cassie. "I'll stay with you in the kitchen, OK?"

Cassie relaxes, and Ryan squeezes her hand. *When did they start holding hands? Have they been holding hands this whole time?*

"I'll set places by the fire," Cassie says, half to herself. "It'll be warm there. I just need . . ." Cassie's gaze goes dark when she looks at me again. She turns away. "I'll get blankets from the other closet."

Cassie and Ryan head down the hall. I'm still looking after them when Theo says, "Don't worry about it. Cassie's just spooked after going through the labyrinth again. Everything has her on edge. She'll be back to herself soon, especially now that Ryan's here."

Ryan glances back at the sound of Theo's voice. I wonder if he can hear what Theo's saying, then I stop wondering because Theo squeezes my arm. As soon as he does, my gaze skips to his. He's giving me that same reassuring smile he offered on my first night in the labyrinth.

Before I can decide whether to slap him away again or not, Theo's hand drops from my arm, and he says, "Need anything else?"

I need to know if I can really trust you.

I shake my head, and Theo bids me good night. After he's gone, I check out the storage room. It's all medical and cooking supplies, along with some linens. They must keep the weapons elsewhere. I try the door, but there's no way to lock it. I contemplate barricading it, but the door opens outward, so that wouldn't work. As a last resort, I grab a few empty jars off the shelves and break them against the wall, then scatter the shards in front of the door.

Finally, I return all my weapons to their rightful places, then bunch up the bag and use it as a pillow, since there isn't one among Cassie's blankets. Kleos must not have pillows either. It's a small, petty thought, but it makes me feel better.

I wake up to hushed curses. I'm up in an instant, axe unsheathed. I swing for the intruder, but he grabs me by the arm, halting my swing and shoving me back against the wall. With my other hand, I slash my dagger toward his side.

"It's me," Ryan says.

I manage to stop myself before cutting him, though I do slash his tunic. It takes me a moment to catch my breath, still easing down from the panic.

"If I let go," Ryan says, "are you still going to cut off my head?"

His breath puffs against my cheek. I can barely see him in the darkness, but I can feel him, inches away. He's warm. From the fire in the kitchen. Maybe from Cassie.

The thought shocks me, and I shove it away immediately, saying, "I wasn't going to cut off your head. I was aiming for your arm."

"My mistake." His voice is heavy with sarcasm.

He lets go, and I put away my weapons, then roll my shoulders. I can't seem to unwind. My heart hasn't calmed yet either. I wish Ryan would take a step back, but I don't push him away, even though I keep thinking I should.

"Why the glass?" Ryan says. "Don't you trust our hosts?"

The way he says it gives me pause. "Do you?"

"They've been good to Cassie," Ryan says carefully. "They haven't given her any problems. She says it's better here than at Fates."

He didn't answer my question, but that can wait. "Did you tell Cassie what happened between us?"

Ryan's quiet a moment, then he says, "Which part?"

"I don't know. All of it. The parts that would make her stop hating me."

"All I told her was that you drugged me and then tried to return me to Fates."

"Why?" My voice goes shrill. "She's going to hate me forever like that! Why not just tell —"

Ryan presses a hand over my mouth, shifting closer to me in the process. My face flames.

Before I can slap him away, he says, "We have to be quiet. Gammon's got people patrolling the base."

"And why would that bother you? You'll side with them, won't you, since they've been so good to Cassie?"

I can hear Ryan's scowl in his voice. "We both know the labyrinth isn't that simple. Have you told them about the map?"

"Of course not."

"What about Theo?"

"No." *Not yet.*

"I haven't told Cassie either. That's why I didn't tell her about what really happened with us. I think it's better we keep the map to ourselves, for now."

I think so too, but . . . "Why do you think that?"

Ryan hesitates a moment, then says, "We made a deal, right? I translate the journal after we find Cassie. We found

Cassie, and I'll come through on my end — just give me the week. As for the map, keep it. You should get to decide what to do with it, but we both know these guys won't see it that way."

"Why not tell Cassie? She'd keep it secret, if you asked her to."

"In the past, maybe . . ."

"What's changed?"

Ryan still doesn't answer right away. Finally, he says, "She thinks you've brainwashed me."

"What? That's ridiculous! How could I? *Why* would I?"

"I don't know, but I can't trust her with this right now. She'd just tell Theo or Kyle or that Jack guy, and then Gammon would find out."

"What do you think of him?" I ask, curious about someone else's opinion of Kleos' leader.

Ryan's response is immediate. "He's arrogant, and he doesn't know when to shut up. I don't like him."

This is reassuring, as I feel the same way, but then I remember that Ryan doesn't like most people. Theo seems to like Gammon.

Which reminds me . . . "When you and Andrea went looking for us at the watering hole, why didn't you tell me Theo was there too?"

"Does it matter that I didn't?"

So Theo *did* try to find me. "Of course it matters. Why didn't you tell me?"

"I didn't leave it out on purpose."

If that was true, he would have said that right away. And he's not even trying to say it in a convincing tone.

"You *did* do it on purpose. Why? If you'd told me, I wouldn't have…"

"Wouldn't have what?"

Thought the worst of Theo. "Jumped to conclusions." Pausing, I add, "Jumped to *your* conclusions."

"Which have to be wrong, right?" Ryan sneers. "Because Theo's such a nice guy."

"Why are you acting like this? You two were on a team together!"

"Exactly. I know what he's like. But you don't, and you won't see him for what he really is until . . ."

"Until what?" I snap.

"Never mind."

I grab him by the arms when he starts to back up. "Finish."

"Why should I? You believe him, that's obvious. I knew you would. Even if you've wised up to the labyrinth, you're as oblivious as ever when it comes to people."

I push him away, not caring if he stumbles onto the glass again. I was going to ask if he'd cut his feet, but I don't care anymore. I hope he cuts them again.

I say, "The only person I've judged wrong recently is you. You're as mean and impossible as I first thought."

"I don't know what I did to make you think that changed."

"Get out."

I think I hear Ryan scoff, then he turns and slips out through the door. After he's gone I slowly sink back onto my bed. I try to figure out how we went from talking about keeping the map a secret to arguing, but I'm too flustered to think properly.

Still, I'm together enough to realize I still need Ryan to translate the journal. And I've just told him how mean and impossible I think he is.

In the morning I'm exhausted, my muscles are cramped everywhere, and I have a pounding headache. I blame it on the inferior pillow.

In the hall, I pass a young Kleos member. He gives me a wide berth. His gaze doesn't leave the hilt of my short sword. He should be watching the chain.

In the main room, Gammon and Silas are already at the table talking. When they see me, Gammon smiles. Silas offers a grimace of greeting before ducking his head.

Gammon waves at the bench. "Please, sit."

"Have you decided what to do about Harmonia?" I ask, not sitting.

Silas rubs both hands over his face, muffling his words. "We only got up half an hour ago. We're not all super-energetic at dawn."

Seeming to remember who he's talking to, Silas freezes. Slowly, his hands slide down his face, revealing his eyes. He blinks at me, looking as if he's just stepped next to a digger, and he's not sure if it's sensed him yet.

"We were discussing Harmonia," Gammon says. "We've made progress. Care to join us?"

Again, he indicates the bench. Begrudgingly, I sit.

"We've made *some* progress," Silas says, "and really, that depends on your definition of progress. We have ideas. Musings, more accurately. Poorly drawn musings."

"I do wonder sometimes," Gammon says, looking at Silas, "if something were to happen to me, how would you rally Kleos? Because — I'm sorry, Silas — but I don't believe you have the knack for motivational speeches."

"Your ideas," I cut in. "What are they?"

"There's one," Gammon says. "We were discussing it just now. Silas is right; it's not very developed, but it's shaping up to be our best bet."

"Let's not talk about that now." Silas's gaze darts between Gammon and me. He drops his voice: "She won't like it."

"I don't see why she wouldn't," Gammon says. "It's more or less her plan."

"Explain," I say.

"As you did for us," Gammon says, "we were thinking of sending Harmonia a new recruit. To assess the current situation."

"I've refused them already," I say. "They think of me as an enemy now."

"They'll change their minds," Gammon says, "given the proper prompting. They know as well as we do that after our fight another territory war is inevitable. You just have to go to them acting like you did yesterday, believing that Kleos may have been behind the incident at Fates. They'll latch on to that in order to convince you to side with them. They know you'd be a valuable ally against us. They won't pass up the opportunity."

"And if they do? I could find myself with an arrow in my throat."

"We'll be there to back you up," Gammon says. "At a distance, naturally. And you'll also be armed. If they haven't killed you yet, I doubt they'll manage to do so. At least, I doubt they'll try to, not when they can so easily acquire their very own secret weapon."

Is that how Gammon thinks of me already: a secret weapon? *Kleos'* secret weapon?

"I'll think about it," I say, just as Cassie appears with two plates. She pauses when she sees me, then completely ignores me as she hands the plates of breakfast to Gammon and Silas.

Theo comes out behind Cassie, followed by Kyle. When Theo sees me, he immediately looks at Kyle, whose jaw has clenched. I think Kyle's going to say something, maybe lash out, but he just turns on his heel and walks back the way he came. Shortly after, a door slams.

Theo sighs. "I'll go talk to him."

"If we're going to be working together," Silas says cautiously, "perhaps it's best they hash it out themselves?"

"You agreed to the plan?" Theo asks me, surprised. "To be honest, I thought you'd take some convincing. I did. I'm still not sure I'm convinced."

"I haven't agreed yet," I say, immediately giving myself a mental reprimand for adding the "yet."

"I don't see why any of you need convincing," Silas says. "It may just be the start of a plan, but it's an extremely logical plan."

"It's a dangerous plan," Theo says. "If these girls really attacked Fates, why wouldn't they do the same to Cla — to, um, her."

"Because there are politics at play," Gammon says. "Besides, our Fey Bell can handle a few Harmonians."

Theo is clearly even less convinced. He looks to me searchingly, as if waiting for me to tell Gammon he's wrong or crazy.

Instead, I hear myself say: "I've faced worse."

Theo is surprised, and I don't know if it's because I agreed with Gammon, or because he still can't believe that I can take care of myself. Gammon, on the contrary, is very pleased that I've finally sided with him.

"So you'll do it?" Silas asks. "We need to know, because scouts have to be sent out well in advance to try and locate a group of Harmonians close enough to our territory for backup."

"That's a waste of time," I say. "If I do it, I can find the Harmonians myself."

"But you can't go alone," Silas says. "We have to know what happens to you in the encounter."

"I'll go," Theo says immediately.

"Good," Gammon says. "We'll send Jack too when he finally gets up."

I almost remind Gammon that I haven't agreed yet, but I keep my mouth shut, because I know I'm going to do it. Not for Kleos or for Fates but for Elle.

After breakfast, I insist on leaving right away. When Silas tries to make a case for sending out scouts again, I break in and say that if Jack's coming with us, someone had better wake him up before I do. Gammon says he'll do it and suggests Theo take this chance to talk to Kyle before we leave. In short order, I find myself alone with Silas at the head of the table. While most of Kleos have left for the day, those who remain keep their distance from me.

Silas keeps peeking at me but, whenever I look at him, his gaze drops back to the table. He's started rubbing his nails against the pads of his fingers. It's a strange, fidgety action that's also uncomfortably familiar. My father used to do something very similar when he was nervous, usually when he was talking to a neighbor who was older and better spoken.

Silas blurts out, "Do you really think you can handle Harmonia?"

"If you don't think I can handle them, why pick me for your plan in the first place?"

"It was mostly at Gammon's insistence. Look, I don't doubt your skills; I doubt you truly understand what Harmonia's capable of doing."

"I saw what they did to Fates. What else do I need to know?"

"Gammon hasn't told you, then."

"Told me what?" I ask testily.

"What happened between us and Harmonia."

My annoyance is instantly replaced by curiosity. Since learning of the two groups, I've wondered what caused the hatred between them. Not that I ever intended to ask about it. If Gammon knew how curious I am, he'd likely feel he'd won against me in some way. I know I'd feel as if I'd lost.

So to Silas, I simply say, "I don't know what happened between you two."

"You should, before deciding if you can take on this job."

"You almost sound concerned."

"I am. If you mess up my plan and Harmonia catches you, they'll guard themselves even more tightly than before. They may even launch an attack against us. What happened at Fates was unprovoked; I don't want to think about what they'll do if we provoke them."

"Then tell me what happened," I say, hoping my impatience masks my burning curiosity. "What did Harmonia do?"

"I suppose some would say it's what we did to each other." Silas winces, then continues, "We were all part of one big group in the beginning. We united on our Fallen Day, and we managed to survive together. Harmonia's leader, she thought we should all follow her, just because she was the first of us to kill a monster. Some of the girls bought into that, but the rest of us could see her single victory didn't make her a leader. Then Gammon joined us."

"He wasn't with you in the beginning?"

"Gammon had the same Fallen Day as us, but his group of Icarii were released in a different part of the labyrinth. He'd lost the rest of his group during a monster attack. When we found him, he'd already been on his own for a long time." Silas shakes his head at this, as if he can't imagine it. "I'd never be able to survive alone like that."

The Executioner had been alone for years.

"We were lucky to run into Gammon," Silas says. "Without him I'm sure our group would have fallen apart. He grew up in the tower where they train the priests of Icarus. He probably would have become one himself if he hadn't become an Icarii. Gammon grew up surrounded by leaders and people learning to become leaders. He was what we needed."

I'm surprised by Gammon's upbringing. I didn't think Icarii were sent from the priests' tower. On Fallen Day, we would watch from our windows as swarms of Icarii made their way through the city, but none ever came from the tower of the priests. I asked my parents about it once. My father explained that the children of the priests' tower are destined to serve Icarus in his temples rather than take the labyrinth test.

"After their service is over," my father said, "Icarus himself comes to guide them through the labyrinth to Alyssia."

I guess Icarus forgot to come for Gammon.

"It's thanks to Gammon that we found this place." Silas gestures around us, indicating the base. "But the leader of Harmonia and her followers, they resented Gammon. I think they believed he stole their power. They argued with him about everything, and they'd slack off and complain when the rest of us voted for Gammon's plans. Then one day they found the place they're now using as their base. We didn't know about it until half the girls disappeared — with as many of our supplies as they could carry. Later the leader of Harmonia called a meeting with Gammon and set out their territory. She said if they ever caught us hunting on Harmonia's lands, they'd shoot us.

"I don't think, at that point, any of us thought they'd actually do it. Even though we'd had our disagreements, we'd all survived together. Surely that had to mean something? But then in Kleos we started to run out of game. In retrospect, we should have seen it coming. Until we split into two groups, we'd been hunting in the same area for almost double our current numbers. But how were we to know Harmonia would form and lay claim to the best hunting grounds for miles? We had no choice but to start hunting in their territory, but we always kept to the edge. We didn't go in any farther than we had to. That didn't matter to Harmonia. They shot one of us."

Before I can ask about the victim, Silas plows on, as if he can't bear to dwell on it. "After that, we knew they meant their threats. We stayed out of their territory as long as we could, but we'd hunted the game in our area to exhaustion. We couldn't live on berries and herbs. We decided to try and reason with the leader of Harmonia, but our envoys were attacked on the way to their base. They had to fight back to escape, and they ended up wounding a Harmonian. So the Harmonians came after us again, for payback, and they killed a boy.

"From then on, we refused to stop hunting in their territory, and they refused to stop attacking our people.

And when we were attacked, we defended ourselves. We didn't want to kill any of them — we didn't even want to hurt them. We all used to be part of the same group! And it wasn't supposed to be anyone's territory. It was supposed to belong to all of us."

"After all that," I say, "how did you work out a truce?"

"A stinger showed up. It was wandering through our territories, killing people from both sides. Gammon managed to convince Harmonia's leader that we had a better chance of defeating it if we weren't fighting among ourselves. The stinger's gone now. But it's only a matter of time before Harmonia tries something or until our game thins out again, and we're forced back into their territory."

I knew Harmonia was hostile, but I never imagined they could do this sort of thing. Then again, was Fates any better? Maybe Polina is more like Collin than I realized.

The thought makes me shiver, and I almost regret agreeing to my mission. But I push all that away, because I can't lose my resolve. Besides, there's still something Silas hasn't explained. "You said that only half the girls joined Harmonia. What happened to the ones that stayed with Kleos?"

"It turned out a few of them were Harmonian spies, and they ran off when the fighting started. As for the others, Harmonia tried to recruit them, but they refused. Even though they hadn't been part of Harmonia in the first place, the leader of Harmonia called them traitors. The next time the girls went out hunting, they didn't return. Just within Harmonia's territory, we found them — well . . . what was left to find." Silas averts his eyes again and folds his hands in his lap where I can't see them. "There was a message left with them, carved in the labyrinth wall: *We feed traitors to the monsters.*"

After a moment's hesitation, Silas says, "I know you've agreed to the plan so you can help your friend, but do you honestly think you can handle Harmonia? Their leader was unstable after our first few weeks in the labyrinth, but she's become bloodthirsty and cruel since. She's capable of anything, and Harmonia will do whatever she says."

"I can handle it," I say. Although seeds of fear are growing rapidly in the pit of my stomach, that fear is just as much for Elle as it is for me.

A half hour later finds me walking through the labyrinth with Jack and Theo. Jack is walking ahead, making a show of stretching and yawning every three minutes. His golden hair looks like a halo in the sunlight, and it doesn't suit him at all.

I don't tell Jack to put up his hood. I'd almost like a screecher encounter right now. Anything to distract me from Silas's words, which still echo through my head. But no screechers grace the sky, which is clear for once. The mist seems to have moved on too.

Jack stretches his arms behind him at an awkward angle. Something in his back cracks. I feel a hand on my elbow and immediately jab backwards, reaching for my axe with my free hand.

"Not again," Theo says. "Please. No axes."

I release the weapon. "Sorry."

"You're really wound up."

"Stretching helps," Jack calls back to us.

Theo frowns, and the next time he speaks his voice is hushed, so only I can hear. "Are you really sure about this?"

"Of course," I say. "I have to get Elle back."

"I know, but you just seem a little off. I thought maybe you were having second thoughts."

I don't want to get into my discussion with Silas. "I'm fine."

"It's OK, you know, if you're having second thoughts. After what Harmonia did to Fates . . ." Theo touches my arm again, like last night, but lighter. "This isn't going to be like fighting monsters."

"I learned how to fight people before I learned how to fight monsters." I speed up, walking out of Theo's touch.

"I'm sorry," Theo says, hurrying to catch up. "I didn't mean to —"

"Hey," Jack calls back. He waves his spear at us. "Labyrinth voices, kids. We're almost out of Kleos."

Theo falls silent, thankfully, and he's not walking right beside me anymore. But I'm still frustrated. How could he think I'd back out of this after surviving for so long on my own? Doesn't he think I'm strong enough?

As I think this, it occurs to me that maybe I wouldn't be so hard on Theo if it weren't for Ryan. It's because of Ryan that I have this doubt, but how much can I really trust either of them? This is just another reminder that there's no room for trust in the labyrinth. It belongs within the walls of Daedalum, between the performers in the Dance of the Angels, trusting each other to bend and sway in tandem, to achieve perfect synchronization. The only performer with no one to trust is Icarus.

Maybe it was a hint. Maybe all along the Dance of the Angels was a hint to us Icarii.

I take the lead as we enter Harmonia's territory. I'm even more alert here than in Kleos' land, especially after learning Harmonia's tailed me in the past. I won't let that happen again.

It takes two nerve-wracking hours to find a group from Harmonia. They aren't as predictable in their day-to-day hunting as Kleos. When we find the Harmonians, I give Theo and Jack quick instructions on which way to go. By the way Jack nods along without really listening to my directions, I know he's been in this part of Harmonia before. He probably trespasses all over Harmonia whenever the urge strikes him.

Jack heads off, but Theo makes no move to follow. When Jack glances back at him, Theo waves him on, whispering that he'll catch up in a minute. Jack shrugs and rounds the corner.

Theo takes a step closer to me, but when I tense, he goes no farther. He rubs the back of his neck awkwardly. "I shouldn't have said that stuff earlier. I don't think you'd actually back out. I know you're not a coward. And I know you can do this too, it's just . . ." He shrugs. "It's dumb, but the last time you went off into the labyrinth, I didn't see you again for almost five months. What if it's longer this time?"

"What does it matter if I'm gone a while?"

Theo studies my expression a moment. He says, "We're friends, aren't we? I mean, we were before. I thought we were."

I don't know how to feel about his use of "friends." Can we be friends if I don't trust him? Do I even want friendship from Theo?

"I'll come back," I say, finally. "We've arranged check-ins, remember?"

"Yeah. And I know you'll take care of yourself. I just hope Kleos can put up with me being a nervous wreck until this is over."

When Theo grins, I find myself grinning a little too. My grin freezes in place when Theo takes my hand. He gives it a quick squeeze, smiling at me in such a soft, warm way that my heart does a little backflip. His palm is warm, and my skin tingles where his fingers press in.

Then he pulls away and follows Jack. I'm left staring dumbly after him. Abruptly I curl my hand — the hand he took — into a fist.

Aware that I'm on my own now, I get a ghostly feeling of panic, like when Ryan left me at the wall on my first night. But it's gone almost instantly, as if it was never fully there to begin with, and I'm back to being the sure, solitary Fey Bell I have to be.

My calculations for reaching the Harmonian pair are off; instead of two turns, I run into them after one.

Immediately, we have arrows pointed at each other. I know I have to start things off like this. If I came in with my hands up, they'd shoot me and be done with it. This way they'll hold, knowing if they release I will too, and even if one of them gets away, the other won't.

I don't know the name of the girl to the left, but I recognize Celia as the one on the right. I was hoping if I ran into a familiar face it would be Risa.

"I thought you understood our warning," Celia says. "You're trespassing."

"I'm looking for answers," I say. "Harmonia might have them."

"If you'd accepted Polina's gracious offer, you'd know."

"It's about a common enemy," I say. "Kleos."

Celia doesn't reply right away. I take this to mean I've caught her attention. "I thought Fey Bell liked to stay neutral."

"Not when one party harms people I care about. Do you know what happened at Fates?"

"I didn't realize Fey Bell cared about anyone apart from herself."

"Fates. Do you know or not? I think Kleos was involved. I'd like to be sure before I make my move."

"And what move would that be?"

"If you were more hospitable," I say, "I might tell you."

Celia's silent a moment longer. The other girl seems to be growing anxious. I hold my ground, trying not to let my own anxiety show. A sweat has broken out at my neck, making my hood feel even stuffier.

"The clearing where we spoke before," Celia says. "Be there an hour before sunset. I won't promise answers, but be prepared to give answers yourself. We'll hold a temporary truce for that hour only. No weapons."

If she thinks I'm agreeing to that, she's insane. Still, I offer a single, stiff nod. Negotiations complete, Celia slowly starts backing up, keeping her arrow trained on me. The other Harmonian follows her lead. Once they're around the corner, I lower my bow and flee back the way I came.

Since Harmonia didn't accept me right away, I'm supposed to meet up with Theo and Jack. Before reaching them, however, I realize I'm being tailed. I don't know which Harmonian it is, but that doesn't matter; whoever it is, I have to lose them.

I start weaving through Harmonia's twisting halls, picking up my pace. I don't even come close to my base, afraid the tail may find it. Several mossy areas go by, a collapsed hall hosting a watering hole, a half-crumbled wall I sometimes use for climbing. I still feel like I'm being watched. Why can't I shake them?

A plan starts to form in my mind. I'll stop by one of the mossy areas. Hopefully, they'll get bored of watching me rest. Or maybe they'll confront me. Anything would be better than this.

I catch a flash of movement out of the corner of my eye, in the sky. I instantly grab for my bow as I turn, thinking it's a flock of screechers. But the creature leaping off the wall is wingless.

My bow skitters away as I hit the ground hard. The creature is clinging to my upper torso and head. My eyes and nose fill with something, and I'm overwhelmed by the scent of rich earth. I'm confused, but that doesn't stop me from unsheathing the daggers in my belt and stabbing at the creature's back.

It leaps off me seconds before my blades come down. Grit fills my mouth, making me cough as I hop to my feet. I spin around and see that the mud monster running at me is humanoid. It swings at me, and two large claws cut the air, inches from my eyes. I take my chance and swipe with both my daggers, high and low.

It — she — jumps back, then to the side. She starts circling me, but before I can fall into the rhythm or join in the circling, she strikes. I lean out of the way just in time, at which point I realize she doesn't have claws. Between her fingers she's holding arrow shafts, the arrow heads pointed out for stabbing. On her back, coated in the same dirt as the rest of her, are a bow and quiver.

She's so quick, so aggressive, I have trouble keeping up. I don't think she's as strong as the Executioner, but there was something orderly and clean about the Executioner's way of fighting. This girl's style is chaotic.

She's hitting me, I realize, as little pricks of pain start to register. She's aiming where my clothing's weak, easiest to tear. If I looked, I'm sure I'd barely be able to see the holes in my leggings and sleeves, but they're there, and underneath I'm bleeding from a dozen tiny gashes.

I try to study her, but she's so fast it's hard; most of my concentration is on dodging. I can barely fight back. But if I don't fight back, she's bound to land a troublesome wound eventually.

Study her: the mud, at first glance, obscures her figure. Look at it long enough, and the outline of clothes and bones becomes visible. She's thin, wiry, and I think she might be tall. It's hard to tell, since she's constantly crouched or pouncing. Her clothing: focus on that. She's either not wearing sleeves, or they're tight-fitted — same with her leggings. She seems to be wearing something over her chest — maybe a guard? Her midriff, however, doesn't seem as well covered. The mud even bumps over muscles in her stomach, and there's a hint of a dent that might be her belly button.

Her hand and arrow-claws whiz past my head. I feel a rush of air, a burst of sun, as my hood falls back. She bobs away from me and out of stabbing distance, as she's been doing. In and out. This time, I follow her out.

I rush her, mustering all my speed in one quick burst. The moment I make contact, I throw all my weight into her. Even if she's taller than me, I'm broader, so we're fairly evenly matched. We crash into the labyrinth wall together, and she starts swiping at me furiously. Her eyes are impossibly cold and unblinking throughout her assault.

I bear with the pain, even as it gets sharper, quicker. I jab my dagger at her shoulder, but before I make contact, she grabs my wrist. All it takes is one quick twist, and I scream, surprised at the pain. I cut off my own scream, biting my tongue, not letting myself be distracted as she is; this is when I make my real attack.

I thrust my other dagger into her midriff. Mud cracks, cloth tears then, finally, flesh breaks.

Before I can push the dagger in deep — because I certainly intend to do so — her knee connects with my gut. I gasp. She shoves me back, and I stumble, releasing my dagger and losing my footing. I fall on my backside as my dagger clatters to the ground in front of me. It's not even bloodied halfway, and I can't see blood on her. I can, however, see where I chipped away the mud around her stomach. For whatever reason, this gives me some small satisfaction.

My satisfaction is short lived, because that's when her knee connects with my chin. When I fall back, my head clips the stone, and everything blurs and darkens.

I black out but only for a moment. Immediately I come to, shoving myself up and reaching for the daggers in my boots. But she's not in front of me anymore. Looking around, I'm just in time to see her muddy shoulder disappear around the corner.

For a long moment, I stare after her. Then I collect my daggers and bow and, yanking up my hood, start the trek back to Kleos.

Theo runs over when he sees me and catches me by the shoulders. His face is ashen. "What did they do to you?"

"I'm fine," I say. "I was tailed, by a Harmonian, then attacked."

"You kill her?" Jack asks, leaning on his spear as he looks me over.

"No. She got away."

"She kicked your ass, you mean."

"*Jack.*" Theo's hold on my shoulders tightens, making me wince. He wouldn't know, but he's touching some of my cuts.

"She ambushed me," I say.

Jack lets out a low whistle. "Fey Bell was shown up. Gammon's never gonna believe this."

"Let's try him," I snap, pulling away from Theo more sharply than intended. I speed past both of them. The sooner we get back to Kleos' base, the sooner I can clean up and prepare.

Theo catches up with me quickly. "Are you sure you're all right?"

"Yes." This time my tone comes out harsher than intended. I take a breath. "Sorry. I'm just not used to this."

"You never really get used to it," Theo says. "Fighting other Icarii always feels wrong."

I'm confused. Then I realize Theo has misunderstood what I said. I wish he hadn't. I wish what I'd really meant was that fighting other Icarii — other humans — felt strange. Because the truth is that thought, from the fight to seething after the fight, never crossed my mind. What I meant was I'm not used to *losing*. Not anymore.

I don't correct him.

When we reach Kleos, Theo tries to convince me to see to my wounds before talking to Gammon. He and Jack can explain what happened, he says. I have to look after myself first. I tell him I'm fine, and before he can argue, I go straight to Gammon.

Jack's wrong; Gammon believes I was beaten. He believes it almost too easily. Despite the fact I don't want his praise, I feel insulted when he brushes aside my defeat.

"So I take it," Silas breaks in, "that the meeting is off?"

"No," I say, at the same time Gammon says, "Not necessarily."

Silas doesn't seem to know who to look at. Theo is shocked, focused entirely on me as he says, "You can't meet with them after they attacked you!"

"Harmonia has a strange way of doing things," Gammon says before I can reply. "They've been known to test potential new recruits in unconventional manners. The fact Fey Bell here was left alive could mean they intend for the meeting to go ahead. This could be a good sign."

Theo is livid. "How is her getting beaten up a good sign?"

"She's alive," Gammon says. "It means that if that was a test, which it almost certainly was, then she passed. If she'd failed, she would have been killed."

"It *is* in keeping with their traditions," Silas says, half to himself. To the group, he clarifies, "So it's going ahead?"

"Yes," I say before Gammon can. Theo says, "No."

When I frown at him, he says, "I'm sorry, but this is ridiculous. It could have been a warning just as much as a test."

"Harmonian warnings," Jack says from around the rim of his cup, "involve an arrow in the face."

"It wasn't a warning," Gammon says to Theo, "because it was the Mud Maid who attacked her."

At our confused looks, Silas explains, "It's what Harmonia calls her. She's their greatest weapon — ruthless, bloodthirsty, and wild. More a monster than an Icarii at this point. She never gives warnings. The only reason she wouldn't kill was if she was ordered to release."

Gammon has been nodding along with this. When Silas finishes, he says to Theo, "This is why we can be sure that, for tonight at least, no harm is likely to befall Fey Bell."

"When you say it like that, nothing sounds sure." Theo appeals to me. "You don't have to do this. We can find another way to get information."

Fury rockets through me. Theo said before that he believed in me, but now he wants me to back out again?

Gammon starts to speak to Theo, but I cut him off. "I'm going tonight. Where are your medical supplies?"

"Silas can show you," Gammon says, clearly pleased.

"I'll show her," Theo says, clearly displeased. As he leads me down the left hall, Gammon and the others start a discussion at the table.

"You've changed in more ways than I thought," Theo says, not looking at me. I get a sudden pain in my chest. Is he disappointed in me?

I squeeze my axe hilt. It doesn't matter who is and isn't disappointed in me. As long as I don't disappoint myself. Except I did disappoint myself. Today, with the Mud Maid. She could have killed me if she'd wanted to.

Theo ducks into the supply closet where I spent the night. He reappears a moment later, confused. He tells me to wait a sec and heads down the hall. I follow. We reach a kitchen smaller than the one at Fates but with double hearths. Cassie has just hefted up a platter of leftover hare when she sees us and freezes. Ryan just glances at us, then returns to what he was doing. He's sitting at the kitchen table, one leg up on the bench beside him so that he can access his half-bandaged foot. A box of medical supplies is on the table beside him.

"It's fine, Cass," Theo says, gesturing to the medical box. "We're only here for that."

"Ryan needs it."

"I don't think he needs all of it." Theo glances at Ryan's foot. "What happened?"

Ryan ignores him. Theo doesn't seem surprised and shoots me a look as if to say, "I tried." How long has Ryan been acting like this toward Theo if Theo's used to it already?

"Don't let us stop you." Theo waves at Cassie's platter. "Jack's probably going to come in and raid the food store in a few minutes. The whole way back he was complaining about missing breakfast."

Cassie contemplates the platter a moment, then goes to one of the bins against the left-hand wall and pulls out an odd, flat, round object. It takes me a moment to realize it's bread. Half-burned, malformed bread but bread all the same.

Kleos can make bread.

Cassie adds that to the platter with the meat, then heads for the door. She pauses by Ryan, giving him a concerned look.

"I'm fine," he says, not returning the look, just focusing on changing the bandages on his foot.

Cassie hesitates a moment longer before going. She puts as much distance between us as possible. Once she's gone, Theo rounds the table to access the medical box from the other side. He waves me over to stand with him.

I examine the bottles of salves in the box. There are two or three different kinds, all familiar. None are as potent as the recipes taught to me by the Executioner. This makes me want to grin.

Uncapping the strongest of the salves, I push my sleeves back up and rub the cream into my wounds. Theo fishes through the box, pulling out any cloth strips he can find.

"It's all right," I say. "I'm not bandaging them."

"Why not? Some of them look kind of deep."

"I'm fine," I say to Theo. "They'll be able to tell if I'm wearing bandages. If Gammon's right about them testing me, I have to show I can handle it."

Theo still doesn't look happy. He glances at Ryan, whose back is to us, then tugs me to the other side of the room. He leaves his hand on my arm.

"What happened to you out there?" Theo asks, keeping his voice as low as possible. "It's like you're an entirely different person sometimes."

Sometimes? We only reunited last night. He can't have decided that about me already.

"You've gotten harder," Theo adds.

I should be glad to hear this, because it's what I wanted. Instead, hearing it from Theo, in that tone, makes me feel as if I've made a mistake. "Soft things don't survive in the labyrinth."

"They can," Theo says, "if you protect them."

I think about Gina, soft and delicate and broken. Not even the Executioner could protect her.

"I understand you had to become like this to survive," Theo says, and I feel his hand slide down my arm, his fingers locking with mine. It's incredibly distracting and confusing. "But is this really who you want to be? If it is, then I'm happy for you. If not, then you don't have to be alone anymore."

"Why are you saying this?"

"Because you have options now, and I don't think you realize that."

"What options? Whatever happens with Harmonia, when it's over I'm back to being on my own."

Theo looks at me, bewildered. "You can't be serious."

I look away from him, clenching my jaw. Ryan's stopped working on his foot, and I'm sure he's eavesdropping. Has he heard us? The thought makes my cheeks heat, and I find myself disentangling my hand from Theo's.

"What about Elle?" Theo asks. "Do you really think you can look after her on your own?"

I hate that the thought gives me pause. I hadn't gotten that far in my plan. Once I rescue Elle, what then?

"I'll protect her," I say, because of this much, I'm certain.

When Theo speaks, I have the feeling he would have said this no matter my reply. "I know, when we get Elle back, Gammon will let her join Kleos."

I'm sure he will. Elle is beautiful.

"Gammon will let you join too."

My gaze cuts to Theo. Now that he has my attention, he hurries to explain. "Kleos is safe and stable, and even if some of their younger recruits aren't comfortable around you yet, they'll learn pretty quickly how sweet you really are. Kyle will get over his issues and so will Cass. You and Elle can go back to the way things were before, except it'll all be so much better. If you stay. If that's what you want."

I don't say anything. I feel as if I'm in a daze, as if I'm the one eavesdropping, hearing Theo's words from afar, muffled and distorted.

"I just think you should know you have this chance here," Theo says. "It's the chance Fates used to give new Icarii — what you were supposed to be given. You could do more than survive here. You could relax. Maybe you — all of us — could even be happy."

Happy? When was the last time I was really, truly, happy?

Clara's face flashes in my mind, leaning in close as she ties my hair into braids just like hers. I remember my joy, in that moment, was so pure. I can almost see the smile I would have worn, the bright blue of my eyes.

And then I realize why I can see them; that smile, those eyes, were Clara's. The joy was hers because she was finally entering the labyrinth to be reunited with her brother.

"You made it bleed."

I'm confused by Theo's sudden change of subject, but then I realize I've unconsciously scratched an itchy spot on my cheek. My fingers have come away smeared with red. I didn't even realize the Mud Maid hit my face. It must have been during our close tussle. I was so hyped on adrenaline in that moment I barely felt a thing.

I feel the heat from Theo's hand all too well when he turns my face toward him. He takes the salve from me, and I let him, watching with a sort of detached interest as a bead of cream sticks to his finger.

"Do you mind?" he asks, reaching for my face. It takes me a beat longer than it should to shake my head, then he leans in and brushes the cream over my cut. The salve is cool, but his finger is warm as he tentatively strokes my cheek.

"It shouldn't scar," Theo says. "It's not deep. Lucky. You must have dodged just in time."

Luck had nothing to do with it. If the Mud Maid wanted to knit her arrowhead through both of my cheeks at once, I'm sure she could have.

Theo finishes and rubs his hand on his trousers. My cheek tingles where he touched me, which is probably the salve already taking effect. I take the bottle back from him and say, "Thanks. I can finish on my own. You go and eat."

"I don't mind waiting."

Theo smiles at me, and I return it tentatively, but I don't meet his eyes. I can feel my face heating again as I say, "It's OK, you go. I have to get the other cuts now and um . . ." I gesture to my tunic. "It's easier if I take this off."

"Oh, uh, right." It's Theo's turn to avert his gaze. He turns from me, saying loudly, "C'mon, Ryan. Let's give her some privacy."

"The kitchen," Ryan says dryly. "How private. But I guess it's better than the middle of the labyrinth."

Theo is confused by this, and I hope he doesn't notice how my blush has deepened.

"It's OK," I say to Theo, then I gesture to the medical supplies. "He'll leave when he's finished."

Theo still seems hesitant to leave me, but I need a minute alone with Ryan before Cassie gets back. I give Theo's arm a light touch, like he's been doing to me lately, but I also give him a light, prompting nudge.

"I'll save you something," Theo says, heading for the door. "If Silas hasn't eaten it all . . ."

I'd have figured it would be Jack, out of all of them, who would have a big appetite — not scrawny Silas.

The moment Theo's gone, I round the table and straddle the bench, so that I'm face to face with Ryan. He ignores me, like before, until I pull the journal out of my jacket. I slide the journal along the table toward him.

"You really trust me with that?" Ryan demands.

"We have a deal."

Ryan shoves to his feet. He walks past me without a glance at me or the journal, heading to a pile of blankets by the fireplace. His and Cassie's bedding, I realize. I catch myself squinting at it, trying to discern if it's enough for two beds or one, when Ryan blocks my view. He's retrieving his jacket, laid atop the blankets. Instead of putting it on, Ryan returns to the bench, unsheathing his dagger as he goes. He cuts a slit in the inside material of his jacket, then fits the journal in. His jacket's baggy enough to obscure the shape of the journal.

"What?" Ryan asks when he catches me staring.

"It's just . . ." *That was smart.* "You'll translate it?"

"What I can. Like you said, we have a deal." Ryan cuts off the loose end of the bandage on his foot, tucking it into the rest of the bandage.

"What did you tell Cassie?" I gesture to his foot.

"One of those Kleos idiots left their spears lying around. It was dark. I stepped on it."

Is your foot OK now? I don't ask this, I just rub some excess salve out below my elbow, flattening the sun-bleached hairs on my arms.

I glance up when Ryan slides the medical box toward me. He's already turned away, heading for the door.

"You don't have to go," I say. "I don't need to take my shirt off to reach the cuts." I finger the little slits in my tunic. Just big enough to access my torso with a fingertip of salve. "That was just an excuse so I could give you the journal."

"So you still haven't told Theo about it?"

"No," I snap, "and I'm not getting into this with you again."

"Relax," Ryan snaps back. "I was just asking. I wasn't going to get into anything. I warned you, and that's more than I'd usually . . ." He clamps his mouth shut, looking almost flustered. "It's pointless for us to talk about anything other than the translation."

"I couldn't agree more." I shove to my feet, ignoring the stinging feeling in my chest.

When I head for the door, Ryan says, "What about your cuts?"

"I can leave the rest. They're shallow."

"Yeah, and what about infection? The wound doesn't have to be deep for that. Haven't you learned anything?"

Before I can snap at Ryan, Cassie comes in and tells me I'm wanted in the main room. She doesn't meet my eyes when she speaks to me, nor when I thank her.

In the hall, I'm shocked to find Kyle just a step away. He's perfectly still, watching me with cold, empty eyes. His hand is resting on the hilt of his short sword. I tense, ready to grab one of my own weapons.

And then he just walks past me toward the kitchen. As he goes, he hisses, "You can't hide your true self forever."

I insist on going to Harmonia alone. Gammon insists on me taking backup. We compromise: my backup will come halfway, to the edge of Kleos' territory.

Jack says, "Try not to get your ass handed to you again."

I glare after him as he starts back the way we came. Theo lingers, as if he wants to say something, but he stays silent.

"I'll be all right," I tell him.

"I know. Just . . . what we were talking about earlier, you joining Kleos, after this. You'll give it some thought, right?"

"I . . ." My mouth goes dry. All I can get out is: "I have to go."

When I try to escape, Theo grabs my arm. He eases his hold when I stop. He starts to say something, then seems to change his mind and just says, "Good luck."

On my way to the mossy area, I keep an eye out for monsters. The labyrinth's empty but for a few tendrils of mist blurring the rapidly descending sun. I wonder if the mist is returning or if these bits are stragglers, rushing now to meet up with the rest of the bodiless Fey.

Someone starts tailing me for the last ten minutes of my journey. I don't try to lose them or confront them. There's no reason to at this point. If it turns out I'm walking into a trap, then I'll just have to handle it.

Typically, I'd avoid potential traps at all costs. I'd avoid fellow Icarii at all costs. And now here I am, working with one group to infiltrate another. Why?

To save Elle.

But is that all there is to it? There might be a part of me that wants to have a group for whom I can fight and to whom I can return. I think about Fates and how, if Collin hadn't turned out to be the way he is, I'd probably still be there. And would that be so bad? I was comfortable there and safe. I had Elle and Theo and Andrea and Felix. Cassie didn't hate me. Addie's stories were always interesting, and Gus was always kind. I could have helped him guard the door. I could have taught Gina how to spell the names of all her favorite toys.

I come upon the mossy area so suddenly it startles me. Just as I'm about to approach the entrance, I realize my hand is clamped around the bell at my throat. When I release it, my fingers ache, cramped from being in the same position for a while.

The mossy area is empty. I'm not surprised. My tail, or tails, will let Polina know I've arrived. That or the ambush will start.

They arrive around ten minutes later.

Celia enters with her bow drawn. "No weapons, I said."

"Where's your leader?" I ask.

"Not far," Polina says, stepping into the clearing behind Celia. The Mud Maid shadows her, her wild blue eyes pinned on me.

"Celia," Polina says. "Disarm her."

Celia lowers her bow. She ducks forward and unclips my weapons belt, which she attaches to herself. It fits snugly around her hips, as it does mine. While she takes my bow and quiver I realize she and I are actually nearly the same height. We're a similar build too. Her face, however, is quite different, and her hair's a few shades darker. Her eyes are the same grayish-brown as the Mud Maid's second skin.

Celia pulls away from me after she's taken the daggers from my boots. She looks like a weapons rack with my belt and the two bows and quivers. Still, she's carrying them properly, at least. Nothing's getting tangled or clinking together.

Polina's voice rings clear through the area. "Celia tells me you know about Kleos' attack on Fates. Why do you care?"

"I spent time at Fates," I say. "There are people there I don't want to see hurt."

"Yet you're no longer with Fates. Why?"

"I've answered your question," I say. "Answer mine: what do you know about the attack? Why did Kleos target Fates?"

"Harmonia doesn't speak for Kleos, but I can tell you this much: they're the ultimate scavengers. If there's something they need or want, they'd much rather steal it than make it for themselves."

I remember Silas's comment about Harmonia stealing from Kleos. Polina is clearly a practiced liar; her tone doesn't waver as she accuses Kleos of what her own people do.

"I'm guessing you want revenge," Polina says, "but you're laughably outnumbered. Now do you wish you'd joined us?"

"Yes," I say, although it pains me to do so. I need to appeal to Polina's pride. It works to some degree, because Polina smirks.

"Tell me, then," Polina says, "how do you plan to get your revenge?"

"Their leader's been trying to convince me to join them for a while. If I join, that should get me close enough. What I do then is going to depend on the excuses he makes."

Polina's lips quirk. "Maybe we passed you over too soon."

She says that as if *they* were the ones to reject *me.*

"You've got the right spirit," Polina says, "but I just don't see how your plan can work. Even if you get close enough to Kleos' leader to try something, he'll easily overpower you. Infuriating as he may be, he's a skilled fighter. The way you are now, you'd never beat him."

I don't even have to pretend to bristle. "I'm stronger than I look. There are dozens of ways I could finish him off."

"But you want more than that, don't you? You want answers. You can't get those from someone you've stabbed in the back out of fear he'd beat you in a head-on conflict."

"He won't beat me."

"Of course he will," Polina says. "Our Maid beat you easily."

The Mud Maid's eyes crinkle, and her teeth flash, bright against the dirt caked on her lips.

I say, "Maybe I could get to Gammon, with your help. You have more experience with Kleos than I do."

"I won't argue with that." Polina looks me over, considering, with that arrogant glint in her eyes. "Just this once, I'll make an exception. Join Harmonia, as a guest. We'll prepare you to face our common enemy. And who knows? If you somehow manage to survive Kleos, maybe we can remain on peaceful terms afterward. What do you say?"

"Thank you," I force out. "I'll be your guest."

Polina's smile blooms in full, every bit as cruel as I imagined it would be. "In that case, welcome to Harmonia."

CONQUER

Polina doesn't let me have my weapons back.. I can't say I'm surprised. Celia isn't aiming an arrow at me anymore, which I guess is an improvement. Still, she walks behind me on the way to Harmonia, and I know if I make one wrong move she'll shoot me in the back. If the Mud Maid doesn't get to me first.

I walk up front with Polina, but she doesn't speak. I don't know if it's because we're going through the labyrinth and she's being cautious, or because she doesn't have anything else to say to me.

We reach Harmonia's base half an hour later. We could have gotten here more quickly, but they tried to throw off my sense of direction by taking a longer route, as I did to Ryan when I kidnapped him. They still think their base's location is a secret from me.

When we reach the base, Celia ducks ahead to the door, where she starts knocking out a code. I glance around the hall as covertly as possible. There's an archer, fairly well hidden, atop one of the walls nearby. If I wasn't used to running the walls myself, I likely wouldn't have noticed her. I'm sure Harmonia always has such sentries posted when their people are in the labyrinth. There may be more than one guard.

The door opens to a Harmonian with short brown hair. Her dagger is unsheathed. Seeing us, she offers Polina a deferential nod and steps out of the doorway. Polina is the first to enter.

There's no foyer. Instead, the base starts with one long corridor, lit by three candles in alcoves on either side of the wall. It reminds me of the Executioner's first base, near Fates, where I'd have to light candles in the stairwell.

I follow Polina, and the others take up the rear. The door shuts behind us and locks are put in place. Harmonia is more cautious with their base than Kleos. They're more like me.

At the end of the hall is another door. Again, Celia steps forward to open it. As she does, Polina says, "You're under our roof now, Fey Bell."

I don't know if it's a welcome or a warning, but it hardly matters, because that's when Celia opens the door.

The room beyond is large and square with the same dirt floor and low wooden ceiling as Kleos. At the center of each wall is a door. The one directly across from us is open a crack, spilling light and noise. On either side of the doorway in which we stand are wooden racks, half filled with bows and quivers. There are boxes of arrows and daggers, as well as other closed crates, but these are shoved up against the walls. The center of the room is empty, apart from a circle drawn in the dirt and two figures standing side by side within the circle.

The girl with her back to us laughs, and when she speaks, I recognize her voice. "You're not going to break it," Risa says. "Just pull the string back as hard as you can."

"But if it breaks," a soft voice says, "it's going to make a loud sound."

Risa laughs again. "I promise it's not going to break."

"Risa," Polina says, her voice steely. Risa snaps to attention and whirls around.

"Wow," Risa says. "Sorry. I totally didn't hear —"

"Clara?"

Confusion crosses Risa's face as she turns to look at the girl behind her. But the girl has already pushed past her, is already running to me, throwing her arms around my neck.

"Clara, Clara," Elle sings into my hair. "You took an awfully long time, didn't you?"

"You know her?" Risa asks.

"Oh, yes." Elle pulls back from our embrace, but only so she can hug my left arm. "Clara's my sister." Elle leans forward a bit, glancing at my hands. "She forgot the water, though."

"Your sister?" Risa exclaims.

"I see," Polina says. She doesn't sound surprised, but I wonder if she's just gotten good at hiding such reactions. "In that case, Risa, you and Elle can give Fey Bell a quick tour. Starting today, she's our guest."

"Uh, great?" Risa blinks hard as if that can distill her shock. "I mean, yeah, that's awesome. I'll show her around. You can count on me."

"I certainly hope so," Polina says, then to me, "I'll leave you to catch up. Risa will run through our rules with you. In the morning, you'll start training."

I nod, and Polina takes her leave, exiting through the door to the left, followed by Celia. The Mud Maid is nowhere to be seen. Did she even enter the base with us?

Risa wets her lips. "So, your name's Clara?"

"No, no," Elle says, leaning her head against my shoulder. "Clara's dead. But doesn't she look like a Clara?"

"Uh, sure." Risa picks up the bow Elle dropped when she saw me. "I'll just put this stuff away and then show you around, I guess."

While Risa goes to the weapons racks, I whisper to Elle, "Are you all right?"

Elle laughs, causing Risa to look over at us. "That's a silly question." Elle suddenly starts picking at the rips in my sleeve with a deep frown. "Why are you wearing scavenger clothes? You're not planning to go outside, are you? You promised you'd stay inside with me. Is someone making you go?"

"Nobody's making me go."

"Risa." Elle leans around me to call to her. "You'll make sure nobody makes Clara go scavenging, right?"

"Right," Risa says, coming over with a gentle smile. "Don't worry, Elle."

Elle beams. Still clinging to me with one arm, she reaches out with her other, stroking the side of Risa's face. For a moment, Elle seems to be fully focused on Risa, then her hand falls away, and she's smiling at me again. She says, "Are you hungry, Clara?"

"We'll get dinner," Risa says. "There's not actually that much to the base, tour wise. While we eat I'll explain the rules."

"The rules are fun," Elle says to me. "You'll like the games they play here. No one's ever bored, and you won't even have to sew. Oh!" Elle grips my arm so hard her nails open one of my cuts. "Clara, they have pillows! Clara can have a pillow too, can't she, Risa?"

"Of course," Risa says as she leads us across the room.

"If there aren't enough left," Elle whispers, "you and I can share. They're wonderful. You just have to hit them against the wall a bit to get the lumps out. I don't mind, though."

Risa leans against the cracked door. It opens fully to reveal a room roughly the same size as the one we're leaving. There are two long tables filling the space and hearths on either side. Harmonians are dispersed throughout the room, sitting together in groups and eating from clay bowls. Others are around one of the hearths, taking turns revolving two skewered rabbit carcasses. The members glance at me before returning to their own tasks and conversations, nonplussed.

"Oi," Risa calls to the group at the hearth. "Still not done?"

One of the members offers Risa a rude hand gesture. Another calls back, "Think you can roast it faster, huh?"

Risa holds up her hands in a show of peace and turns toward the other hearth. "Stew it is."

There's a pot over the fire, in which simmers a brown, chunky sludge. Risa fills a bowl and passes it to me, which I take in my free hand. Elle remains glued to my left side. Risa fills two more bowls and leads us to a free space at the end of one table.

"Sorry if they stare," Risa says to me. "Not everyone's used to seeing you up close."

"'Not everyone?'" a brunette calls from down the table. "No one's used to it, Ris, not even you!"

Risa flaps a hand at her, then pushes one of the bowls across the table to Elle. Elle turns to me. "Want to go eat in our room?"

For a moment, Risa looks hurt. Then she speaks to Elle in a gentle tone, "Nobody's going to hurt her. It's safe to eat here."

"It's what we do," Elle says to Risa, as if she doesn't get it. She looks at me again. I feel her tug my arm gently. "Come on, Clara. It's quieter."

"Elle." I run a hand through her hair. Soft and clean. She's been bathing here. "We should stay."

Elle pouts. She releases my arm but doesn't touch her stew. After a moment, she leans her head back on my shoulder. Risa watches us with an odd expression that I can't quite place. She blinks hard and looks at me.

"So, the rules. Yeah, basically, don't take stuff unless Polina or Celia gives you clearance. By stuff, I mean weapon stuff. Obviously take food stuff when you're hungry and water. As for blankets and medical supplies, they're out in the main room. I'll show you where. And you saw all the doors, yes?" Risa juts her thumb over her shoulder. "The one that way leads to the washrooms. It's divided for pissing and bathing. It's sorta obvious which side is which."

"You bathe in here?" I ask.

"Yep. We bring the water in on bath days. It's safer than bathing in the mossy areas. No offense. I guess if you're on your own, you can't really transport that much water back to a safe place."

"Not exactly," I say, surprised by the edge in my voice.

"This is boring," Elle says. "I promised Clara she wouldn't be bored."

"I'm not bored," I assure Elle. She frowns at the table.

"We'll do something interesting after dinner," Risa says to Elle. "Promise."

Elle smiles a little and picks up her wooden spoon. She doesn't start eating, though. Instead, she turns the spoon around and around, examining both sides as if hypnotized.

"You know," Elle says, "I think I might start dreaming of metal spoons soon. I have pillows now, so maybe metal spoons. I used to like staring at my face in them. Both faces were always so different. I wonder what happened to those faces. Do you think they're still out there, Clara?"

I nod, unsure what Elle wants me to say.

"What were they like, Elle?" Risa asks. "The different faces."

"One was stupid," Elle says. "Very stupid, but she was kind. And a little naive. The other face was always tricking her. The other face was horrible and mean. She was ruthless, but she always got what she wanted, because I'd look at her longest."

"Why?" Risa asks, seeming genuinely intrigued.

"Because she was beautiful," Elle says wistfully. She cringes. "Except her nose was squished. Maybe that's why she was so mean."

"I'm sure she wasn't as mean as you think," I say, and I'm not entirely sure why.

Elle looks up at me, her eyes so wide and dark and focused, it makes me think she's fooled us all. That she's the most together, most complete of us all.

"Oh, Clara." Elle smiles. "She was mean to the metal."

After dinner, Risa shows me through the other door in the main room. It leads to their sleeping quarters, which turn out to be a large room with blankets and pillows strewn all over the place. If the rest of Harmonia is order, this single room is chaos. Hammocks hang from between the wooden support poles in the room, sometimes on top of each other. When I stop to examine the hammocks, trying to determine how Harmonia made them, Elle says, "No, no, Clara. Those aren't ours."

"I told you," Risa says to Elle, "if you want a hammock, I can sort it."

Elle is shaking her head before Risa's finished speaking. Then she points to the corner of the room, where a blanket bed is almost entirely covered by lumpy pillows. "There, Clara. Come on."

Elle pulls me over and then down onto the pillows. Risa stands in front of us, at a loss. "Are you going to bed already?"

"Do you want to go to bed, Clara?" Elle asks.

"Is there more you need to show me?" I ask Risa.

"It can wait 'til tomorrow," Risa says, her gaze constantly wandering back to Elle. "If you guys want some time alone, I can go."

"OK," Elle says brightly, smiling at Risa. "See you."

Risa seems surprised, then she turns and quickly leaves the room. Although this is only my third time speaking to Risa, I still want to call her back in, explain to her that it's in Elle's nature to be this dismissive. It's no reflection on Risa.

But at the same time, I do want to talk to Elle alone.

"Elle," I whisper, taking her hands to get her attention. She likes this and twines our fingers together as she starts humming. "Has Harmonia done anything to you?"

"Who?" Elle asks. "Risa?"

"Risa or any of the others. Have they hurt you?"

Elle giggles, pressing our palms together. "Clara, you're being so silly today! I think it's to do with the clothes. Let's not fix them when you take them off. Let's just tear them apart and burn them, so you never have to wear them again. Scavenging clothes are dirty and disgusting. They'll kill you."

"So Risa's been nice to you?" I ask. "Everyone here has been nice to you?"

"They've existed quietly," Elle says. "Only Risa's been loud. But it's a lovely loud. Isn't Risa a lovely loud?"

"Risa's lovely," I say. I force our hands up between us. I want Elle to look me in the eyes. "Elle, what happened at Fates? Did Risa and the others take you here?"

Elle hums for a moment longer. Then she pulls her hands free, only to reach for my face. "Clara, there's something in your hair. Have you been washing it?"

I try to pull away, but Elle's fingers are already digging into my right braid — into the metal spikes in my hair.

Elle yanks her hand back. A bead of blood blossoms at the tip of her finger. She scrambles away from me, and in seconds, has buried herself in a fortress of pillows.

"Elle, I'm so sorry." I touch her shoulder, but she jerks away from me.

Her voice comes out muffled yet all too clear. "This is because you went outside. You're bleeding, Clara. You're dying."

"I'm not dying, Elle. That's your blood. I'll get you a bandage."

But Elle isn't listening. "When you went outside, you breathed them in, all the bad things, and they sharpened your bones like I knew they would, and now your bones are cutting you up from the inside. And you're so pale, Clara. Soon there won't be any blood left. It's all going to be gone."

I know I should reach for Elle again, try to get through to her, and it's more than because I still need information on Harmonia. I missed Elle, in an odd sort of way, and I've been so worried for her: now that we're back together, I want to take care of her. But after what she's just said, something stops me from touching Elle's shoulder.

"I'll get that bandage." I push to my feet. "I'll be back in just a second, OK? Then we can talk. Or we can sleep if you want."

Elle hugs her pillow, every muscle in her back tight. I feel horrible for hurting her and now for leaving her, but I know she needs to calm down — and, in a way, so do I. Plus, even if the cut is shallow and will have scabbed over by the time I get back, I want to bandage Elle's finger, since I caused the injury.

The training room is empty apart from Risa, who's lingering by the weapons rack. When she hears me enter the room, she glances over, surprised. "Done talking already?"

I shake my head and go to the medical supply crates. Risa comes over. "What do you need? Is it your period?"

I blush, surprised Risa would bring it up so casually. Then I realize it must not be a big deal here like it was back in Daedalum. There are only girls in Harmonia, and all in close quarters. Someone must always be on their period. Their large crate of old rags suddenly makes sense to me. I thought it was a bit much for pure bandaging purposes.

"Elle touched my braids before I could stop her." I'm telling Risa, because I don't want Elle to bring it up later in a way that might make the Harmonians think I meant to hurt her. When Risa still looks confused, I part one of my braids enough to show her the spikes the Executioner taught me to weave into my hair.

Risa's eyes widen. "Is Elle OK?"

"Just startled," I say. "It was only a scratch."

Risa nods to herself. She's quiet for a moment, then she says, "Y'know, I always wondered why you bothered with the braids. They're an easy target, right? That's why we all either go super-short or tight bun, though sometimes Polina lets us away with high ponies." Risa gestures to her own hair. "Gotta say, now that I know what's up with the braids, it's brilliant. False sense of security. Lure those idiot Kleos in for the sting, right? I might mention some new lethal hairdos to Polina or Celia myself — er, if you don't mind copycats?"

I shrug, although really I'm wishing I hadn't shown Risa the spikes. I tell myself it's because I've given away a secret to Harmonia, when really I'm pushing down memories of the Executioner tying these into my braids.

"Can I ask you something?" I say. "It's about Elle."

"Sure, though I bet you know way more about her than I do."

It seems like an odd thing to say, but instead of thinking about Risa's comment, or her not-quite begrudging tone, I press on, "How did she end up here?"

"Oh." Risa scratches the back of her head. "Well, you obviously know what went down at Fates — again, you probably know more than us or me at least. Elle hasn't exactly said much about it, and I don't wanna push her. But finding her, right. Kleos was dragging her through the labyrinth on the way back from Fates. I heard her screaming while Celia and I were patrolling near the territory border. Her screams carried right through the labyrinth. Before we could get to the group, she went quiet, but we tracked them down eventually. They'd knocked her out, and someone was carrying her over his shoulder. There were a bunch of them, too many for Celia and me to take on our own, but we couldn't leave a girl with Kleos like that. So we backtracked to this stinger we'd avoided earlier — my plan, not one Celia was too keen on — and we lured it right to Kleos." Risa grins evilly at this part. "They scattered, Elle got ditched in the havoc, and we picked her up and got back here fast as we could. Polina wasn't even that pissed at us after we told her about the stinger bit. So, anyway, Elle's with us now."

"Why don't you bring her back to Fates?"

Risa shrugs. "That's Polina's call, and she says she's not risking any of us on that kinda trip, and she's not gonna let someone as . . . *defenseless* as Elle try it on her own. Anyway, Elle doesn't seem too bothered about staying here. She hasn't mentioned going back to Fates at all. Actually, after her first night, she, uh, asked me if she could stay here forever." Risa reddens a little as she says that, and although her smile is tiny, she looks extremely pleased.

I can't blame Elle for wanting to stay here; it seems much better than Fates, and she probably has no idea her caretakers were behind the attack, especially if she was drugged for the trip through the labyrinth.

Risa leans closer to me, suddenly dropping her voice. "Hey, um, I'm not sure if I was supposed to tell you all of that. I don't see why not, but rules are always changing, and no one ever tells Ris 'til she breaks them. I'm like the rule tester, but it's a blind test or something like that . . . uh, ignore me. On the test thing. Not on the keeping-quiet-about-me-telling-you-this thing. Or have I said that part yet?"

"I won't bring it up," I say. Risa looks relieved. She starts to turn away, and I find myself adding, "But thank you. For looking out for Elle."

Risa smiles at me, which I don't expect, just like I didn't expect I'd thank her. But it's what I would say if I didn't know the truth about what happened at Fates, and I have to play the part.

"It's easy to look out for Elle," Risa says, then gestures to the gauze in my hand. "Maybe not always easy, but it's easy to want to, y'know?"

"I know."

"Tell me if you need anything else. Today or tomorrow. Whenever, I mean. You or Elle. I'll help until someone gets pissed at me for breaking the new 'no helping' rule. Sorry, I'll shut up and let you get back to Elle. You've seriously got to believe her, though."

I stop on my way back to the room. "About what?"

"The pillows," Risa says. "They're the best thing outside of Daedalum. Now that I know you've been going without for so long, I can see why you've always been so cold. Comfort deprivation."

"Must be it," I say, but as I do my voice turns into a mumble. I turn away before Risa can see the expression on my face, because I'm not sure what it might be.

Back in Daedalum, then again at Fates, I was used to people calling me shy to my face or behind my back. It didn't matter. That's what I was, and a part of me was glad everyone could understand that without me having to do anything. I was shy and most would accommodate it.

But despite all the comments I've gotten about my new self, from Ryan and Theo's statements of how I've changed, to Gammon and Jack's snide remarks, I don't think I've ever been called cold.

Hearing that makes me *feel* cold all over. As I curl up against Elle's sleeping form, even her warmth can't penetrate this layer of ice inside me.

Maybe Elle was right. Maybe the labyrinth is slowly draining all my blood, leaving me a cold and lifeless Icarii husk.

The next morning, while Elle is still sleeping, while the majority of Harmonia is still sleeping, Celia wakes me up. With sharp, silent gestures she directs me into the main room.

"This is the start of your training," Celia says as she gears up. "Take a bow, full quiver, and three daggers. Arm guards and knee guards."

"I have my own equipment."

"You should feel honored to use Harmonia's equipment."

"I'm grateful, but I don't need it."

"You think yours is better?" Celia moves faster than I expected, unsheathing my axe. I grab her wrist, and she levels me with a cool gaze. "Guests of Harmonia don't harm their hosts. Shall I tell Polina you no longer wish to be our guest?"

Glaring at her, I release her wrist. Celia weighs the Executioner's axe. "You're right. This is better."

Celia whirls and hurls the axe at the wall. It embeds in a roughly drawn chalk circle — for target practice, I assume. It's not dead center but only a ring away. Celia's aim is good, and seeing how deep the axe is in the wall, her arm is strong.

"Better weapons require less skill to handle." Celia tosses me one of her daggers, which I nearly catch by the blade. "Leave your gear."

Celia takes the lead once we're in the labyrinth. She keeps her bow drawn, so I do the same, trying to ignore the foreign feel of it. It never occurred to me before that, despite all the Executioner's training, all it would take to throw me off was a new weapon.

I don't ask Celia about the training since we're in the labyrinth. I'm not sure she'd explain even if I did ask.

We walk for a while, and I get used to the feel of the bow. I itch to fire, to practice with it, but Celia keeps her arrow loose against the bowstring. I assume we're hunting, though I'm not sure why she'd consider that training; I've hunted enough on my own. Besides, they think I'm training to fight Gammon. He won't exactly run from me like a boar would.

When we start pushing the borders of Harmonia in the direction of the deeper labyrinth, I'm on high alert. I'm not as familiar with this part of the labyrinth. I've only been here once or twice before backtracking, since I couldn't understand the symbols on the Executioner's map. The map I don't have with me right now.

I just have to focus and find landmarks. I won't get lost.

Celia turns another corner and suddenly we're on the doorstep of a roofed hall. The wall has caved in, allowing entry to the dark, roofed area. It reminds me of the watering hole where Felix died.

But as Celia picks her way inside, her foot lands on solid ground. No water. We're not going fishing.

"What are we doing here?" I whisper.

Celia turns to me with a stern, silencing look, then speaks as lowly as I did. “Hunting.”

“What?” I mouth, but she waves away my question and raises her bow, edging deeper into the darkness. Not knowing what else to do, I heft my own bow and follow her in.

I can barely see Celia a few steps ahead of me; only her vague outline is visible, growing darker by the second. A strange panic squeezes my chest. This is what it would have been like traveling underground toward the hundred-headed monster if not for the Executioner’s candles. For a split second, I close my eyes, willing the monster’s blue fire to burn against my eyelids, but I don’t get so much as a flicker. Everything is shadows, and when I glance behind me, I can barely see the morning glow of the exit. I hear Celia’s soft, slow footsteps and follow, relying on my ears now more than my sight. It’s almost easier this way, like tracking a digger.

A strange smell tickles my nose. As it gets stronger I fight the urge to gag. It’s disgusting. It smells stale . . . but no, that’s not quite right. It smells like wet dog and bad meat.

I’m just about to head back when we round a corner, and a light appears ahead. A hole in the roof, spilling sunlight into the hall. But we’re not in the hall anymore; we’ve come out into a room of some sort. It’s hard to tell how big it is since the hole doesn’t light the whole room. When I take a step forward, the smell rolls over me, so strong that bile rises in my throat.

I force it back down and listen for Celia. She’s not walking anymore. Tentatively, I reach toward the spot where I last heard her, but my hand meets air. I was distracted by the light and smell, so I must have missed her most recent movements. Where is she?

"Celia?" I whisper, my voice barely more than a breath. There's no response, but then I hear another fainter breath in the room. I take a step toward the sound, speaking only a decibel louder: "Celia?"

There's a whoosh of air right past my head — an arrow, I'm sure — then the soft, almost muted thud of it hitting its target. But what *is* its target?

The thought's barely formed when a roar shakes the room. I go stock still. That's not a human sound, and it's not the sound of a monster I've ever encountered before. But it's familiar. I've heard it before, back in Daedala, on the computers in the library. They had audio recordings of extinct animals, and the teachers would play them for us when we were in level one to teach us about the animal kingdom. This roar is close to that sound, but there's something strangled about it, higher-pitched and more guttural. Something mutated and even more terrifying.

A strangled growl reverberates through the room, and then there it is, half in the light. Its coat is the same color as the shadows, so the two blend seamlessly. The one visible eye is like a drop of blood, its pupil so thin it's barely there. Yet it feels like the monster's staring right at me.

Leo nemeum. Temple lion.

I fire instinctively. The arrow hits and bounces harmlessly off the creature's dark fur. The lion snarls, its yellowed saber teeth flashing in the sun, then it darts back into the shadows. I can barely see its outline cutting through the darkness. I throw myself out of the way just as I hear it leap.

I land on something that almost makes me throw up. The scent is everywhere, and my shoulder is digging into something squishy. My fingers brush what I'm sure is bone covered in gristly bits.

I hear the lion growl, too close. I can barely see it weaving through the shadows. I can't see Celia at all. Where is she?

It doesn't matter. All that matters is the monster in front of me.

I grab the bone. It's connected to more bone — a set of ribs? — but it's still light enough for me to toss at the lion. The creature snarls, but I know I haven't hurt it. My initial panic, though still simmering, has worn off enough for me to think. The Executioner's journal. Ryan read me the entry. *Leo nemeum* are impervious to everything but bronze beaks and their own teeth and claws.

I reach for my bronze-beak dagger, but what I pull out instead is Celia's dagger. Sweat breaks out at the back of my neck. In the shadows, I see the lion leap, and I roll out of the way. Its teeth or maybe its claws scrape off the bones of the animal corpse.

Everything in me screams to flee. For a moment, I almost do, but then my brain kicks in. The way in here was too long, too dark. The lion has night vision. I don't. It will catch me. I have to fight it here.

But how, without my dagger?

The lion rises and starts to shake itself off. I reach for an arrow. Even if shooting at it won't cause any harm, it will cause a distraction. Maybe enough for me to get away . . .

Rather than my arrow, my fingers brush something squishy. Part of the corpse, I realize, and it doesn't disgust me as much as before. A bit of dried flesh or organ. It must have stuck to my arrows when I fell.

That's it. The corpse. The journal said that if temple lions run low on their preferred game, they're inclined to turn on members of their pack.

I shoot the lion, then turn and run along the wall. The lion roars, and I hear it coming after me. As I draw another arrow, I try to scan the shadows in the room, looking for corpses. There. In the corner. A pile against the wall.

I turn and shoot the lion again, distracting it from another pounce. Then I run for the pile. The smell is at its strongest here, but as my fingers sift through squishy flesh and brittle bone I feel nothing but determination. I've gutted enough animals to get through this. Hopefully I've taken down enough monsters to survive this too.

The lion is getting closer, stalking me. Is it taking its time now because I'm cornered, or because I've fired at it enough to make it wary? I don't care, because that's when I slice my finger on something sharp.

It could just be a broken bone, I know, but as I grope along the hard surface, I find my fingers quickly met by matted fur. A split second more of exploration, and I know I've found a clawed paw.

The claws are long and deadly sharp, but they're not big enough to take down the lion. I try pulling out the paw but it's attached to the rest of the corpse by bone. I rise enough to stomp the bone in half. The sound makes the lion growl again, and I turn just in time to see it charge me.

Gripping the grisly paw to my chest, I roll out of the way. The claws dig into my jacket, tearing strips almost to my flesh. The lion crashes into the pile of corpses, sending bones flying. A larger corpse lands with a thud beside me. I reach for it, and my fingers brush a sticky mane. The dead temple lion's head.

I immediately force its jaw open. The dried, shriveled inside of its mouth feels like the putty we used for arts and crafts when I was a child. I focus on that memory as I take the claws to the flesh around the dead lion's saber teeth. The skin tears easily under the claws, and I fleetingly think that I should use these claws for arrowheads. Then the lion's roar shakes the room, and it pounces. Just a cut or two more and I'll have the tooth —

The lion lands on top of me, the corpse between us. The corpse takes the brunt of the lion's claws, but I take the brunt of both their weight. The lion snaps its teeth at me, but the corpse keeps it momentarily at bay. All I get is a shower of spittle. Before the lion can recalibrate its attack, I jab the claws into its shoulder.

The lion roars again, this time in pain, and rears back. I take the chance to roll out from under the corpse. The lion's shaking itself, trying to dislodge the claw. Just as it does, I throw myself at it, sending us both rolling into the light. The lion roars in fury and swats at me. I gasp as three deep gashes open in my left arm, but the gasp is more in surprise than anything else. I don't feel the pain yet. I'm too high on adrenaline.

The lion is about to swat at me again, aiming for my head and neck this time. If it can't dislodge me, it'll just kill me. But not if I kill it first.

I slash the saber tooth along its stomach. For a moment, nothing happens, and a cold sweat covers me. The Executioner was wrong and now I'll —

The lion's stomach opens in a gush of blood and guts, just like the rabbits I've bled out for dinner. The lion goes slack, its limbs curling at awkward angles as it lets out a last hiss of breath. The breath is so long, I start counting the seconds it takes for the lion to give up on living. Twenty-three. I stop counting after that.

In the end, I bandage the wound in my arm. Even if Celia didn't let me take my weapons, she let me take a small pack of medical supplies, since she did as well. As I tie the bandages as tightly as possible, to stop the blood flow until I can clean out the wound, I think about Celia and Harmonia. Was this a skewered kind of training or an attempt to feed me to the monsters? If the latter, and I go back, they'll attempt to kill me again.

I could just return to Kleos. I know the interior of Harmonia's base, and I know they have Elle. We can storm the base, save Elle, and I can repay the Harmonians for the gift they've given me.

But as I stare at the tooth resting beside me, I find myself hesitating. The story Risa told me, about how they found Elle, has been nagging at me. It could easily be fabricated, and I knew they'd make up something, but I can't find any holes in it, and Risa seemed so genuine. She's also been good to Elle, and Elle clearly likes her — at least, as much as she can like someone who isn't Prosper. Or me.

Now that Harmonia knows Elle is my sister, or thinks that she is, will they still look after her? Even if Risa would, she's not in charge. Polina could easily get rid of Elle, just like Celia may have tried to do with me.

I can't abandon Elle. Not again.

Despite this decision, I don't return to Harmonia right away. I stay in that dark, foul-smelling den until I get used to the smell. I cut the lion apart with the teeth of its last meal. My wound starts bleeding again, and I take the time to rub in some salve and change my bandages. Then it's back to work.

On my way back through the labyrinth, the lion's pelt is heavy on my back. I'm glad I memorized landmarks on the journey. I'm not sure I'd last the trip to my base if I had to waste time wandering the labyrinth. My Kleos base is actually closer, so I sneak into their territory and luckily, don't run into any of Gammon's scavengers. I'm not ready to report right now, and besides, I don't want Kleos taking the pelt.

I collapse the moment I'm locked inside my base. Then I start smiling into the grisly pelt and hug it to me. When I've rested enough, I drag myself to the hearth and start a fire. I boil some water and then set to cleaning my wound. I have to grit my teeth against the pain and push down panic when fresh blood starts flowing again too quickly. I start growing light-headed. As soon as I've cleaned out the wound, I apply some medicinal leaves and bandage my arm. Once that's done I gulp a full flask of water. I stopped for drinks through the labyrinth but never long enough to drink my fill. I didn't want to risk being spotted by Harmonia or Kleos or a monster that might be attracted to the smell of the lion's pelt. Then again, maybe it was that same smell that kept the monsters away.

I return to the pelt and drag it to the far side of the room. I'll try to turn it into a jacket, like the Executioner wore. I know it'll be uglier than hers, and if I can't manage it I'll just make a cloak, but I have to try. This material is almost impenetrable. It's the ideal armor for traveling through the labyrinth.

I don't know what I'm going to do with the map yet, but I need to start preparing, just in case.

I decide to spend a few hours on the lion's pelt. I have a meal in my base as well, since Celia dragged me away before I could eat. I also change, for once grateful for all the doubles and even triples in my clothing selection. My outfit is the same as before, minus the blood. When I'm ready, I pack up, leaving my loot from the battle behind, and return to Harmonia.

There are sentries by the base entrance now, unlike when Celia and I left. They're evidently startled to see me, as is the girl who opens the door to the base. In a shocked voice, she mumbles for me to wait and disappears inside. A few minutes later, she returns and leads me in.

Polina is waiting in the main room, Celia standing beside her. Celia's scowling at the ground, while Polina's gaze is on me. Her attention flickers to the bandage on my arm, but she doesn't comment.

Polina says, "Celia told me about what she did. I'm sorry, Fey Bell, on behalf of Harmonia. We don't condone such training methods, and we're glad you've made it back. How did you defeat the lion?"

"I distracted it with arrows and ran as fast as I could."

"You escaped it, then. Though not unscathed, I see. I believe Risa showed you our medical supplies. They're at your disposal."

I nod in thanks.

Polina isn't done. "You escaped the lion this morning."

She doesn't actually ask, but I know what she's implying. *Where were you?* "It took me a while to find my way back." I glare at Celia. "I wasn't familiar with that part of the labyrinth."

Polina's expression shifts so subtly I almost miss it. She believes me, and she's pleased that I don't know all of their territory. It makes me wonder if Celia really did act on her own, taking me to the den. Maybe Polina wanted to test me in more than one way.

"Your official training," Polina says, "starts this evening when the scavengers return. Until then, please rest."

I nod again and pass Polina and Celia, heading for the medical supplies. Although I've already seen to my wound, I'll have to pretend to do so again, for show. Polina says something quietly to Celia, who gives a single clipped nod and takes off for the exit. Polina gives me a broad smile that meets her eyes in a mean way, then heads into the dining area. I hope she hasn't sent Celia to check on the den. As hard as she seems to be, I don't think Polina would risk her second-in-command like that, in case the lion really is still alive. But I could be wrong.

I take the medical supplies into the sleeping quarters, assuring myself it'll be fine. Even if Celia finds the corpse, I can play it off as another monster attacking the area. Perhaps I saw something heading that way when I made my escape?

I've barely made it two steps into the sleeping quarters when Elle launches herself at me. I drop the supplies and catch her. She squeezes me so tightly my wound screams with pain.

Suddenly, Elle goes rigid. She jerks away and looks at me with piercing, accusing eyes. "You smell like you're rotting from the inside out."

Before I can think of a reply, Elle grabs my hand and tugs me back into the main room, then toward the bathing area. "This is what happens, Clara, when you go off on your own. You come back smelling like dead people. I would have thought you'd understand that by now. Didn't I tell you? You die in the labyrinth and so does everyone else. You said you'd stay inside."

I said that a long time ago. But I don't remind Elle of what's happened; it wouldn't do any good. I just let her continue her tirade as she drags me into the bathing room. There are buckets of water, all cold, but Elle still insists I let her wash the smell off me. When I tell her I'm fine, she starts yelling and pulling at her hair, so I finally relent and undress. Elle drops my jacket unceremoniously into one of the buckets of water, but when she turns to snatch my tunic from me, she sees the bandages on my arm.

"It's just a scratch," I say, "but we shouldn't get it wet."

Elle purses her lips and nods. She grabs a rag from a pile near the wall and soaks it in the chilly water. "Sit down, Clara. I'll wash your back."

I sit on an empty bucket turned upside down. Elle scrubs my back viciously, soaking the material of my chest-band and almost tearing through it. When she rubs at my neck, water splatters my front and dampens my hair, but I don't complain. I start to shiver. Elle doesn't notice. She's talking about the ways I could have died in the labyrinth. Detailing them.

"Is that what you want, Clara? To be swallowed by one of those disgusting worms? Their bodies go on forever, you know. Silly people from Fates try to say otherwise, but if you ask them, they'll admit they've never seen the full body before. They can't, because the body doesn't end. You'll just get swallowed and keep falling and falling in the dark and you'll be covered in spit and dead things, and every now and again you'll touch its tongue, which never ends either, and its tongue is made of bumpy spikes that cut you, and they're covered in something like acid that burns but never burns all the way. You'll wish it could, so it could burn you away to nothing, but it never will. It wants you to fall toward nothing, forever, and that's just what will happen if you go outside, Clara."

I let her rub my shoulders raw for a moment, then I say, "Please stop calling me that, Elle. It was my late friend's name."

"If she's dead, she doesn't need it anymore," Elle scoffs. "Honestly, Clara. I thought you were more sensible than that."

A few minutes later, after Elle has told me about the "shiny-beaked birds" that like to "eat a bit of you, then let it grow back, then eat the bit again and do that forever and never let you die," I feel her fingers in my hair, around my crown.

"Won't you undo these grungy braids, Clara? They don't suit you anymore, especially with those stupid accessories, and I need to wash your hair."

I ease away from Elle's hands and turn to face her. "I'm cold, Elle. I need to go and warm up. What if I get sick?"

Elle's a flurry of concern at that, wrapping me in towel after towel from the pile near the door. Then she pulls me back to the sleeping quarters and cocoons me with her pillows.

"Is that better, Clara?" Elle cups my face in her freezing hands.

I nod and capture her hands in my own, trying to warm them up.

"Good," Elle says. "I'm glad you understand now what happens when you go outside. You almost get sick, and you get cold and uncomfortable, and you smell and look terrible. Being inside is much better, especially when there's so many pillows. Why would you ever want to leave?"

"I'm a bit hungry," I say. "What about you?"

The distraction works. Elle yanks her hands from mine and hurries to the door, calling over her shoulder that I should stay here and warm up, that she'll bring back the food. Once she's gone, I slump back onto our bedding, trying to squeeze the water out of the tips of my braids.

Why *would* I ever want to leave?

True to her word, Polina summons me later that evening for my training. This time it's not Celia who retrieves me, but Risa, who's still dressed in her scavenging gear.

"Clara can't go," Elle says, waving to the grid we've traced in the ground and the little rocks dispersed within. "We're not done our with checkers game."

"It's OK, Elle." I touch her arm. "Polina just wants to talk to me about my leaving this morning, probably to tell me what a bad idea it was."

"I've already told you that."

"Yes, but Polina's in charge here. You know how Col —" I swallow. "How the leader of Fates always liked to deal with things himself."

Elle cocks her head to the side, giving me a curious, measuring look. I begin to get unnerved and wonder if it's too late to come up with a new excuse.

"I'll play checkers with you, Elle," Risa offers.

Elle looks her over, then wrinkles her nose and says, "All right. But only if you put your bow and arrows somewhere I can't see them. They remind me of a useless person who wouldn't stop bothering Clara."

Risa grins a little and agrees. As she swings her quiver free, I slip away, while Elle's still distracted by Risa. I'm glad Elle's found someone other than me who can distract her.

When I enter the main room, I'm surprised to find many of the Harmonians gathered there. They form a semi-circle around the ring in the center of the room and, when they see me, they part to reveal Polina. She smirks and indicates that I should join her.

"How is this training?" I ask out of the side of my mouth, when I'm standing beside her. I hate the way the Harmonians are watching me, their gazes hungry. "Am I supposed to fight you?"

"Not me." Polina steps back, out of the circle, and someone else slinks forward in her place. The Mud Maid.

"These are the rules," Polina says. "The first to land three hits or knock her opponent out of the ring is the winner. No weapons, no armor. Everything goes."

I removed what equipment I did have earlier, before settling in with Elle. The Maid doesn't look armed either but, then again, she hid her claws well in our first fight.

When Polina tells us to begin, we start circling each other. The Maid is caked in dirt, as usual, obscuring the thin line of her mouth and the curve of her brows. It's hard to read anything in her masked expression. Even her eyes show nothing but cold focus.

The lion showed me more than this. Rage, bloodlust, pain. All of my enemies, up to this point, have shown me more, whether human or monster. But the Maid is impossible to read, and it's not just her emotions.

When she strikes, I don't see it coming. The Harmonians cheer, then boo as I manage to dodge the strike, but the Maid throws another at my side. I block her just in time, but then she knees me in the gut. The room swells with cheers as Polina announces the first point. The Maid returns to her side of the circle, and I do the same, even though I'm still catching my breath. How did she get me so quickly?

Because you're not used to fighting people, let alone with your fists. You've never even hit someone before.

But I have, I realize, as the Maid and I start circling again. I hit Ryan, when he jumped me in my main base. I was so mad and so desperate that I didn't even think about throwing a punch at another human; all that was on my mind was winning.

I try to muster that same determination now, as the Maid darts in again. *Think about fighting her the other day. How it felt to lose. The sting of every little cut she delivered, every little failure. Think of Celia, leaving you to die with the temple lion. That's the face of Harmonia. You're fighting Harmonia.*

I block the Maid and manage to stave her off, but only for a few seconds longer than before. I think I'm doing better when a swift kick to my side sends me reeling, almost out of the circle.

"Second point!" Polina gestures to the Maid.

As the Maid returns to the other side of the circle, her teeth flash at me in a quick, feral smirk. My fury soars.

The second we start, I charge. The Maid ducks away and I almost stumble out of the circle, but I thought she'd dodge, so I'm ready to change course, spinning just as she aims a punch at my back. I block her and try to knee her in the gut, as she did me, but she twists out of the way and leaps back. That's her tactic, I remember. In and out.

Before she can come in, I go out. Like before, it works, but only for a moment. I swing for her but she ducks, and the next thing I know I've been swept off my feet. My back hits the ground, and a second later, the Maid's foot grinds into my stomach. I gasp. Spittle flies into the air and hits my cheek.

"Third point!" Polina declares. "The winner!"

The Harmonians cheer, but the Mud Maid ignores them, staring down at me, unblinking. As I push myself up, she abruptly crouches, bringing our faces even closer. She continues to stare, and the room goes silent.

Finally, the Maid lurches to her feet, looking away from me with such disinterest I almost can't believe her previous stare. The crowd parts for her, and she disappears into the dining hall. The Harmonians start chatting again, and after a moment, flow into the dining hall after the Maid.

Only Polina remains. She watches as I get to my feet.

Polina finally says, "I expected more. The Maid said you did better during your first match against her."

"I had my weapons."

"You might not have your weapons when you face the leader of Kleos."

I glare after the Maid. "He's not that fast."

"He's faster than you'd like to think and than I'd like to admit."

That gives me pause. "You've fought him before?"

"Not quite, but I've seen him fight — both humans and monsters. If you can't last five minutes against the Maid, you'll never beat Gammon."

I open my mouth to tell Polina I've survived a monster with a hundred heads and that, next to it, Gammon would be nothing. But I don't say it, for two reasons. One, I don't want Polina to know about the hundred-headed monster. I don't want to ever speak of it again. But the second reason is the Executioner's lessons. I might like to think I'm more powerful than Gammon because I survived such a terrible monster, but it was the Executioner who actually defeated it, not me. Even if I had, and even considering the lion I beat today, I know it's not the same as facing Gammon or any human. Just like every monster in the labyrinth takes a different strategy to defeat, every human does too.

So I say nothing, and Polina turns away. "Your training continues tomorrow. Lessons during the day and another match at night. Unless you're not up for it?"

Polina glances over her shoulder as she says this. I scowl at her, but that only makes her smirk broaden. She heads into the dining hall without another word.

When Celia comes for me again the next morning, I'm tempted to draw on her. But then I realize it's much later than it was yesterday, and most of Harmonia is awake. Half of them have already left for the day, including Risa, who had been keeping Elle company until I woke up.

Now that I'm up, Elle wants to play, but Celia insists we need to start our training. Elle thinks this means I'll be going outside and makes a fuss until Celia says, impatiently, that we'll be training indoors.

This piques Elle's interest. She follows us into the deserted main room, where Celia reaffirms the lines of the target in the wall. Then she goes to the weapons rack and retrieves a belt full of small sheaths.

"Dagger throwing?" I ask when Celia sets us up in front of the target.

"Polina insisted." I can tell by Celia's tone and her expression that this is the last thing she wants to be doing.

"I thought I had to learn to fight with my hands."

"Considering how well you're doing with that, Polina thought a backup tactic might be required."

I'm about to say I have my own tactics, all of which are much sharper and more proficient than dagger throwing, but then I remember Elle. She's standing to the side, watching us with a hooded gaze.

Celia throws a few daggers, which meet the center or close to it every time, then passes me my belt. She waves for me to try, without as much as a word of advice. That's fine. I know how to throw daggers. It was one of the things I taught myself in the long hours I've spent on my own. But Harmonia doesn't know about my proficiency at this, which I intend to keep hidden as long as possible. Plus it's a chance to study Celia's form.

"Do you want to try?" I ask Elle at one point, worried she might be bored. It's not just that. After seeing Risa teaching her how to hold a bow, a small part of me hopes that Elle might be opening up to the idea of learning how to fight. If I could teach Elle to defend herself in the labyrinth, like the Executioner taught me, then our problems would be solved. We wouldn't need Kleos or Harmonia to keep us safe. We could protect each other.

But Elle gives me one of her fake smiles, which makes my gut twist. "It's OK, Clara. You have fun."

Ignoring the underlying venom in Elle's voice, I return to training. It's painful and long. Celia offers no helpful words but plenty of useless criticism. It's different from training with the Executioner. While the Executioner didn't cut me any slack, she'd still do everything slowly enough for me to study her movements, to understand what was key. Celia seems to be throwing fast on purpose, and sometimes she'll even wait until my gaze strays to Elle.

By midday I allow myself to hit the wall hard enough for the daggers to stick. Elle has disappeared. She slipped out when I wasn't looking. I feel a bit guilty about boring her, but I push that feeling back. I'm doing all this for her.

We break for lunch. Celia waits until I've sat down with my food, then sits at the other end of the dining hall. I eat quickly and return to the main room, hoping to have a moment to look through their supplies before we return to training. But Celia reappears almost immediately, scanning the room as soon as she enters, as if expecting a surprise attack. Maybe I should have planned one.

When Celia is lining up one of her throws, I say, "Did you hope the lion would kill me?"

A part of me wanted Celia to miss, but instead she stills, dagger still clutched expertly between her fingers. Then she lets it loose. It hits the bull's-eye.

Celia unsheathes another dagger, but instead of aiming to throw she turns and takes a step toward me, raising the weapon between us. "You don't deserve Harmonia's help, and we don't need yours. We're perfectly capable of handling Kleos on our own. Polina knows that. She's only playing with you because Gammon thinks of Fey Bell as his toy. It's only to get to him. When she's had enough of that, you're gone."

I hope my expression is neutral. Celia's expression is anything but. I hold her gaze, watching the dagger in my periphery. "What about Elle?"

"So you were in Fates together. She'd forgotten about Fates before you showed up, and she'll forget them again. We know you're not sisters. You look nothing alike."

"We had different fathers," I say, which isn't a lie.

I can tell Celia doesn't want to believe me, but this gives her pause. Finally she scoffs, frustrated, and whirls to throw her dagger at the target. It hits the outer rim. She doesn't turn to me, but I see her shoulders tense. So Celia's the type to lose her mastery when angered.

"We can stop here for today," I say. "I can continue on my own."

"Polina's orders were to practice for the whole morning and the whole afternoon." Aggressively, Celia yanks her failed dagger out of the wall. "The afternoon isn't over yet."

It turns out the training regime Polina has created for me isn't a one-day thing. Every night she has me square off with the Mud Maid, who never says a word. Every night I lose, but I last longer each time, which is what I'm focusing on. I wanted to beat the Maid that first night, but now I know what I really need to do is study her. Study her tactics and skills and show her the bare minimum of my own. Try different moves, however risky they might be, knowing I'll fail, but doing it to see her reaction. It's taking longer than it would with most, but bit by bit I'm beginning to see the human below the mud.

My daytime training alternates. Every other day, Celia trains me with her daggers. Between that, different members of Harmonia take me out hunting. Polina says this is to keep my instincts sharp for when I enter Kleos, and also so that I can contribute to Harmonia, but I know there's more to it. She's having the Harmonians watch me every time I go out to collect as much information as possible. Like I'm doing with the Maid.

Risa wants to hunt with me, but when Elle makes a huge fuss the first day I go out, Risa opts to stay back at Harmonia with her. Elle still throws a tantrum every day I leave, but Risa manages to calm her down, and I feel better knowing someone's there to look out for Elle while I'm away. At the same time, it feels hauntingly like the days the Executioner and I would leave Gina.

Every day I go out, I try to find an opportunity to slip away, to meet up with Kleos. We decided on a time and a spot where someone would wait for me every day. But whenever that time rolls around, I'm either too far from the spot or unable to lose my companion.

Finally, after almost a week with Harmonia, an opportunity presents itself. We're in the midst of hunting a stray, wily doe. I get the chance to shoot it, but I deliberately miss. We're nearing the direction of the meeting spot. If I can just get away . . .

And then it happens. My companion shouts for me to go cut off the doe and rounds a corner, out of sight. Not about to let the opportunity slip away, I take off, faster even than when we were chasing the doe. Although we're close to the meeting spot, it's still five minutes away, being right on the line between Kleos and Harmonia's territory.

When I reach the spot, a collapsed wall, I check the sun's position in the sky. It's a little past the meeting time but not by much. They should still be here, or nearby, at least.

I start searching the area, quickly but quietly. I don't want regular Kleos members to spot me and mistake me for a Harmonian. They'd attack, and that might cause enough commotion to draw my Harmonian companion if she's chased the doe to a nearby area.

I turn down the next hall and spot a figure, back to me, heading toward the other end. At my approach, the figure turns around, raising his sword. When he sees me, he lets his weapon fall to his side, but the slight frown on his face remains.

"It's been six days," Theo says.

I'm surprised by his tone, his expression. It's not at all the warm welcome I was expecting. Thrown, all I can manage is, "I couldn't get away."

"And now? You didn't blow your cover, did you?"

"Of course not," I say, irritated. I'd actually been happy to see him.

I tell Theo how I got away, and he says, "We don't have long, then. Tell me what happened as quickly as possible."

I know he's right, that we can't linger, but part of me is hurt by his dismissive attitude. Still, I was prepared for a short talk, and I quickly relay what's happening at Harmonia. Their response to my story, the fact that they're training me, and Elle's safety in their hands.

"She might seem safe now," Theo points out. "What has she said about the night she was taken?"

"She won't talk about it. I think she's trying to block it out."

Theo nods, unsurprised. "Just like when Prosper died." Theo glances to the sky. "Kleos thinks you should stick with Harmonia a little longer. Silas is sure they're planning an attack. See what you can find out."

I nod, and Theo starts to turn away, saying, "Meet us again when you can. Same time, same place."

Before I know what I'm doing, I've grabbed his arm. "What's wrong?"

"Nothing." Theo pulls away. "We don't have time for this."

"Have I done something?" I ask, some frustration seeping back in. He was so kind to me before, and now, in the time I've been gone, he's acting like this? "Is it because I couldn't make it to the meeting spot earlier?"

"Of course not," Theo snaps. "I was worried — *we* were worried — but we knew there was a chance you wouldn't be able to get away"

"Then what is it?"

Theo's silent so long I think he won't answer, so I turn to go.

"It's stupid," he says, "with everything else that's going on, but I can't stop thinking about . . ."

Again, he falls silent for a long stretch. This time, I wait for him.

"It's something Kyle saw when he was patrolling the base one night. Ryan, going into Cassie's room. He was in there a while, so Kyle thought they were . . ." Theo rubs the back of his neck awkwardly. "The point is, Kyle didn't find out until then next morning, but Cassie wasn't in her room. That was the night before you left. He told me after."

It takes me a moment, when he's done, to fit together what exactly he's trying to say. When I do, my face flames. "You don't mean . . . you don't actually think that I would with . . . with . . ." I can't even say Ryan's name. My tongue ties, and I flush even more.

"Kyle said Ryan was in there for a while, and before you left for Harmonia, you spent a while with him in the kitchen. You even got rid of me to do it."

My mind races. Should I just tell Theo the truth about the journal and the map? A part of me wants to, but the rest of me is too wary, especially seeing the way Theo's acting right now. But I don't want him thinking there's something between Ryan and me. If Kyle's theory gets back to Cassie, Ryan might tell her the truth to get out of it. Considering Cassie's current opinion of me, what if she takes the journal to Gammon?

"That first night," I say, "Ryan wanted to talk to me about Cassie. I wanted to know what happened when he reached Kleos. I didn't think we were talking that long."

We weren't. I'm sure of it, because we got into a fight, and he stormed off. But I'm sure when Kyle realized it was me in there, he twisted the details for Theo. Maybe Kyle knew it was me in there all along.

Theo says, "What about the kitchen?"

"I wanted to talk to Ryan about you." My cheeks redden when I realize how that might sound, and I quickly add, "About his attitude toward you."

"And?"

"And we got into a fight." This much, at least, is true. "He can be such a child."

"What do you expect? He's only fifteen."

"He's sixteen."

Theo had started to relax, but this makes him frown again. I hurry to add, "Which makes it even worse. He could be a bit more mature by now."

Slowly, Theo starts to grin. Then he shakes his head.

"What is it?"

"I'm just trying to imagine you getting in a fight with someone. I saw you yelling when you first got to Kleos, and you've got all these weapons now, but it's still hard to imagine. Speaking of, where *are* your weapons?" Theo looks me over, focusing on my Harmonian equipment. "Toning it down?"

I blush. Did he think my previous inventory was overkill? "They're training me, remember? According to their leader, that requires the bare minimum of equipment."

"Interesting approach. Not one I've ever taken in training, but I guess each group has their own way of doing things." Theo sighs. "I wish we had longer to talk, but you really should get back. It was my fault for being a jerk for so long. I'll be better next time, promise."

I nod, and with a tentative smile, Theo takes off. So do I, in the opposite direction, notching an arrow as I go. Maybe I'm not too late to catch the doe.

A couple of days later, my training with Celia changes. Although my aim still needs work, I don't miss my target anymore, and my daggers always stay in the wall. Usually, I hit somewhere within the deepest three rings. According to Polina, this is enough for me to progress to the next level of training, which involves dagger throwing on the move. Celia and I go hunting in the labyrinth with nothing but our daggers. I try not to let on how nervous I am. Without as much as a bow for backup, I feel naked.

Luckily, Celia sticks to the safest hunting grounds in Harmonia's territory. We catch a rabbit the first day thanks to Celia. Our next day out, I lose one of my daggers in a boar, which a different scavenge team brings back for dinner, full of arrows. My dagger is missing. Celia says I should give up one of my own daggers to replace Harmonia's borrowed equipment. Evidently, Polina doesn't agree, because Celia doesn't press the matter.

My third day hunting with Celia, we go farther from Harmonia's base than usual.

"Aren't we near the edge of your territory?" I say.

"A small herd of deer were spotted in this area yesterday. Polina decided we would check. They're bigger than your usual targets, so maybe you'll hit one today."

I bristle, about to remind her that I did hit the boar, and maybe if she'd backed me up we would have caught it. But then I hear something out of place. I still, trying to pick up the sound again. A digger? We're a bit far from digger territory, but it could be a baby straying. Definitely not screechers. I haven't seen any of those for more than a week and a half, not even in the distance — my longest stint in the labyrinth without seeing them.

Celia turns to scowl at me, but when she sees how I've tilted my head to listen for something, she does the same.

The sound doesn't come again. Celia gives up first, continuing down the hall. Gripping my daggers tightly, I follow her.

It happens the instant we reach the corner: a spear comes flying at Celia. She jumps out of the way, and then there's a boy between me and her, advancing on her with another spear. He's holding his shield so I can't see the front of it, but I know what symbol I'd find there. Kleos.

I raise my daggers, but then I hesitate. Who do I attack?

Before I can decide, another Kleos boy appears at the corner, weaponless. He must have been the one to throw the spear. He sees me and immediately tackles me to the ground. We're too close for me to dodge, and I drop my daggers, not wanting to risk cutting him.

We hit the ground hard. The boy keeps me pinned and whispers in a shaky voice, "I know who you are. It'll be done soon."

What will? I almost ask, but then my gaze lands on Celia. The other boy is pursuing her aggressively, not giving her the room she needs to launch her daggers. His spear and shield keep her from fighting in close quarters, so all she can do is dodge each of the boy's hits. Celia has more stamina and speed than the boy, but she's also using up more energy dodging, and the boy is quickly backing her into a corner.

I could just let this happen. I should. I'm working with Kleos, and they're clearly planning on taking out Celia. No, not taking out. Killing. Like Celia hoped the temple lion would kill me.

I think about the lion's blood flowing around me as I stare at the boy attacking Celia. He's not hesitating in his thrusts. He knows he'll kill her or cripple her when he lands a hit. He's willing to do that. Why? Because of Kleos' past with Harmonia? Because the stinger's gone and they need to break the truce before Harmonia breaks it?

I don't like Celia. I don't trust her. But I don't trust Kleos either, especially when they try something like this.

Sliding out a dagger from my belt, I press it to the boy's neck. His eyes widen, and he looks at me for the first time.

"Tell Gammon this is a stupid idea," I hiss. "Get off."

He does, right away. As I rock to my feet, I grab my fallen daggers. Celia has since lost one of hers. I see it on the ground behind the boy. She tried to throw, despite their close quarters. She's getting desperate. Her back hits the wall as the boy raises his spear.

I throw my dagger at the boy's back. It embeds to the hilt, and he yelps, dropping his spear. The boy whirls to face me, and behind him, Celia grabs his fallen weapon. Before I can do anything, before it even occurs to me to do anything, Celia has put the spear through the boy's gut.

The boy's staring at me when his eyes go wide, and his mouth opens in a soundless gasp. His shield clatters away as he looks at the weapon protruding from his stomach. He touches it, tentatively, then his eyes roll back in his head, and he faints. He's going to die unconscious.

The boy next to me suddenly scrambles to his feet. He takes off down the hall. I want to scream at him to stop, but it's too late. Celia unsheathes a dagger and throws it at him. The sun glints off the blade seconds before it embeds in the back of the boy's head. He hits the ground face first.

Celia's panting, her hair wild out of its bun, but there's nothing wild about her eyes. They're as focused as ever. It gives me chills.

"You should have gotten him," Celia says, gesturing at the far boy with her dagger, "before you tried to help . . ."

As Celia trails off, her gaze narrows on my expression. She scoffs and heads back down the hall at a clipped pace. I can't follow her right away; I'm shaking too much. I have to press my hand to my mouth to keep from vomiting.

When I catch up with Celia, she says, "If you can't stomach the deaths of two Kleos grunts, you'll never be able to take on Gammon."

"That's going to be different. I didn't know those boys, but I hate Gammon. He's responsible for what happened to Fates."

"Gammon may be the leader, but all of Kleos is responsible." Celia's hold on her daggers tightens. She's already wiped off the blood. "If there weren't so many of them, Kleos wouldn't have the nerve to do the things they've done."

"And what exactly have they done to deserve to die like that?"

Celia gives me a sharp look, and I worry I've overstepped the mark. But it's hard to play my part when Celia's just murdered two boys.

"They were trying to kill us," Celia says. "Isn't that reason enough to kill them?"

"The last boy gave up. He was running away."

"To regroup. To try again. They always try again."

I think Celia will leave it at that. She resumes walking, still gripping her daggers. I soon realize she isn't leading us back to Harmonia.

"Where are we going?" I ask guardedly.

"There won't be any temple lions this time."

Because she thinks I can get away from them now?

I withdraw my daggers as I follow Celia. She glances back when I do, but she doesn't comment, and soon her attention returns to the hall ahead. I'm surprised she's putting her back to me when I'm armed. Does she trust me now, or does she just think I don't have it in me to attack her?

Celia comes to an abrupt stop in the middle of a small stone clearing. I scan it for a threat, but there really doesn't seem to be anything amiss. This isn't even digger territory. The only noteworthy thing here is a section of wall coated in dried mud, as if it has been smeared there.

Celia grits out, "You want to know why Kleos deserves to die?" and she goes to the labyrinth wall and claws off the mud. Below it are letters, carved deep into the stone.

We feed traitors to the monsters.

"Harmonia and Kleos," Celia says, "we used to be part of the same group. In the weeks following our Fallen Day, we came together to try and survive. Some of us died, some of us were killed. We were on our own, so Polina became our leader. She took charge. She gave us courage. Then Gammon showed up.

"He said his friends had left him for dead when a monster attacked. Polina welcomed him. She didn't see what he was doing to the group until it was too late. She couldn't see how he undermined her. Insulted her behind her back." Celia snarls. "She was so good to him, so good to all of them, and yet . . ."

Celia breaks off. When she continues, her voice is even again. "By the time we made it this deep into the labyrinth, Gammon and Polina were co-leaders. We found Kleos' base first. We hadn't been there a week when Gammon started convincing the group that hunting more than once a day was a good idea. Polina tried to get it into his thick skull that we couldn't over-hunt if we wanted to preserve resources, but he belittled her in front of the whole group, and he won. His idiot supporters liked the idea of feasts and celebrations more than surviving. So Polina and I tried pushing further into the labyrinth for more resources. That's when we found the second base. Gammon still wouldn't see sense. We knew he'd waste the resources we'd found. The only way for any of us to survive was to split the group, so Polina formed Harmonia. Most of the girls came with us. Some stayed with Kleos.

"Gammon and Polina negotiated territories. Neither group would infringe on the other's land, in hunting or harvesting. But as Polina always warned them would happen, Kleos exhausted their resources. They started poaching in our territory. We'd remind them of the deal, first with words, then with the threat of our arrows, and they would pretend to comply. But they always came back. So finally Polina told us that the next time it happened, we should give them a warning shot. And we did. One of the boys, in the leg. Two days later Kleos captured one of our girls and sliced her leg open as payback. They dumped her just inside our territory. The wound was infected by the time we found her. She was dead within two weeks."

Gina's face flashes in my mind. I grab at my bell.

Celia doesn't notice, so absorbed is she in her memories. "The next time Kleos trespassed in our territory, we got our own payback. A life from Kleos to match the one they'd taken from us. At first, Polina was angry about what we'd done. She hated Kleos as much as the rest of us — more than the rest of us — but she still saw them as her people. She didn't want to see any of her people die. But when Kleos came for revenge and killed two more of our own, she understood: we're not a united group anymore. There's Harmonia, and there's Kleos."

"What about the girls left with Kleos?" I ask, thinking about Silas's tale.

"Two of them defected to Harmonia. They could finally see Gammon's cruelty, and they said they were scared. They had a right to be. After they ran away, Gammon convinced the rest of Kleos, and maybe himself, that they'd been spies for us all along. He didn't want to take that risk again with the girls who stayed." Celia stares hard at the message in the wall when she says, "This is where we found what was left of them."

I'm at a complete loss. Celia's story is so much like Silas's, yet totally different. Who killed those girls? Who left this message? Harmonia has already proved their coldness, their cruelty. They attacked Fates, and Celia herself tried to feed me to a lion. But Risa's a part of Harmonia too, and she's so kind. And the way Celia's looking at those words, carved in the stone . . .

Who's telling the truth?

"You want revenge against Kleos," Celia says, "for Fates. You won't be taking it for Harmonia, for my sisters, or for Polina. You haven't earned the right to kill Gammon. I don't even think you can." She looks me in the eyes for the first time since she brought me here. "This is between Harmonia and Kleos. There isn't room for a scared little girl who cries instead of finishing off the person who's trying to kill her."

I didn't know the boys Celia killed. I wouldn't have recognized them as members of Kleos if it hadn't been for their weapons and shields.

Harmonia feels faceless too when I'm surrounded by them like this, when they're watching me with hungry eyes. They never get tired of watching the Maid crush me. Celia is here somewhere too, probably behind Polina, but when I'm focused on the Maid like this, I can't even pick out Harmonia's leader among the mob. It could be a flock of screechers surrounding me for all the distinction. They certainly make as much noise.

I hit the ground for the second time this evening and just lie on my back, staring at the dirt ceiling. It's so much like Fates and Kleos. It's not stone, not dark and damp, like my bases. It's the wrong kind of familiar.

If I was back home, I'd be staring at a white ceiling and Mother would come in with a basket of fresh laundry, and it would smell wonderful, and I'd say, "Today I saved one person so that she could kill two people."

Mother would say, "Icarus will forgive you."

And I would say, "I'll never forgive Icarus."

"Are you forfeiting, Fey Bell?" Polina's voice cuts through my daydream. My eyes snap open, and I rock to my feet. The Maid's already circling again. I stand where I am, watching her. For once I'm not tense. I let my muscles relax, let my heart calm down, let my breathing even.

The Maid isn't fazed. She walks a semi-circle around me, back and forth. I stop looking at her directly. I stare ahead, into the crowd, searching it for something human. Instead, I find Celia. We look each other in the eye, and in that moment, I hate her more than anything. I hate that she showed me the pain in her face when she told me about Harmonia's and Kleos' past, yet she showed no shred of pain or regret after hurting those boys. Even now, the remorse in my eyes isn't reflected in hers. Would that Kleos boy have felt remorse if I'd let him kill Celia?

Did the Executioner feel remorse when she killed the man who took her daughter from her?

The Maid strikes. I usually block with my arms. This time I lean out of her hit without fully dodging. The fury I'd been keeping locked away bursts free, and I grab the Maid around the waist, putting all my weight into throwing both of us out of the circle. This is what I've learned about the Maid: she's fast and powerful, but she's light. Her baggy clothes hide her thinness. I'm heavier than her. Stronger than her. If I can't beat her speed, I've got to use my strength. I just needed the chance to do it.

The Harmonians break and scatter just in time to make room for the Maid and me. We hit the ground outside the circle, me on top. Polina doesn't call it. Just as I start straightening up, the Maid kicks me in the gut. I grunt but grab her ankle, twisting it so hard the Maid grits her teeth. She kicks at me with her other foot, this time aiming for my leg to throw me off balance. I let her trip me up, and fall directly on top of her. She gasps as my weight pushes her harder against the ground. She hits me right across the face and tries to buck me off, but I won't be moved. I keep her trapped below me, locking our legs together so it's even harder for her to break free. She tries to choke me. I respond by pressing an arm to her neck. I can push all my weight into it so, if we really were to go all the way, she'd give her last breath first.

"Clara!"

The screech distracts me, but I don't release the Maid. Then I feel someone grabbing at my shoulders, nails digging into my flesh.

"What are you doing?" Elle shrieks. "Stop it stop it stop it!"

Finally, I let Elle pull me away. As soon as I begin to rise, however, the Maid flips me. Elle shrieks again, but the Maid ignores her and punches me in the gut once, twice. Then she just sits there, staring down at me, her head cocked to the side. Studying. Like that first night. Elle's still screaming at the Maid, but Risa's arrived to hold Elle back.

The Maid reaches for my neck again, but she doesn't squeeze it. She touches the bell at my neck.

I grab her wrist, forcing her hand away. "Touch that again, and I'll replace all that mud with your own blood."

The Maid does the last thing I expect; she laughs.

"Enough." Polina's voice rings through the room. "The match is finished. Everyone out."

"It's not finished," I call. "It's two to one."

"The Maid won," Polina says. "You're disqualified."

"For what?"

"For bringing weapons into the ring." Polina gestures to my braids. I seethe. The Maid didn't even touch my braids. Polina has to have known about the spikes for a while, probably since I told Risa. She's just been waiting to use them against me.

The room begins to clear. The Maid rises and looks down at me until Polina and Celia pass by, then falls into step behind them. Once everyone's gone, Risa releases Elle, who throws herself at me.

"How could you do that?" Elle screams inches from my face. "Clara, this place is lovely and peaceful! You can't attack people like that! What if they throw us out? We have to stay here, Clara. We can't go outside."

"It's not so bad outside," I say.

Elle slaps me. I'm so shocked all I can do is stare at her.

"You don't know," Elle says, her eyes wide and wild. "You haven't heard them, Clara. The labyrinth's thoughts. They're dark and twisted, and every time you go out they try to burrow inside you, and they'll grow thorns in you and rip you up from the inside. It took me forever to pull out all the thorns after the last time. But they're gone now. Don't let the labyrinth back in. I don't want to hear the lies it tells me."

I reach for her hands. "What does it tell you, Elle?"

Elle turns away from me and glares at Risa. Looking hurt but taking the message, Risa heads into the dining hall, leaving us alone. Elle tilts her head toward mine, speaking so low I can barely hear her.

"It tells me awful things about Prosper. Dirty, false things. But I won't listen. I know it's only thorns."

My heart speeds up. "When did the labyrinth tell you this?"

"When I was coming here, naturally. Really, Clara, it's obvious. The labyrinth knew how lovely this place would be, and it tried to cut me up before I arrived, because it was jealous of the pillows. It's terribly simple."

"Of course." I try not to squeeze Elle's hands too tightly. "Elle, was the labyrinth's voice male or female?"

Elle twines our fingers together. "It was the voice of a dead boy."

I wake up in the middle of the night with a hand over my mouth.

"Your name isn't Clara," an unfamiliar voice hisses in my ear. "You were kicked out of Fates for pretending to be the leader's little sister. Because of you, a boy and a little girl were killed. Water diggers got one, screechers got the other."

"Where did you hear that?"

A crooked grin flashes in the darkness, and the shadow figure slinks away. By the movements, I'm sure it's the Mud Maid. Careful not to disturb Elle, I follow the Maid out of the sleeping quarters.

All of Harmonia is dark, but this doesn't perturb the Maid. She doesn't say a word as she heads into the dining hall. I grab my chain and spiked ball and axe before following. She goes to the far wall and pushes a few crates out of the way, revealing a small tunnel. She disappears into it, and after a moment's hesitation, I follow.

After a few seconds of crawling, the Maid stops, and I hear an odd grinding sound. Then moonlight seeps into the tunnel. Seconds later we're standing in the labyrinth, and the Maid is putting the bricks of the labyrinth wall back in place. A secret tunnel. Just like in Fates.

I follow the Maid through the labyrinth, keeping an ear out for bats. I know she could be leading me into a trap, just like Celia did, but I need to find out how she learned all that about me. She could have heard some of it from Elle but not the parts about how Felix and Gina died. The only one I've told that much to is Ryan.

The thought sets my heart racing. Did they capture him, somehow? Have the Harmonians raided Kleos?

I manage to keep a lid on my panic until we reach a collapsed wall. The Maid climbs up, and I follow, and then we dart along the ledge. After we turn a corner the Maid crouches, keeping as close to the ledge as she can get. I follow suit. There must be something ahead that could attack us. I reach for my axe. I don't hear any bats, but the Maid might have caught something I missed.

The Maid starts to slow, then waves me ahead, indicating we've almost reached the spot. I follow her gesture and see a pair of figures up ahead, one standing on each side of an entrance to a mossy area. I can't recognize them from here, but there's something off about the closest figure. When we get nearer, I realize what's wrong: the figure's a boy.

What's a boy doing in Harmonia?

The boy keeps stealing glances at the girl, who has an arrow notched in her bow. She doesn't have it aimed at him, though, and after a moment she returns his stare. He looks away quickly, but I'm more focused on the girl. Thanks to the moonlight, I can make out enough of the face to recognize her. Celia. She scowls at the boy, then returns to her previous position. They're keeping watch. But why?

The Maid starts moving again, very carefully now that we're this close to the pair. She pauses when we're close enough to see the mossy area. There's another pair in here as well, another boy and girl, but they're not standing a doorway apart. They're kissing.

They pull apart for a moment, and my heart jumps into my throat. The girl is Polina. The boy is Theo.

I'm frozen. Even when the Maid pushes me back the way we came, I can't move. An odd pain is spreading through my chest, as if I've been struck there. And then the Maid does strike me, in the side. She gives me a venomous look until I start moving, numbly, back down the wall.

I pause before we clear the mossy area entirely, glancing back to study the guard beside Celia more closely. He keeps looking over at Celia, and when she outright glares at him, he looks away again. This time, he turns enough for me to see his surprisingly sheepish face. Kyle.

The Maid gives me another shove, and I escape down the wall.

After we've returned to the ground floor of the labyrinth, the Maid goes in front of me again. I think she's leading us back to base until we reach another mossy area, this one deserted.

"Why did you show me that?" I ask, trying to keep the quaver out of my voice. I'm still a mess of shock and confusion.

"Polina thinks those Fates boys have joined Kleos to be her informants. She's blinded by the older one. She can't see that they're toying with her. She won't even entertain the thought that they might be Kleos spies."

The Maid's voice is strange. It seems disembodied. Probably because it sounds so normal, yet it's coming from a crouching mud monster.

The Maid looks at me sharply. "You're ready to be sent into Kleos, but Polina won't agree to send you. She wants to drag it out so she can continue her midnight meetings. Her indulgence is putting Harmonia in jeopardy."

"What do you want me to do about it?"

"If you appear to beat me fairly, in front of all of Harmonia, Polina will have to send you. We're going to stage our next fight." The Maid rises from her crouch but still stays slightly hunched over, as if ready to take off on all fours. "Do you still want to avenge Fates?"

"Of course."

The Maid cracks her feral grin again. The moon glints off her canines. "Then let's begin."

I follow the Maid's instructions to a T. We practice most of the night, and the next day I'm exhausted. It doesn't help that what sleep I did get was fitful. I kept thinking about Theo with Polina. Or maybe I dreamed those parts.

The next day I request to stay at base with Elle to help soothe her after last night's fit. Polina agrees, and I can't help but wonder if she does it to prolong my training.

I catch up on my rest during the day, and Elle doesn't seem to mind. She's just happy to have me to herself for the day. When I wake between naps I often find her combing her fingers through my hair or curled up beside me, also asleep. At one point I find her missing, only to discover her in the dining hall. The scavengers have started to return, and Elle is eating with Risa. Risa spots me before Elle and for a split second looks disappointed, then smiles as usual and starts to wave me over. Before Elle can notice, I shake my head at Risa and slip out of the room. I'm glad that Risa likes spending time with Elle. I won't infringe on their meal.

Finally, it's time for the fight with the Maid. I'm glad I rested, because I need all my energy now. Despite the fact the Maid got even less sleep than me and was out all day, she's as fast as ever. If I slip for even a moment in our choreography, she'll land a hit, and the plan will be ruined.

When the fight does start, I almost mess up a few times, but the Maid improvises feints that still look natural — calculated, even. The Maid gets the first hit and I the second. Polina calls it begrudgingly. She ignores my next hit, which the Maid expected, so we worked several hits into the routine. Finally Polina has to call it or risk looking as if she's rigging the match. The Maid gets another hit, which Polina calls right away. The last hit is a blow to the gut that sends the Maid reeling; a hit Polina can't breeze over. The match is mine.

I thought winning a staged fight would leave me hollow or bitter, but I'm actually proud of myself. Not because I won, but because I executed the choreography with no real hitches. Maybe I could have joined the Dance of the Angels after all.

I get up early the next morning, long before Elle rises. I hate disappearing on her again, but I can't stay to say goodbye. She'd cause too much of a scene.

Polina sees me off. She's sending Celia and another girl as my escorts to make sure I get into Kleos unharmed.

"Good luck," Polina says with a stern expression. I can't tell if her words are sincere or not.

We're just about to leave when a frazzled Risa runs over. By the state of her messy hair and clothes, it's clear she's just got up.

"I'll look after Elle," Risa blurts, then quickly adds, "So you just, uh, look after yourself. And come back, OK? Basically everyone else got to hunt with you, so I want my turn."

"All right." I can't help smiling at Risa. I don't feel as anxious about leaving Elle since Risa's here. She's taken better care of Elle than anyone at Fates ever has. Better than I did.

I follow the very impatient Celia out of Harmonia, trying not to think about the fact that the next time I return, it might be to battle them.

It takes us an hour to find a group from Kleos. It's unnerving how similar the Harmonian tactic is to Kleos' tactic in terms of planting an insurgent spy. Celia and the girl part ways with me near the group to watch from a distance and provide backup if I need it. A part of me wonders if they'll really help if I get in trouble. For all I know, Polina has ordered Celia to let Kleos get rid of me. No Fey Bell, no spy to kill Gammon, more time for her and Theo.

I know Theo must be a double agent for Gammon. But, if so, why didn't Theo tell me about it? Why didn't anyone tell me? It's the kind of thing I should have known, going undercover in Harmonia.

I shouldn't dwell on this. I'll confront Theo later. Right now there are more pressing issues. Like whether Gammon's boys will remember that they're not supposed to hurt me, yet still draw on me and pretend I'm not working with them.

As I approach the spot where the boys were wandering, I start feeling a little apprehensive. What if Gammon has given the boys new orders? What if, after his two assassins didn't return, he assumed I've started working for Harmonia?

Have I?

After Elle's confession about the voice in the labyrinth, I'm more confused than ever. On her way to Harmonia, she said the voice she heard was male. That could have been in her head, but if it wasn't . . .

Yet Theo, Cassie, and even Ryan seem to trust Kleos, at least about the attack on Fates. And if Kleos were truly behind the attack, would they really send me to Harmonia, knowing I'd find out information that contradicted them?

How do I know who's telling the truth? Kleos or Harmonia?

For now I'm going along with the plan. Kleos and Harmonia expect me to go to Kleos now, so that's what I'll do. I can't risk either of them questioning my loyalties until Elle is safe.

As soon as I step in front of the boys, they whirl around and draw on me. I raise my hands and go over my half of the script. I want to take Gammon up on his offer and see Kleos for myself. They hesitate. I say they can check it with Gammon if they want to, that I'll wait here. They decide not to risk leaving me on my own and agree to take me to Gammon if I give up all my weapons. This part doesn't get any easier no matter how much I do it.

Weaponless and with my hands still raised, I let the Kleos boys lead me back through the labyrinth. I doubt Celia and the other girl follow us all the way to the base, but it's not until we're inside that the boys lower their weapons.

The main room is empty, which isn't much of a surprise. Most of Kleos is probably out hunting and scavenging. There might even be someone waiting at the meeting spot since there was no way of warning Kleos when I'd be returning. Theo might be waiting for me right now.

Or maybe he's planning another meeting with Polina.

One of the Kleos boys uncertainly tells me to wait here, then disappears down the hall to the right of the hearth. I've never been down that way before. Judging by how few rooms are in the left hall, the right must be the one that leads to Kleos' sleeping quarters.

I refill my flask while I'm waiting for the boys. They return a few minutes later without my weapon bag.

"Is Gammon here?" I ask, immediately.

"Um, no. Silas said to just wait out here."

"Where are my weapons?"

"Silas said to put them in the storage room for now."

"Where?" I demand, advancing on the boys. They start cowering.

One of them still manages to say, "I don't think you're allowed —"

I grab the boy by the collar. His friend reaches for his spear, but I don't as much as glance his way. "Which room?"

"Second door on the right." The boy gestures wildly back the way they came. I release him and head down the hall. It's almost a mirror image of the left hall. I expect the room the boy indicated to be as small as Cassie's closet, but it's actually rather large and filled with weapons racks and crates of supplies.

I find the bag containing my weapons immediately, resting against one of the crates. I curse when I find they've tangled my chain again. I'm in the midst of straightening it out when I notice something out of the corner of my eye.

From this angle I can see that the room is even larger than I first thought. The weapons racks have been set up in a way that divides the room. It's probably as big as the sleeping quarters back at Fates.

While the first half of the room contains food and medical supplies, as well as clothing, linens, and weapons, the second half of the room is solely an armory. Curious, I leave my weapons and edge into that part of the room.

There's a crate full of shields and a rack full of spears, some in much better condition than others. There's also a crate of daggers and broken spears. But what surprises me the most is the rack of short swords at the back of the room. Some have been hung up, but for the most part they're scattered on the floor. Then I notice the crate beside this rack. It's full of arrows. Tentatively, I pick one up and roll it between my fingers. Wooden shaft. Black feathers at the end. A stone arrowhead. Just like the ones I used to make back at Fates.

I drop the arrow and step away from the crate. My gaze returns to the swords and widens. Andrea used a sword. Theo still uses a sword. I saw Theo's when I first got here, and it looks just like these weapons.

I check the other crates. Bows. Clubs. More daggers. All weapons Kleos has never used. All weapons used at Fates.

And then I find a familiar weapon, in with the clubs. Nails are driven through the side, poking out to make spikes. Theo's club. The one Sybil helped him make.

He told me he left it back at Fates.

My breath stalls in my throat. I think back to Harmonia. I saw all of their base, all of their weapons. I recognized nothing. No loot.

Kleos attacked Fates. Kleos took Elle. Kleos killed Gus.

I can't breathe, and then I'm breathing too quickly. I grab my bag and rush from the room, only to run into someone in the hall. Instinctively I reach for my axe. But it's still in the bag.

I'm glad it's still in the bag. When I look up, I find Ryan in front of me.

"They said you were back . . ." Ryan starts to say, but he trails off and then he frowns. "What is it?"

I grab his arm and tug him into the storage room. As soon as we're inside, I shut the door behind us and lean hard against it, still catching my breath.

"What's going on?" Ryan demands.

Leaving my bag, I gesture for him to follow me to the back of the room. "Check the crates," I say. He gives me a confused look but does so. He picks up an arrow, like I did, and goes still.

"Kleos doesn't use bows," I say, "or swords or clubs."

"They're from Fates." The arrow falls from his hand, clattering softly back into the crate.

Everything comes spilling out of me. "Harmonia told me they saved Elle from Kleos. I didn't believe them at first, but then Elle told me a boy spoke to her when she was coming through the labyrinth. I thought maybe it was just one of her delusions but with this . . ." I wave weakly at the weapons.

Ryan curses. "What do we do now?"

"I don't know." My mind's still reeling. "I've already given Kleos information on Harmonia. They know the location and layout of their base. If they attack, Harmonia might fall."

Ryan curses again. He hits the crate so hard I think he must hurt his hand.

"We need to tell the others from Fates," I say as my head starts to clear.

"You want to tell them?" Ryan demands. "They're probably in on it."

"How can you say that? Do you really think Cassie would help attack Fates?"

"*She* wouldn't, but the others might if it meant they could get into Kleos."

"Gus was *killed*. Theo would never —"

"You've seen how far people are willing to go out here."

"Why are you so suspicious of Theo, but you're sure Cassie wasn't involved?"

"Because I know both of them," Ryan snaps. I think he's about to say something else, but then the door creaks open. Ryan clamps his mouth shut, and I tense. Thanks to the dividing weapons rack, we can't be seen from here. The person takes one step into the room, then another. I hear faint rustling. They must be getting supplies.

I don't dare move a muscle while we wait for them to leave. If Ryan and I are found right now, what do we say? I decided I wanted to try a new weapon, so I went snooping through Kleos' supplies, and Ryan is helping me pick out a good bow?

My mind stops racing for an excuse when the door creaks as it closes. I let out a silent sigh of relief. But the door doesn't click shut. Instead, footsteps sound, coming back in the room. I hear something faint near the door. The clinking of weapons.

My bag.

The door shuts, but Ryan and I stay silent. Footsteps come deeper into the room. Toward us. Are we going to have to fight our way out? Is that even possible? I don't know how many people are in Kleos right now, and there's Cassie to worry about. We can't fight. We can't run. What do we do?

An idea strikes me, and if I had longer to dwell on it, I'd never do it. But I don't think. I just grab Ryan by the front of his shirt and pull him to me. He's surprised, but he doesn't fight me. I angle us so he's in front of me, his back to the front of the room. Then I loop my arms around his neck and pull him down so that my lips are inches from his cheek. From this angle it will look like we're kissing.

Ryan has frozen. I move enough to whisper in his ear, "Put your hands on my waist."

If possible, he gets even tenser, but then his hands fall on my hips. The contact makes my face flame. I'm glad we're too close for him to see. But it's because we're close that there's a problem.

"That's not my waist," I mumble into his ear.

His cheek brushes mine as he tilts his head to reply. "It was your stupid idea."

His voice sounds strange, huskier, but it might just be because he's whispering. So there's no reason for me to be blushing even more. Or for me to feel the heat of his palms so acutely through the material of my leggings.

I tilt my face away from his ear, trying to angle myself to better listen for the intruder, but our faces have gotten too close. In the process of turning, my lips brush his cheek.

I still and so does he. I wait for him to pull away or shove me back, to give up the charade. I wait to do it myself. But my instincts must be delayed, because I don't move and neither does Ryan.

His skin is softer than I expected against my lips. Not rough with the start of facial hair. Not yet. He's still only sixteen. I'm only seventeen. This is the closest I've come to kissing a boy in two years.

The thought makes me embarrassed, but there's more than that. There's curiosity too and an odd warmth, a tingling that's covering my body, stemming from where Ryan's touching me, where I'm touching him. Experimentally, I brush my lips along his jaw. Ryan's hold on my hips, once tentative, tightens so suddenly my heart skips a beat. It hurts, but it's not a bad pain. I'm not sure if he pulls me against him, or I pull him against me, but I know that now we're touching even more, and my lips are at the corner of his mouth.

And then something clatters to the ground, and we jump apart. My heart drums in my ears as I frantically search for the source of the sound. A spear that's fallen from the weapons rack. That was pushed down. By Kyle.

"I knew it," Kyle says, disgusted. Then he says to Ryan, "You should have picked Cassie."

"Get out," Ryan growls. His voice is rough, throaty. It sends a shiver up my spine, and my face is on fire again, now mostly from embarrassment. What did we do? What did *I* do?

Kyle glares at us a moment longer, taking his time. Then he says to Ryan, "Theo wants her."

Ryan stiffens, and I redden even more. Then Kyle adds, "He's looking for her. He wants to talk."

Ryan glares at Kyle, and if I weren't so embarrassed I'd probably do the same. Kyle doesn't make any move to leave, and neither does Ryan, the two locked in a battle of dirty looks.

"I should go," I say. Without looking at Ryan or Kyle, I hurry from the room, almost forgetting my bag.

In the hall, I have to stop for a moment to try and pull myself together. I feel cold in the spots where we were touching, but the rest of me is burning.

I don't pull it together, but I can't risk loitering in the hall any longer in case Kyle comes out. In case Ryan comes out, and I have to face him.

It was just to trick Kyle. That was all it was. And it worked.

It *definitely* worked, a small part of me says, and I catch myself touching my lips. Shaking my head to try to clear the thoughts, the feelings, I head to the main room.

And run into Theo right away. When he smiles at me, I feel a strange sense of guilt. Why should I feel guilty? Theo and I aren't together, and more importantly, what happened with Ryan was just a show.

Then I remember what the Maid showed me, Theo and Polina in the mossy area. I sober.

Or I start to, but then Theo gives me a hug. I go rigid in his arms, but he doesn't seem to notice. Or maybe he just thinks that's my natural reaction.

"I'm so glad you're back safely," Theo says. He sounds so genuine that I start to relax. That's right. Theo could never attack Fates. Ryan was just being his typical neurotic self.

Theo pulls back a bit, but his arms remain wrapped around me. He speaks to someone over my head. "Hey, have you welcomed her back yet?"

I glance over my shoulder, only to see Ryan staring at us from the hallway. The moment our eyes meet, he looks away and mutters, "Yeah. I greeted her."

It's easier to tell, in this light, that Ryan's blushing. He turns his face to hide it and crosses to the left-hand hall, heading to the kitchen.

"As sociable as ever," Theo says, rolling his eyes. Then he releases me, only to take my hand and tug me to the table to sit.

"Can we talk outside instead?" I ask quickly. "I could, um, use some fresh air."

I can't stay in here. It's too warm, and Ryan's just down the hall. Besides, I don't want my talk with Theo to be interrupted. I have to ask him about a few things.

It's a bit cooler outside, but the sun feels scalding, and I can't seem to get comfortable.

"So . . ." Theo grins at me playfully. "Now you assassinate Gammon, right?"

"Why have you been meeting Polina?"

Theo's smile freezes on his face. It takes him a moment to reply. "How do you know about that?"

"The Mud Maid showed me. She thinks you're a Kleos spy."

"Well, yeah, obviously. What exactly did you see?"

"Enough."

He winces at my tone, which surprises me. I may sound accusing to him, but talking about this isn't nearly as hard as I thought it would be. I just feel kind of numb about it all. No, not numb. Distracted.

Inwardly, I shake myself and continue. "I was already spying on Harmonia. Why did Gammon send you too?"

"Actually, Kyle and I have been spying on them longer than you, just by a couple of days. I ran into a Harmonian my first time out, and it ended up being Polina — er, the leader of Harmonia."

"It's fine. Just call her Polina."

"Polina would have killed me if she knew I was with Kleos, so I told her half the truth. Kyle and I were sick of Fates and left, looking for something better. We got talking. She decided that if I acted as her spy in Kleos, she'd eventually accept us into Harmonia. Kyle and I have been feeding them fake info ever since."

"Not all fake," I say. "Not the parts about me."

"Thanks to Elle, she knew you were from Fates, and since she knew we were from Fates, she wanted information. If we'd lied, and Elle had contradicted us, she might have gotten suspicious. We couldn't take any chances."

"That makes sense," I say, but I think, *it's easy not to take chances when the price is someone else's secrets.*

"I'm sorry," Theo says. "We should have told you. The others wanted to, but I insisted there wasn't any need. I was being selfish. The stuff with Harmonia's leader . . . that's all to keep her trust. I don't feel anything for her."

"How can you not?" I demand, my mind wandering despite myself, back to the storage room. Ryan and I weren't even close to doing what Theo and Polina did, but I still felt something.

Stop thinking about it.

"I'm going about this all wrong," Theo says, frustrated. "It's just a role with Polina. It isn't real."

Just a role. Just like with Ryan.

I blink, hard, and say, "You don't need to make excuses to me."

"But I do! There was a reason why I didn't want to tell you. I was afraid you'd feel the same way I did when Kyle told me there was something between you and Ryan. At the same time, I was kind of hoping you would feel that way."

Panic stirs in me, sudden and insistent. I can't ignore it this time. What Theo's saying, the way he's looking at me, his tone — it's the kind of thing I've seen before, on other boys, toward Clara. This is the kind of situation she'd tell me about. I'm used to being told about it. Being at the center of it just makes me want to run away.

"I was jealous," Theo admits, not awkward this time, but resolved. He takes a step toward me. "Were you?"

I don't say anything. He kisses me. It's happening before I realize it's happening. And my first thought is: *so this is my first kiss after two years.*

Theo's arms go around my waist, but I clam up. Does he notice? Maybe he thinks I'm in shock, and that I'll respond in a minute. I *am* in shock. Maybe I will respond if he keeps kissing me like this. He knows what he's doing. It would feel nice, if it weren't for the panic cutting off my windpipe. Or is that the kissing? Is that why I'm breathless?

When Theo pulls back, he smiles questioningly. He searches my expression, and it occurs to me that he's looking for a sign of rejection.

I return his smile instinctively. Theo's worry disappears, and he takes my hand, giving it a quick squeeze. It's a gentle gesture. Something about it is easier to accept than the kiss, but it doesn't burn in the same way. My lips still tingle pleasantly, and I feel warm all over.

I embrace that warmth and ignore the numbness simmering underneath it.

Silas must have sent out scouts to collect Gammon, because half an hour later the leader of Kleos returns, Jack in tow. All three sit at the table with Theo and me. Just after we've taken our seats, Theo's hand moves toward mine under the table. I pull my hands onto the table, clasping them and hoping the pose looks natural. I still don't know what to think about that kiss, but I know this is much too fast for me, and I have more important things to focus on. Like the fact I'm part of a war council with the enemy.

Gammon starts with a request to hear everything I've learned about Harmonia. Silas takes notes as I talk. I reiterate everything I said to Theo but give them no more. When they ask for specifics about the dimensions of the base, I make it sound smaller than it really is. No matter his relationship with Polina, Theo won't have been allowed into the base, so he won't be able to contradict me. Near the end of my explanation, Silas asks if there are any secret exits.

"None," I say.

After that they move on to discussing the plan from here. Jack has since wandered off, bored by my description of Harmonia. He returns from the kitchen with a lumpy loaf of bread, takes a big bite out of it, and drops onto the bench next to Silas, interrupting the smaller boy. "We at the good part yet?"

"You're just in time," Gammon says and waves for Silas to explain.

"We're going to have a siege," Silas says.

"A siege," Jack drawls. "How exciting."

"It means," Silas says, "we'll be surrounding Harmonia's base and waiting until they either give themselves up or run out of food and water."

"Never mind." Jack tosses a handful of bread into his mouth. "Not exciting."

"It should only last a couple of days at most," Silas explains. "We can take turns, in large groups, guarding the entrance. They'll run out of water quickly, as they don't have our advanced system."

The system Silas is talking about isn't really that advanced, just convenient. The roof of Kleos is bent in a way so that when it rains, fresh water flows down to a hole near the front of the roof. It drops down through a pipe, which is attached to the water barrel. Although Silas would like to lay claim to its design, I've since learned that the barrel and roof were set up like that when they arrived. Kleos just needed to clear the pipe, as it had clogged up. The original builder came up with the clever design. Whoever the original builder was.

Jack is still quite bored by the prospect of a siege and is more focused on tearing apart his bread. The boys keep talking for a while to figure out logistics and decide on a date. In two days, Gammon says. That will give them time to stock up on supplies and prepare the troops.

"What happens after Harmonia gives up?" I ask.

"We escort them out of our new territory," Gammon replies. "Back toward Fates or deeper into the labyrinth. We'll leave it up to them."

"They won't just go," I say. "Even if they do, what's to stop them from coming back?"

"An example," Gammon says, and Silas starts to fidget nervously. Jack even pauses in his meal.

I ask, "What's that supposed to mean?"

"Let's just say the leader of Harmonia won't be going with her people, nor her second-in-command."

I remember what Gammon said to me during one of our first encounters. He told me if I were to kill him and Silas, Kleos would fall apart.

"They'll elect a new leader," I say.

"In time. But that new leader won't forget what happened to the old one. Harmonia's present leader is too proud for fear, and her second-in-command is too senseless. The rest of them, when it comes down to it, are simply little girls."

The rest of them are around my age.

"We should move on," Silas says hastily. "We still need to assign the boys their tasks, choose party leaders —"

I break in. "I should go back to Harmonia." I've got all the information I need, and I'm anxious to be done with Kleos.

Gammon raises an eyebrow, mildly curious. Silas balks at me. Jack's barely paying attention. Theo exclaims, "Why would you do that?"

"For two reasons." I address the next part to Gammon, knowing he's the one I need to convince. "I'd be more useful on the inside. Being locked in there will chip at their morale, but they're tough. Some of them trust me now. I can work on the weak links, and if we're lucky, Polina will have a mutiny on her hands."

"The other reason?" Gammon asks, a light smile playing on his lips.

"The Maid," I say. "You know how dangerous she is, and she wants Kleos destroyed even more than Polina does."

"And what will you do about the Maid, Fey Bell?"

"She trusts me. I'll use that and do to her what she wants me to do to you. I'll stab her in the back."

I can tell Gammon's bought it. Silas still looks skeptical, but I think that's because he wishes he'd come up with this plan.

"You can't," Theo insists. "There are too many ways this could go wrong. And if they don't surrender, you'll be trapped in there without any food or water. If they try to fight, you could get caught in the crossfire."

"I'll be part of the crossfire," I say, just catching myself from snapping it. *Even now, Theo still doesn't trust me on my own?*

"Theo's right," Gammon says. "There are many ways this plan could go wrong. There are also many ways that it could go in our favor. But we wouldn't be putting our lives on the line in there. The decision is yours, Fey Bell."

Theo puts a hand on my knee and squeezes it, his gaze imploring. I ignore him. To Gammon, I say, "I wouldn't have suggested it if I hadn't already made up my mind."

I'm to sleep in Cassie's room again tonight. She doesn't appear, so I assume she's set her place in the kitchen like before. Ryan's probably in there with her.

Theo walks me to my room, frowning the whole way. I'm just about to say good night when he says, "This is a really bad idea."

I sigh. I was hoping we wouldn't have to go through it again. "It's my choice."

"But I don't understand why. Silas's plan is going to work, whether you do this or not. It may just take a day longer."

"Or more," I say. "If I do this, I could help save people on both sides. If the Maid gets out, she'll kill someone."

Theo glances up and down the hall, then leans in and says, "I don't care as long as it's not you."

That should make my heart skip a beat. It would have, I think, when I first entered the labyrinth. Back in Daedalum. But now it just irritates me.

"I'm not going to sit on the sidelines when I can change things."

"You can change things outside Harmonia. You can join our forces for the siege."

"*That's* the sidelines. I can do more within the walls."

"But you don't have to. We'll get Elle out. We might even be able to negotiate for her. You don't need —"

Theo clamps his mouth shut when Jack comes down the hall.

"Oh, good," Jack says. "You're still up. I forgot to tell you not to let the diggers bite."

I scowl at him, and he grins lazily, then nods at Theo and continues to the kitchen.

"You won't change my mind," I tell Theo. "I'm going to bed."

"Wait. We shouldn't go to sleep on this kind of note."

I wasn't aware we'd ever gone to bed on any sort of note. But then Theo gives me a soft smile, and I know he's talking about *us*. This. Is it a relationship? The start of one? I don't know, but Theo seems to have some kind of idea. The thought of asking him puts me on edge, and the panic from earlier starts to wake up, so I force a weak smile and say, "We're OK. But I really am tired. Being with the enemy was exhausting."

"I know what you mean." Theo reaches out and strokes the side of my face. I stiffen, but as usual, he doesn't seem to notice. "You're really beautiful, you know? Did I ever tell you that back at Fates? I thought it when I first saw you. Well, when we got back to Fates, and I saw you properly. I guess I never said it out loud. Typical."

Beautiful. I'd always wanted someone to call me that, someone other than my parents or my aunt. Not that they said it much. I wanted Clara to reassure me, tell me I was half as pretty as she was. When I got older, I wanted the boys to pay attention to me and think I was beautiful. And now here Theo is, telling me just what I've always wanted to hear, and all I can think about is that, two weeks ago, Ryan told me he thinks my hair looks bad. Up or down.

Theo's hand is still on me, but now it's slid to the back of my neck. He's going to kiss me again. Is this how it works? You kiss, and then you keep kissing that same person whenever the mood strikes? I thought it went slower than that. A first kiss. An awkward conversation post-kiss. More time together. A second kiss.

But why should this be normal in the labyrinth when nothing else is?

I let Theo kiss me. I'm not panicked like before, but I still can't get into it. Maybe it's a matter of practice?

After a moment I pull back, mumbling something about being really tired. For a split second, Theo looks disappointed. Then he pulls me to him, kisses the top of my head, and whispers good night. It's so tender that for a moment I regret pushing him away. But once the door's closed and I'm alone, I'm glad. I really am tired. And still reeling. From everything.

It takes me a while, but as I begin to drift off, I'm grateful. When I'm asleep I don't have to think about anything.

When I wake, I check the candle I left lit. It's burned enough for me to calculate that I've been sleeping three hours, maybe four. I'd hoped Ryan would visit me by now, like he did last time. We need to talk about the plan I made with Gammon and my real plan for dealing with Kleos. And I need to know how much headway he's made with the journal.

Is it that, after what happened in the storage room, he can't stand to see my face? Or has he decided not to work with me anymore?

No, he wouldn't be that stupid. But still, the thought makes me uneasy. If Ryan's turned against me, then what?

Then I'll still go ahead with the plan to save Elle and maybe try and find the exit. But for the sake of the journal, I have to find out what's going on with Ryan.

Rolling out of my blankets, I listen by the door for the sentries Ryan told me about. I don't hear anything, so I peek into the hall. Empty, but a dim light comes from the main room. The sentry might be guarding in there, or he might be doing rounds, as Kyle evidently did on my first night. I can't wait, in case it's the latter, and I slip down the hall into the kitchen.

One of the hearths has been left going, but it's died down to a dull glow. I can make out two shapes, one on either side of the hearth. I'm surprised they're sleeping so far apart.

I hurry over to Ryan and crouch by his cot. His blankets are surprisingly messy, half thrown off him, tangled in a fist. He's wearing his ever-present scowl, and I catch myself grinning. Even asleep, Ryan's unimpressed.

I'm a little surprised about the state of his bedding, though. For all the nights he slept in my main base, his blankets were always fairly undisturbed the next morning. Admittedly, that could have been because I drugged him.

I start to press my hand over Ryan's mouth, to keep him silent while rousing him, but when his breath tickles my palm, I hesitate. Earlier today, his breath felt this warm against my neck, then my cheek, then close enough to mingle with my own breath.

I catch myself reaching for my lips again and instead grab my bell for a count of three. Then I wrap my sleeve over my palm and press my hand to Ryan's mouth. With my free hand, I shake him awake. His brows knit more tightly together, and he tries to push me away. I would have figured Ryan for a light sleeper. Annoyed, I shake him again as I lean down to hiss in his ear: "Ryan!"

His eyes flutter open slowly. He doesn't make a sound, so I remove my hand, but just as I do he reaches for me, his hand cupping the back of my head. I freeze, and only then do I notice the unfocused way he's looking at me. Is he still asleep? Does he know who I am?

He mustn't. He wouldn't touch me this gently.

His fingers tangle in the hair at the base of my skull. I find myself swallowing another lump in my throat, and the room warms as if the fire has been rekindled.

"Ryan?" I whisper again, but I don't mean it to be a question.

He blinks, then his eyes snap wide. He lets me go and shoves himself up and away, putting immediate distance between us. Although he's still staring at me in shock, his voice is angry when he says, "What are you doing?"

His gaze immediately jumps to Cassie, who hasn't stirred. The odd feelings his touch inspired die to even less than the dregs of the fire.

"Calm down," I whisper. "We need to talk. The journal — have you finished it?"

"I . . . not yet. I'm close."

I nod and pull my hidden chain out from my shirt and over my head. The Executioner's key hangs on it. "Remember where my base is here? The sliding wall?"

Beginning to calm now, Ryan nods. I hold the key out to him. He frowns. "Why are you giving me this?"

"I'm going back to Harmonia. Gammon and the others think it's to help Kleos, but it's to warn Harmonia and get Elle. Tell Cassie the truth about Kleos if she doesn't know already." Ryan glares at me when I add that. I continue, "While Kleos is distracted with the fight against Harmonia, take her to my base. Elle and I will meet you there as soon as we can."

Ryan still doesn't take the key. "If Harmonia loses, Gammon's going to try to kill you. Or worse."

"Fates prepared me for leaders that don't get their way." I wave the key. "Do you want to keep Cassie safe or not?"

"You should keep it. We might not be able to get away."

That might be true, but Ryan's going to have a much higher chance of getting away with Cassie than I will with

Elle. Despite this, Ryan's right. I should keep the key. Even if my situation's more desperate, I should just be looking out for myself. Like the Executioner.

But that wasn't the real Executioner. The legends painted her as solitary, ruthless, cutthroat. The real Executioner risked a flock of screechers to save Gina and me. She set herself on fire to save me and gave me a map I've been too afraid to use.

I take Ryan's hand. He tries to pull away, but I tighten my grip and press the key into his palm.

"When I'm done," I say, "you're going to be waiting at my base."

"Ordering me around again, huh?"

"Are you going to tell me I can't?"

"Not this time." Ryan pulls the chain over his head. "What happens after we meet up?"

"We get out of the labyrinth."

Ryan looks up at me sharply. He studies me, trying to figure out if I'm serious, if I'm tricking him again. I know he can't trust me, not after I lied to him about this before, but I say, "We're going to find the exit."

I don't realize I'm clutching the bell until Ryan puts his hand over mine. I look at him.

"You'll make it out for her," Ryan says.

"*We'll* make it out," I say, "for all of them."

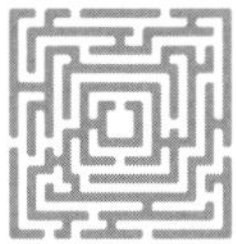

I never thought I'd pretend to run for my life in the labyrinth, but that's exactly what I do later the next day. Gammon assigned Jack as leader of the Fey Bell Hunting Party. Jack gets a little too into pretending to try and kill me. There are a few spear throws that get close enough to brush my shoulder. Whenever I glance back, I catch Jack grinning. I'm sure that's the expression he wears when he's hunting down actual Harmonians.

Has Jack ever killed any of them? He concussed Celia once, supposedly, and he's gotten into other altercations. He even jokes about storming Harmonia as opposed to the siege tactic, so that it'll be more exciting. But has he ever killed someone?

I doubt I'll get the chance to ask him. It occurs to me that this, Jack chasing me with a grin and a weapon, may be the last time I see him. It's fitting, I think.

Finally we reach Harmonia's territory. Since it's Jack, he pursues me over the border, but eventually lets me lose him. I immediately head for the base, but before I reach it I'm intercepted by a pair of Harmonians who heard Jack chasing me. I don't have to act exhausted. In clipped words, I explain to them that Gammon isn't dead, and I need to talk to Polina right now.

They escort me back to Harmonia's base. They still trust me, at least, because I get to keep my weapons. With everything else I have to worry about, this is a huge relief.

"Is Polina here?" I ask once we're inside. The girl who let us in shakes her head, so I say, "You have to call her in. Kleos is planning an attack."

The Harmonians pale. The two who brought me here exchange a look and then return to the labyrinth. The remaining Harmonian looks me over as I work on catching my breath. The Harmonians who took me here tried to keep a steady pace, but I pushed them. The sooner I get to speak to Polina, the sooner we can prepare.

I could just get Elle, and we could escape together. I wouldn't have had to leave my key with Ryan then. He could have met us at the base when he and Cassie could get away. But now that I know Harmonia wasn't involved in the attack on Fates — rather, they saved Elle from Kleos — I can't just abandon them, especially when I spied on them for the enemy.

But why did Kleos take Elle? That's something I still don't understand, and mixed with what one of them apparently said to her in the labyrinth, it's even more confusing. How could anyone from Kleos know about Prosper?

A horrifying thought occurs to me, one I should have considered much earlier. Theo and Kyle know about Prosper. It could have been either of their voices she heard in the labyrinth. Maybe they were talking about Prosper to try and distract her from the labyrinth. But no — she said the boy was saying something horrible. Were they using Prosper to threaten her somehow?

I can't imagine Theo doing that. I couldn't. But how well do I really know Theo? I always thought he was so kind and gentle, and he wasn't afraid to be silly to cheer me up. He always helped me. But that kind of person wouldn't be able to do what he's doing to Polina. If he can lie to her so easily, and lie to me just as easily, then what is he really like?

But he *has* been kind to me. Even his lie was told out of kindness. And his hugs, his little supportive touches, his kisses, those have been gentle.

So is he an enemy, or have I left him with the enemy?

I find Elle in the sleeping quarters. She's taking a nap, her face peaceful, her arms full of pillows. A smile ghosts my lips, and for a moment, I let myself stretch out beside her. I brush a soft, silky curl off her face. Elle is the beautiful one. I always knew it, but at first I thought it was just her exterior. I thought what was inside Elle was cruel. And it is. Elle has a cruel side, an inhumane side, a manipulative side, but that, like her physical beauty, is just something else in the way of the beauty inside. A part of Elle, deep down, is still the child she was when she entered the labyrinth. That child is inside all Icarii, but most Icarii kill that child to survive. Instead, Elle killed her sanity, and used its corpse to shelter the child. Because of that, a part of Elle will always have her innocence. A part of her will always have Prosper.

A part of her will always be in the process of becoming an angel.

Elle wakes up. She smiles dreamily when she sees me, then tosses aside her pillow and hugs me to her instead.

"Elle?" I whisper into her ear. She nods against my shoulder, indicating I should continue, or maybe just snuggling in more. "The labyrinth's voice, the dead boy — did it belong to Theo or Kyle?"

"Don't be silly, Clara. They aren't dead. Though they will be, since they like to scavenge. Remember what I told you about scavenging?"

"I remember. Did the voice belong to a boy named Gammon?"

Elle tenses against me. Her fingers dig into my shoulders so hard I know she'll leave bruises.

"The voice belongs to the labyrinth," Elle whispers. "It just sounded like the dead boy. He's dead. He can't own a voice anymore."

I pull back from Elle a bit, hoping she'll ease her grip on my shoulders. She doesn't. She won't even meet my eyes. Hers are wide and glazed. She's seeing something else now.

I put a tentative hand on her arm, rubbing gently, trying to calm her down. But I can't leave it like this, not when I'm so close. I ask carefully, "Who was the dead boy?"

"A liar," Elle hisses, then she's released me, and she's sitting up, tearing at her hair. "A liar a liar a liar!"

Elle keeps screeching. I try to quiet her, to reach for her, but she just swats me away. She tears out a chunk of her hair, and when it falls against a pale blanket, I see the ends are coated in blood.

I force Elle's hands from her hair, afraid she'll hurt herself badly. Elle stops screaming, murmuring rapidly, too low for me to make out the words. I think she's still saying "a liar," but when I lean closer, I hear what she's really saying.

"It's not Papa's fault."

Elle has finally stopped pulling at her hair, hugging herself tightly instead, when the doors to the sleeping quarters burst open and armed Harmonians come in, headed by Celia.

"What's going on?" I ask, when they surround me. "I need to talk to Polina."

Celia's voice is as cool as ever. "A prisoner is in no place to make demands."

"Prisoner?"

There's a smug glint to Celia's gaze now. "'Traitor' works just as well." Celia gestures to the other Harmonians. "Take the Kleos spy away."

I try to explain, but one of the Harmonians presses a knife to my throat, probably at Celia's order. They take my weapons. Again. Then they lock me in the bathing room with guards immediately outside the shut door. At least they haven't fed me to the monsters. Or will that come later?

I look around the bathing room. There are buckets of varying sizes, some half-filled with cold water. There are clean towels in the corner and a crate for dirty towels. I try to pry a board out of the crate, but I just scratch my fingers, and I know they'll start to bleed if I continue. I try the buckets next, but only a few have iron handles, and when I try to step on them at an angle to break them off, I just bruise my foot. I have nothing. No weapons, no way out. All I could do is throw buckets at the Harmonians.

Eventually I wrap myself in a towel for warmth and sit against the wall. There's nothing to do but wait. Wait and hope someone comes in to question me, or punish me, before Kleos launches their attack.

I'm here for what feels like hours. I nap and drink the water in the buckets. Hunger starts to gnaw at me. I think about my meal last night at Kleos, then again this morning. There was bread. It tasted as delicious as I remember it being in Daedalum. Better even, but I couldn't appreciate it properly. I was too focused on the fact that I was eating with the people who attacked Fates. I was too anxious about today.

I'd appreciate the bread now.

But still, this hunger is nothing close to the time Collin made me go without food. And I survived that.

I'm in the middle of a nap when the door grinds open. I jolt awake. Polina is in front of me, flanked by Celia.

"I can't say I'm surprised," Polina says. "I'd hoped Celia and I were wrong about you, Fey Bell, but we always suspected you were working with Kleos. We thought after their attack on Fates, you'd break ties with them. Or were you happy about the attack? Did you help? We've heard Fates exiled you."

"Who told you I'm a traitor?" I demand.

"An informant. Harmonia has better spies than Kleos."

"If you mean Theo and Kyle," I say, and Polina goes rigid, "then you're wrong. They're double agents, working with Kleos, just like I was."

"If that was true, they wouldn't have betrayed you."

"You're right," I say, "but I'm willing to bet it was Kyle who betrayed me, not Theo. Kyle hates me."

Celia stiffens when I say this. Kyle must have told her I was a spy during their guard shifts, while Theo was too distracted to stop him.

Polina starts to speak again, but I speak over her. "We don't have time to waste. I was a spy for Kleos, because they told me Harmonia attacked Fates. When I returned to Kleos, I found their hidden loot from Fates. I was wrong, and now I'm here to try and help. Kleos is planning a siege, tonight, while all of Harmonia is in for the night. They know the location and layout of your base thanks to me. But they don't know about the secret exit. You have to get everyone out before Kleos arrives."

"Don't believe her," Celia says to Polina. "She's working for Kleos. She'll lead us right into a trap!"

"Why would I?" I say. "It's easier to starve you out, and they don't have to risk anyone doing it. There's no reason for me to come back other than the truth —"

"How do you know about the secret exit?" Polina asks, her tone cold, her expression giving nothing away.

I hesitate. I don't want to reveal the Maid's mistrust of Polina's leadership, not when she might be my only ally here. So I say, "I was snooping, for Kleos, but before I could tell them about the exit I found out the truth about Fates."

Celia tries to interject, but Polina starts speaking, so she shuts up. "If what you're saying is true, why did you come back to help us?"

"I told them about your base. I have to take responsibility for that."

"Honor and goodwill gets you killed in the labyrinth. You must know that. What's the real reason?"

"The *other* reason," I stress, "is Elle. I can't leave her."

"But you'll leave your allies in Kleos?"

"I don't have allies in Kleos. Not anymore."

Polina watches me for a moment, still not giving anything away. Then she turns to leave. Celia shoots me a final, withering look before following.

"You'll get everyone killed!" I yell, which makes the sentries by my door glance in, startled.

"Ignore her," Polina says to the guards, "and don't let her out unless I give the order."

With that, the door slams in my face.

An hour later, the door opens. Polina stands there, alone. She's dismissed the guards. Not even Celia shadows her.

"Kleos is here," Polina says. "Come with me."

She heads back down the hall without waiting to see if I follow. I do, in a flash, and then I'm walking just a step behind her, in the spot Celia usually fills.

"Kleos has set up for their siege," Polina says. "Like you said, the back way is still clear."

I'm about to ask if this means they've evacuated, but when we reach the main room I find it teeming with armed Harmonians.

"You're not escaping?" I demand.

Polina levels me with a stern glare. "This is our base and our territory. We won't just give it up to Kleos."

Another scan of the room shows that, although it's crowded, not all the Harmonians are here. I'd say half are missing, maybe even more.

"You sent them out the back," I murmur.

"Of course," Polina says. "Gammon tried to surprise us. Instead, we'll surprise him."

As we pass a weapons rack, Polina grabs something. The Executioner's axe.

"This was going to happen eventually," Polina says. "I'd hoped to avoid it, but we have to teach Kleos, once and for all, that they can't just take whatever they want. And fighting them here, in our territory, is going to give us the upper hand. If not for your involvement, we might have been at a disadvantage when the time came to battle. I'll thank you for that much. Now . . ." Polina holds the axe out to me, hilt first. "Collect your weapons and your sister and go."

"You know Elle isn't my sister."

"It's my experience," Polina says, "that even though the labyrinth steals one family from you, it gives you another. In Harmonia, we're all sisters."

I accept the Executioner's axe. "Thank you."

Polina inclines her head, a slight smile playing on her lips. For once, it isn't mean. Then she turns back to instructing her troops. I quickly retrieve my weapons, then search for Elle. She's not in the sleeping quarters, so I try the kitchen. She's standing by the secret exit, clutching a pillow to her chest. Risa's waiting with her. When Elle spots me, she breaks into a beam and starts waving me over, as if I can't see them in the empty room.

"Hey," Risa says, relieved, then sheepish. "Uh, sorry about the Harmonian prison treatment. Polina can be a bit . . . drastic."

"I understand," I say. "She's only trying to protect her family."

Risa relaxes. Elle grabs my arm. "Risa says we're going somewhere fun!"

I glance at Risa, and she gives me another sheepish look and a smile, which seems to say: *It was the best I could come up with.*

I turn to Elle, hating that I'm about to break her bubbly excitement. But she needs to understand what's going on, so that I can keep her safe as best I can. "Elle, we're going into the labyrinth."

Elle rolls her eyes. "I know that. But Risa told me your secret, so it's going to be OK." She leans forward, speaking in a hushed, conspiratorial voice. "Risa told me how your special bell keeps the labyrinth's dark thoughts away, so we'll only hear happy ones. Or even our own thoughts. Won't that be strange?" Elle touches my bell, almost with reverence. "Risa told me about your new name too, that you got it because you're the keeper of the bell. Can I call you Bell instead of Clara? Fey Bell is much too long and clunky."

I'm surprised when I feel tears stinging at my eyes. I take Elle's hands and squeeze them. "Of course you can call me Bell."

Elle claps her hands happily. "Oh, it's wonderful, isn't it? Elle and Bell. It's just perfect!"

"It is," Risa agrees, then with a sidelong glance at me, "but we really need to go before Kleos and Harmonia start, uh, *yelling* at each other."

"We?" I ask.

Risa reddens. "I thought you might like another escort to help get you wherever you're going or part of the way, just in case something happens . . . not that it will, since you've got your bell, and you're Fey Bell, I just thought . . . uh, I cleared it with Polina, anyway."

"Can Risa come?" Elle asks me. "Please, Bell. It'll be even more fun with Risa."

I smile at Elle, then at the Harmonian. "Thank you, Risa. We won't keep you long."

Risa nods and heads for the tunnel. Just before she climbs in I catch her by the shoulder and whisper, "Really. Thank you for everything."

"It was fun. No, I mean, it was nothing. But it was still fun. It was no problem, is what I should have said. I'm just going to disappear into this dark space now, OK?"

Risa crawls into the tunnel, and I wave Elle ahead of me. She drags her pillow with her. I could point out that I have pillows for her where we're going, but it might help her to have a comfort item as we go through the labyrinth.

When we get outside, Risa fits the wall back into place. Elle watches Risa curiously, hugging her pillow. I notch an arrow as I scan the area. Risa does the same when she's done with the wall. I tell Elle to stay between us and keep quiet, so that the bell will work. Risa takes up a spot at the rear, and I lead. Calling up my mental map, I chart a route. The fastest one would take us right between the Kleos and Harmonia standoff. We have to go the longer way, even if it'll add another ten minutes, maybe twenty in a group. But that's nothing if we can avoid a fight.

The first ten minutes are fine. Whenever I glance back, Elle is just hugging her pillow and staring at the sky. Her lips are moving like she's saying something, but her words are soundless.

I realize, at one point, that this is the first time I've seen Elle in the sun. Natural sunlight makes her look even more beautiful. It picks up bluish strands in her black curls and highlights the flawless bronze of her skin. Her eyes sparkle under the light, not dull Icarus gray but something alive and blooming. Elle, I think, should always be in the sun.

I round the next corner, only to back up so quickly I knock into Elle. She doesn't say anything, since I asked her not to, but I feel her hand on my shoulder, steadying me. I glance back at Risa, who gives me a curious look. I mouth *Kleos*. Risa frowns, then edges forward to take a peek herself. She pops back around the corner when she sees what I saw. Kleos members, camping in one of Harmonia's potential escape routes.

My mind races as we start back the way we came. Do we try to take this Kleos party? I only got a glance, but it didn't seem like there was any more than four of them. Still, discounting Elle, that's double our numbers. And to be honest, if it came down to it, I'm still not sure that I could kill someone. I can't risk Elle's life on that, nor Risa's.

Another idea occurs to me. The collapsed wall the Mud Maid had us climb to show me the mossy area. I've used that wall myself a couple of times but stopped when I realized how close it took me to Harmonia. But the top of the wall is wide enough that, if we stay crouched in the middle, people on the ground won't notice us. We could sneak right past Kleos' camp.

It's risky, just like the other plan, but this one might not involve a confrontation. And I've sneaked past Kleos before. So has Risa.

"Elle," I whisper, "how would you like to see the labyrinth from the sky?"

Elle blinks at me, then nods rapidly, her chin digging into her pillow.

"OK. Then we'll go a special way. A fun special way. But we can only go that way if you stay quiet, no matter what, all right? If we're not quiet, the labyrinth can't hear the bell, and it might start thinking again."

Elle mouths, "I'll be quiet."

I hate that I'm using her fears to control her. It's like the cautionary tales we were told as children, back in Daedalum. *Once there was a young boy who was so graceful the adults and elders said he was like the angels themselves. Bolstered by such high praise, the boy ignored the elders' warnings about the balconies and danced on their ledges, pretending he was Icarus, flying among the clouds. And then, like Icarus, he fell.*

That story was one of the main reasons the balconies terrified me. I'd think of the boy whenever Clara fooled around on the ledge. I reminded her of the story once, and her response was, "The adults just made that up to keep us from having fun. Besides, if he was really as graceful as the angels, he wouldn't have fallen."

I know Clara was right: that it was a lie to keep us in line. I hated the adults for that, for instilling in me this fear I couldn't shake, when so many other children could. I don't want to do that to Elle, but I want her to live. Maybe that's all the adults wanted too.

If that's what they wanted, why did they send us in here to die?

I push down the thought. I locked it inside me in my early days in the labyrinth. There are no answers here. I'll never know if my parents knew the truth about the labyrinth. If anyone in Daedalum ever did. It doesn't really matter. What matters is getting Elle to my base and doing it right under Kleos' nose.

Quickly and quietly, I explain the plan to Risa. I watch her steel herself before she agrees to it. She collects her courage much faster than I did.

In five minutes we reach the collapsed wall. Risa and I help Elle up, then climb up ourselves. I take the lead again, motioning for Elle to copy my pose. She does so, her eyes glittering as they scan the labyrinth, but soon her attention returns to the sky. She starts mouthing her soundless mantra, and I focus fully on our path.

I'm glad Elle's focused on the sky again, because a few minutes later I spot the bulk of Kleos' forces. They're camped down the hall leading to Harmonia's entrance. They've brought crates of food and water, even bedding for when night sets in. We're only an hour from sunset, I'd say, which doesn't help my anxiety. While I've never encountered a bat in Harmonia's territory, it's Kleos' land we're traveling through later to reach my base, and I've had two bat attacks there. We need to hurry.

Despite this thought, I slow, distracted. While most of Kleos is camped down the hall, a small group stands in the clearing that hosts Harmonia's entrance. Gammon is at the center of the group, surrounded by Kleos warriors with their shields up. All the warriors are wearing gear and hoods, so that it's hard to recognize them.

What surprises me even more is that Harmonia's entrance is open, and Polina is standing in the doorway behind a guard of her own. Each of them have bows raised, arrows ready. Most would probably hit shields, but the moment Kleos breaks formation to attack, an arrow could get through.

As we draw closer, I realize Gammon is speaking to Polina. I wave for Risa and Elle to wait where they are, then creep forward until I'm close enough to make out what Gammon is saying.

"We've had peace before, Polina. Maybe we can have it again. The first step to that is handing over Fey Bell. She tried to kill me and injure Kleos. We have the right to decide her fate."

Gammon doesn't know I've betrayed him yet. That's good.

After a long moment, Polina calls, "We want peace as well. We'll give Fey Bell to you."

A few moments later, there's a commotion at Harmonia's entrance, then a hooded girl is pushed forward. She's around my height, my size, and even has blonde braids swinging out from under her hood. There's a bandage wrapped around her mouth, gagging her, and her bangs are in her eyes, further obscuring her face. Her hands are tied in front of her.

When she hesitates in front of Harmonia, Polina barks, "Move! We've got arrows on you!"

My substitute listens to Polina, but she takes her time, as I would likely do in that situation. Finally she reaches the group from Kleos. They part enough for her to reach Gammon, inside the shield circle. He starts to say something to her, and then a dagger flashes out of her sleeve. I catch my breath as the blade cuts toward Gammon. She's close enough to end it all, in a moment.

But one of Gammon's guards is faster. The hooded Kleos member drops his shield and puts his spear through my substitute's stomach. Her dagger clatters to the ground, and her hood falls back, revealing hair just a couple of shades darker than mine.

Celia's eyes are wide, shocked, as she stares at the boy gripping the spear. He seems to be staring back. When she topples, he quickly catches her, then bends his face close to hers. Blood blossoms over her jacket, around the spear.

I see Celia's eyes close, and then the boy screams, "It was supposed to be *her*!"

I know that voice. I've never heard it this anguished before, but I know it. Kyle.

He keeps screaming, and then he hugs Celia to him, burying his head in her chest and wailing. I thought Kyle had hardened past the point of caring about someone. I didn't know he had sounds like this left in him.

Harmonia starts firing. Kleos raises their shields just in time to block the attack.

"Stop!" Gammon roars, and he has to do it twice more before a relative calm returns. I think it's more that the Harmonians are scrambling for new arrows. "Give us the real Fey Bell and the girl from Fates, and we'll forget about this!"

"We'll never forget!" Polina yells, her voice wracked with grief. "We'll never forgive you! Kleos ends tonight!"

"Just give us the girls!"

"They've already left," Polina replies, a sneer in her voice. "Fey Bell figured you out, Gammon, and she's long gone. Your spy was ours after all."

Gammon is silent for a long time. I can only see the side of his face, but it's turning a fiery red. His voice is tight with fury when he asks, "Where are they?"

"We'll never —"

Gammon shrieks, "*Where is Elle?*"

There's a gasp behind me. I turn. Elle is only a few steps away, Risa desperately trying to drag her back. Elle is fixated on Gammon, her eyes wide with horror and disbelief. Then she slams her palms to her eyes and screams.

Immediately everyone on the ground looks at us. Gammon's murderous gaze sweeps right over me and lands on Elle. Before I have time to react, a spear is flying right at me. I scramble out of the way, only to find myself tipping on the side of the wall, over the enemy. I quickly regain my balance. On the ground, Kyle has wrestled a new spear from a companion and is aiming at me again.

"Down!" I yell to Elle and Risa. My voice can barely be heard over Elle's shrieks, over Gammon and Polina's shouted orders. Harmonians begin flooding the area from the end of the hall opposite Kleos' camps. Kyle's next spear misses, but this one was closer. He's furious with grief and hatred, and it's throwing off his aim. But not enough. He's recovering, quickly.

While some Kleos members face the Harmonians with their shield formations, others turn their spears to us, while others grab bows and arrows from the crates they brought. Weapons from Fates.

We can't stay on the wall. Risa and I realize this at the same time, and with one look we agree. It takes both of us to haul Elle over the other side of the wall. We hit the empty corridor hard. Elle cries out, or maybe she just keeps crying. I drag her into a run as Risa notches an arrow. We're clear for now, but with Elle making so much noise, we'll be easy to track. Kleos just has to catch up. They might even have a camp up ahead, in this hall, which was why I didn't bring us this way in the first place. But there's no avoiding that now. I just hope Harmonia keeps Kleos busy long enough for us to get away.

The sounds of the fight begin to drown out the sounds Elle is making. Risa keeps glancing back over her shoulder.

"Go," I tell her. "They're your people. Help them."

Risa hesitates. She glances at Elle, then sets her jaw. "You guys are kind of my people now too."

I feel relieved but only for an instant. With my free hand, I withdraw the Executioner's axe, and we keep running.

A break in the wall is coming up ahead, opening this hall to the one in which Kleos and Harmonia are fighting. But we should be far enough away by now to avoid the skirmishes. Risa glances quickly through the opening, then keeps running. I push Elle after her.

I've barely made it halfway past the hole when someone rams into me. My hand rips free from Elle's, and I hit the ground. I lurch to my feet immediately, only to find myself face to face with Kyle and his spear. But I've still got my axe.

His eyes are wild, his lips curled back in a snarl. He hates me. I can feel it from here. He hates me with everything in him.

Running footsteps sound from the other hall. Kleos backup.

"Go!" I yell at Risa. "Get Elle out of here!"

Elle screams for me, and I know Risa has trouble dragging her away, but finally she does, right before the backup arrives. When the pair get here, they flank Kyle. One of them raises a crude Fates bow, with an arrow I might have made.

"Don't touch her," Kyle hisses. "She's *mine*."

The Kleos boys give him skittish looks. When they continue to hover, Kyle half turns and screams, "Get lost!"

They do, taking off back the way they came. Kyle turns back to me. His grip on his spear is white-knuckled, and he starts to circle me. Like the lion and the Mud Maid. A combination of human logic and animalistic fury.

I start circling him too, eyeing the spear. Whether or not I'm a better fighter with my axe, it doesn't matter. My axe doesn't have the same range as that spear, and if I try to change weapons, he'll strike.

So I do what the Maid would do: I strike first. I hurl my axe at Kyle. It's an attack that works on screechers and bats but not on a human and not on someone as dexterous as Kyle. He evades the axe easily. But it gives me time to dart in and draw my short sword in the process. I get it out just in time to block Kyle's spear. I wish, fleetingly, that the spear were wood instead of metal, so I'd have some hope of cutting it in half.

"We survived our first night together," I say. It only fuels Kyle's anger, and he shoves my sword away. I barely dodge a thrust of the spear, then block another with my sword. I don't try to get through to him again. I wish I could, but he's blinded by his anger. I just have to keep him from killing me and . . .

And what?

"This isn't a fight to the death," I tell Kyle, just as much to convince myself as to convince him.

"You're right," Kyle says, surprising me, and he gives me the cruelest smile I've ever seen. "It's an execution."

He's almost overpowered me. I have to free my sword and dart back, but this gives him enough room to jab at me.

I manage to knock the weapon away, but each time he strikes he gets closer to landing a hit. And with a spearhead like that, it's only going to take one.

"That was how you got like this, right?" Kyle says. "The one who executes people. The woman we saw on our first night — the one you said didn't exist. She turned you into this."

I try not to pant as I block another strike. I can't let on that this is winding me, otherwise he might charge. It's easier to keep from panting than it is to keep his words from getting to me.

"She died, right?" Kyle says. "I bet that was your fault too."

I want to scream at him to shut up, but instead I demand, "Who told you about her?"

"Theo. Who else? He loves telling your secrets. He won't love it half as much when I tell him about you and Ryan. He'll probably be glad I've killed you. And maybe then I'll kill Ryan too. He's a pretentious prick, always looking down his nose at me, just because I'm the better fighter. I'm faster." Kyle darts forward, locking his spear with my sword. "I'm stronger." With a sudden jerk, he tears my sword from my grip. "I'm *invincible*."

Kyle lunges at me, but I turn and run.

"Didn't you hear me?" Kyle yells. "It doesn't matter what you do! You're going to lose!"

Kyle's right about a lot of things. He's stronger and faster than me. With that much, I'd usually lose. But he's not invincible. There's a way to beat him. I just have to find it.

Kyle doesn't throw his spear, instead pursuing me on foot. I was betting on that. Even if he thinks I can't stop him, he won't risk losing his own weapon in case he misses. Which shows he's doubtful in one area: skill. I've just got to hope the Executioner gave me enough of that to beat him.

Before Kyle can eat up too much of the distance between us, I spin and fire an arrow at him. It embeds in his shoulder, and he jerks back, coming to a stumbling stop. He reaches for the shaft, but I've already gotten another arrow notched. This one digs into his left leg. Kyle cries out in rage and rips it free, then the other, tossing them aside. He turns to attack, but I got the distraction I needed to unsheathe my main weapon.

I let my chain loose just as Kyle realizes what's going on, a moment too late. The chain wraps around his spear, just below the spearhead. I pull the chain hard, trying to dislodge his spear. It doesn't budge. Kyle's grin widens to show his teeth.

"I warned you," Kyle says, giving the chain a quick jerk. Unwilling to release it, I stumble forward. Kyle wrenches the chain again, reeling me in.

"Stronger." Another tug. "Faster." Another.

I'm close enough. I slip the dagger out of my sleeve and, just like Celia, let it fly. It digs into the back of Kyle's left hand.

With a screech, Kyle drops his spear. I quickly yank it and the chain to me, then release them, letting them sail down the hall. I ram Kyle before he can recover, sending us both to the ground, me on top. I shove the dagger from my other sleeve against his throat.

"You're not invincible," I tell him. "Even the monsters in the labyrinth that look invincible can bleed."

"You'd know all about blood," Kyle growls. "You've got enough on your hands."

"I haven't killed anyone."

Kyle's eyes spark. Sudden, sharp pain shoots through my thigh. Kyle has stabbed me with the dagger I put in his hand. The next thing I know, he's flipped me, and now he's the one on top. But he doesn't grab my fallen dagger. He pulls the one in my leg free and tosses it aside. I gasp as blood flows from my thigh, but before I can fully feel the pain, Kyle slams my head against the ground so hard I hear something crack.

"Admit it!" Kyle screams in my face. "Admit that you killed them!"

"I've never killed —"

Kyle's hands wrap around my throat so quickly and so tightly my words are cut off in another gasp. He squeezes with crushing force. I start to gag, then choke.

"Because you exist," Kyle says, "they died. That means you killed them. Felix. Gina. And now Celia."

Kyle's eyes have gone glassy. I can't see the hatred anymore. I can't read anything in them, which is even more terrifying. Then my vision starts to blur. I bat at Kyle's chest, but my strength is draining quickly. I'm seeing dark spots now, and everything sounds very far away. That makes it hard to tell if what Kyle says next is a whisper or not. Either way, his voice is softer than it ever has been when he says: "You just have to stop existing. It won't be hard. You don't even have a name."

I do, I want to say. *I have Clara's name, and now I have the name of the Fey and the Executioner's bell, and I have the name my parents gave me.*

If I could speak, I would tell Kyle what it is, because it's all I have to give him.

That's my last thought before everything goes dark.

It's only dark for a moment.

A scream sounds, and it seems far away, so I don't panic like I should. The pressure lifts off my neck, and I assume it's over. I'm dead now, and it's all just darkness, like the hundred-headed monster's cave. Then I see the blue fire, except it's paler than before, and there are clouds scattered across it, and there's the sun. The gate to the realm of the gods.

I blink, and the last spots clear from my vision. I'm lying on the labyrinth floor, my lungs burning. Alive.

I gasp for air and shove myself up, my shaky limbs searching for purchase as much as weapons. Where's Kyle? Has he decided to prolong our fight? My death?

"You're still alive?"

The voice is weak, defeated. It takes me a moment to recognize it as Kyle's. He's lying on his back, just a couple of steps away. There's an arrow sticking out of his chest and blood blooming over his tunic.

I look around, frantically searching, only to find Risa at the other end of the hall, Elle hovering behind her. Risa's eyes are wide, horrified. Her bow is still raised.

Kyle starts laughing. Broken and hysterical.

"Of course," he says, and I see that he's crying. "I couldn't even kill you first!"

His laughter dies abruptly, his eyes going dull, but he's still breathing. He's even strong enough to look at me.

"Come here," he says.

I crawl over to him, still too weak for much more. Kyle can't hurt me now. He's out of weapons and almost out of strength. Invincible no more.

I reach Kyle's side and lean over him, close enough to hear his small voice, but he doesn't say anything right away. He just stares at me, his slow blinks and gently moving chest the only indication he's still alive.

"Theo," Kyle says. "He knew about the attack on Fates. We both did."

I freeze.

Something flashes in Kyle's eyes. Victory. "It was Gammon's terms. He'd let us into Kleos if . . . if we left Fates open for Kleos to loot. Cassie didn't know about it, but Theo did. Theo agreed to it, and . . . and that's not all."

"You're lying."

"I don't care if you think that. You just have to listen to me. You have to. These are my last words." In a final burst of strength, Kyle grabs my arm, pulling me closer to him. "When Ryan showed up at Kleos, before Gammon went to pick you up, Gammon asked Theo if he would help get rid of you if you didn't agree to his plan to attack Harmonia. Theo said he would."

Kyle's skin is starting to turn pasty, but that's not what makes his smile sick. "He doesn't think of you any differently than he does Harmonia's leader. He's just using you."

"I don't believe you."

"Good," Kyle says. "That means you'll let him use you even more."

He tries to yank me down again, although he's not quite strong enough now. He's fading fast.

Kyle says something, but I can't quite hear it, so even though everything in me says to ignore him, to force his fingers off my arm, I lean down.

"I . . ." A shallow breath, against my cheek. "I should have pushed you out of the shelter."

The air against my cheek goes still. Kyle's hand falls from my arm. I can still feel his fingertips pressing into my flesh. A part of me knows I always will.

Night has just fallen when we reach my Kleos base. When the wall slides away, Elle mimes clapping her hands and Risa breathes, "Whoa."

It's the first thing she's said since what happened with Kyle. Mostly she's kept her head down, a troubled look on her face. She saved my life, and this is what she has to live with. I wish I could take it from her. I wish I'd been strong enough to stop Kyle when I had the chance. Or to let Kyle stop me.

I shake that off and usher Elle into the stairwell. We can't be out here any longer for fear of attracting bats. But Risa doesn't follow us inside.

She says, "I've got to get back to Harmonia."

"Don't be silly, Risa," Elle says. "You can't go back through the labyrinth without Bell's bell, and she can't give it to you, otherwise she wouldn't be Bell. You'll just have to stay here."

"Sorry, Elle," Risa says, with a weak smile. "My sisters need me."

"Stay with us tonight," I say quickly, before Elle can get upset or Risa can leave. "Your sisters wouldn't want you traveling back alone this late. It's a long way. You won't be any help to Harmonia if something happens to you."

Risa's hands clench at her sides. I think she'll still leave, but finally she says, "OK. I'll stay until morning. Then I really must go."

I understand why she's so anxious. Anything could have happened between Kleos and Harmonia in the time it took us to reach my base. There may not even be that many of Risa's sisters left. But if Risa left on her own now, a bat trio could easily pick her off before she makes it halfway home.

While Risa and Elle follow me inside, I light a candle. The wall slides into place behind us. Elle starts humming as we descend the steps, but it does nothing for the dread building in the pit of my stomach. What if the door is locked, and Ryan isn't here?

I try the door. It's locked. I catch my breath but force down my panic and knock. I strain to hear a sound, footsteps or voices, any sign —

The door swings open, revealing Ryan with his bow, an arrow notched. When Ryan relaxes, Cassie peeks out from behind the door. She doesn't look terribly pleased to see me, or maybe it's Elle she's upset about, because her attention is focused on the girl behind me.

Ryan swings his bow over his shoulder as he approaches. For a moment, I think he's going to hug me, and I'm surprised that I hope he does. I want to hug him. I'm glad he's here. I'm glad he made it safely.

But then Ryan says, "Who's this?"

Of course he wasn't going to hug me. He doesn't even care enough to greet me. And I shouldn't care about him not caring. I don't.

"She's my friend," Elle pipes up. "Not my sister. Not like Bell."

"Bell?" Ryan echoes.

"I'm Risa," Risa says, offering a hand.

"Is she from Harmonia?" Ryan asks me, ignoring Risa completely.

"Yes," I say, annoyed by his behavior. "And she just saved my life."

Risa reddens and looks away.

"What happened?" Ryan demands. His expression has shifted. His frown is deeper, and he's scanning me up and down.

"I'm not injured," I say.

"Yes, you are." Ryan's fingers graze my neck. His voice is hard when he says, "Someone tried to choke you."

"A member of Kleos," I say when I notice how warily Cassie is looking at me. Kyle, to her, is an ally from Fates. Someone who helped her escape Collin. If I tell her Kyle tried to kill me, she might use that as more ammunition for her hatred, and I don't want her hating Risa for it.

"From Kleos, huh?" a voice calls from within my base. "Hopefully not a friend of mine, because that would be awkward."

I stiffen. The last time I heard that voice, it was shouting for other Kleos fighters to catch me. I shove past Ryan, only to find the speaker sitting in front of my hearth, eating my rations.

"Nice place you got here," Jack says to me, then with an appraising look at the bone he's gnawing on: "Food's kinda stale, though. I'd give it a three out of five. Maybe a three and a half?"

"What is he doing in my base?" I demand, whirling on Ryan.

Before Ryan can reply — not that it looks like he will anytime soon, avoiding my eyes as he is — Cassie steps in. She flicks a hand toward Risa. "Just like she saved you, Jack saved us."

"You make me sound gallant," Jack says, then tosses the bone in the fire.

"I could have used that for broth," I hiss.

"Nah. I sucked all the good juices out of it."

"Gammon left guards at Kleos," Cassie interrupts, shooting Jack an annoyed "shut up" look. "When we tried to sneak out, they caught us. Gammon left Jack in charge, so they brought us to him. We explained what happened and —"

"We?" Jack asks with a wave at Ryan. "I don't remember that guy doing anything but sulking."

"He wasn't sulking," Cassie says at the same time Ryan says: "I just didn't want to let an idiot in on the plan."

Now Ryan gets Cassie's "shut up" look.

"The point Cass is trying to make," Jack says, "is that I liked the idea of getting out of the labyrinth a bit more than murdering a bunch of girls."

"You mean it was more likely to happen," Risa says from where she's standing in the corner.

"Oh, hey, Harmonian, didn't see you there." Jack gestures to Risa's notched arrow, currently aimed at him. "Charming as ever. You aren't the one I concussed, are you?"

A lump rises in my throat when I realize that was Celia. I didn't like her, but I have to respect her dedication to her sisters. From the way Risa's eyes go cold and she pulls her bowstring taut, she's thinking of Celia too.

"OK," Jack goes on. "Wrong thing to say." Then, under his breath, "Not that there's a right thing to say with this group . . ."

"Jack," Cassie snaps. "Quit it." Then Cassie looks at me. "Get your friend to stop aiming at him. He saved us."

"It sounds like he just got you out of Kleos," I say. "Ryan could have done that."

Ryan stands a little straighter, I think. Cassie bristles. "I know that, but we were attacked on our way here. That's when Jack really saved us."

"Hero-for-hire over here," Jack says.

"What happened?" I demand, looking from Cassie to Ryan. Ryan's not standing up straight anymore. If anything, he's evading my gaze even more than before.

Finally, Ryan says, "It turns out I wasn't being as careful with the journal as I thought. Someone saw me translating it."

"Who?" I demand, my heart speeding up. "Where is it?"

When Ryan doesn't answer right away, I step right up to him and grab his shirt front, ignoring Cassie's protests. "Ryan, where is my journal?"

It's Jack who answers.

"That guy you were kissing outside the base stole it." Jack opens one of my flasks, inspecting the contents. "Theo, right?"

I don't know how I get to sleep that night, but somehow I do. It helps that I'm curled up next to Elle. Risa's on her other side, closest to the wall and as far from Jack, who made a bed against the opposite wall, as possible. Ryan and Cassie are sleeping by the hearth.

Or they should be, but when I find myself being shaken awake, it's Cassie whose face greets mine. She gestures for me to be quiet and tugs me gently away from my bed companions. I let her, and as I go, I glance over at the hearth. Ryan isn't there.

"I don't know where he is," Cassie whispers. "I'm worried he might be . . . maybe going after Theo."

I tense. "How long has he been gone?"

"Not long. At least, I don't think so. When I woke up, his bed was still warm."

I grab my weapons from the nearby crate and quickly slide them into place. "I'm going to try and stop him. I know the area better than he does. Wake Jack and Risa. Tell them what's happened, but don't let them come after me. Someone needs to stay to protect . . . um . . ."

"To protect me and Elle. I know I need protection. I wish I didn't, but it doesn't hurt me to hear it." Cassie ushers me toward the door before I've finished slipping my axe away.

But right before I leave, she grabs my hand. "I'm sorry for how I've been treating you. Ryan told me the truth — that you didn't hurt him in the end, and that you actually saved him and the others from the screechers the day you took him. Please save him now."

I squeeze Cassie's hand. "I'll find him."

Cassie nods and lets me go. I race up the stairs. I've just made it to the top when the dim light behind me goes out as my base door shuts. In seconds I'm in the labyrinth, breathing in the crisp night air, and the wall slides back into place behind me. I glance to the left, wondering which way Ryan might have gone. I glance to the right.

And something slams into my head. There's brief, sharp pain. Then there's only darkness.

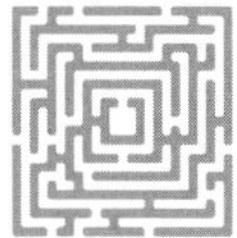

I wake to a splash of cold water against my face. I gasp and some of it gets in my mouth, while more drips down the front of my tunic. Instinctively, I reach to wipe the water away, but I can't. My hands are bound behind my back, while my knees are bent under me. I'm leaning against a wall. A labyrinth wall, because I can still smell the night air, still see the night sky, with its thousands of stars and bulbous moon. But the moon is half blocked out by a hulking figure that towers over me.

The figure takes a step forward and tosses back his hood. I stare up at him.

"You could look happier to see me," Gammon says. "At least pretend. We know, if nothing else, that your acting skills are quite good, don't we, Fey Bell?"

I don't know what to say. I'm shaking and only partially because of the water.

Gammon hunkers down in front of me. This close, I can see there's something wrong with his face. There's a gash running across his temple, scabbed over and ugly. But that's not what's wrong. It's something in his expression. His charismatic mask has finally cracked.

"I bet you want to know how it ended," Gammon says. "The grand battle. Harmonia lost."

I go rigid. Gammon smirks, but there's no humor in it, and it doesn't reach his eyes.

"Kleos lost too. It was a draw, you could say. There isn't a Harmonia anymore, but there isn't a Kleos either. The monster made sure of that."

"Monster?"

"Oh, yes. We thought the stinger was bad, but this? I'd never seen anything like it. None of us had. It massacred us. I don't think any of the Harmonians survived. Polina fell early, trying to save some of the younger girls. The monster got them anyway. An appropriately pathetic end to a pathetic group. But my boys didn't fare much better. And Silas? My faithful second-in-command? He ran away. Don't worry; when I'm done here, I intend to hunt him down. I'm sure someone must have told you what I do to traitors."

I remember the hallway in Harmonia with that message carved into the wall. It was Gammon. *He* killed those girls.

"Where is she?" Gammon asks.

"Who?"

"Elle!" he shrieks, and he grabs my arms so hard my bones throb. "I saw you take her inside that wall! How do I get inside? How do I get to Elle?"

"How do you know her?" I demand.

"Know her? Oh, I don't know her at all. I know *of* her. Her name. Her status. That sickening face. But what do you know, Fey Bell? That's the real question." Gammon leans in close to me. His breath stinks as he hisses, "Do you know the truth about Daedalum?"

"What are you talking about?"

"I'll tell you a story, will I? You always liked my stories." Gammon laughs at himself, then shoves to his feet and starts pacing. "All the little towers in Daedalum have a priest of Icarus, don't they? And all the little priests of Icarus, they report to the head tower, at the center of the city, because under that tower is the resting place of Icarus." Gammon laughs at that too. "Of course the head tower knows the truth. There is no Icarus. The labyrinth is a death trap. The perfect answer for a population constantly exceeding its limits.

"That's what happens when you live in such a confined space. You risk running out of food and water and energy for all the people in the city, so you have to get rid of some of them. But how? How to do that without causing panic, without tempting revolution? You tell them they're becoming angels, of course. You get them while they're young, weed out the weaker ones, the dumber ones, the ones there are too many of in any given year. Boys. Girls. Get rid of them before they're established, vital members of the community. Off them before they've created a space that will need to be filled. Pacify the parents by telling them it's *all for Icarus*."

Gammon turns to me, spreading his hands as if he's a school teacher concluding a lesson. "So you see, Fey Bell, all the little towers and the little priests of Icarus had no idea, but the head tower did, and so did the families in charge of the head tower and the Church of Icarus. And one day, one stupid little man decided he was going to stand up for all the little towers. He was going to risk his status and safety to save all the little future Icarii. But he couldn't do it alone, could he? So he pulled in all the other righteous little idiots — my parents included. Do you know what happens when people are so consumed by their own self-importance that they think they can be the heroes everyone needs — they can be the real-life Icarus? Do you know what happens, Fey Bell?"

Gammon gets in my face again, so suddenly that I jerk back and hit my head against the wall. Gammon cups my face in his hands. His touch makes my flesh crawl.

"When a stupid little man tries to be Icarus," Gammon says, "his children become Icarii. And so do the children of the people who joined his stupid little rebellion. And all the children are sent to their deaths, and they never become angels, but if they're lucky, the angels eat them before they have to start eating each other."

I'm shivering all over. I can't stop myself. Gammon sighs, and his hands drop from my face. "It's the father's fault, you see. But since I can't get the father, the children will have to do, right? Though they've done enough to deserve it themselves. They left me to die when we first entered the labyrinth. Did you know that?" Gammon strokes my cheek, and I recoil from his touch. "Don't worry. My revenge is almost complete. I'm halfway there."

"Halfway?" I echo.

Gammon laughs. It's his typical, deep, throaty laugh. I hate how normal it sounds when he looks like this. The smile he gives me is in no way normal. There's something broken about it yet something pitying. He waves a finger at me. "Now, now, Fey Bell. Did you really think Elle's brother died by accident?"

I go cold.

"Though we did stage it to look that way. It was easy to lure the screechers, then let them have their way with Prosper and his partner. I think they would have beaten the screechers too, even though there were only the two of them. But one well-placed arrow made Prosper screecher food. I don't think Fates ever recovered the body. What was left to be recovered, that is."

Gammon is beaming. I feel like I'm about to throw up.

"I've heard Elle's gone a bit soft in the head," Gammon says, "that she doesn't quite believe her brother's dead. I intend to clear that up for her."

I really am about to be sick when I spot something behind Gammon. A shadow. Moving.

"So, Fey Bell," Gammon says, "how was my story? Do you think Elle will like it?"

There's a whooshing sound. Gammon jolts, ramrod straight. Then, with a sort of morbid shock, he looks at the arrow embedded in his leg. He doesn't even gasp. His face shows no pain as he cranes his head back to take in the shadows of the hall.

"Who's there?" he calls.

The approaching figure tosses aside their bow. It clatters into the light. "Prosper's brother."

Gammon blinks blankly at the shadows. "Prosper didn't have a brother."

"Then your story's missing something." He steps into the light, weapon raised. Gammon starts to push to his feet, reaching for his own sword, but he's too slow. With one furious swing, the figure embeds his sword in Gammon's neck.

Gammon's jaw goes slack, his eyes wide. The figure jerks his sword free, and Gammon's blood showers the ground. Gammon clutches at his neck and starts to keel over, but the figure grabs him by the back of the shirt and hauls him upright.

"The story's not done yet," he says, and he swings again.

The next swing kills Gammon. He would have died anyway, from blood loss, but this one severs his spinal cord. I see the way Gammon's eyes lose focus instantly. There's no slow fading. There's no clinging to life — like the temple lion, like Kyle. Gammon's there one moment, and then he's not.

Gammon's dead, but the figure keeps hacking until his head is severed clean from his body. It lands with a thud between me and Gammon's body, which flops backward. I stare in horror — not at the head, but at the figure, who stands in profile, outlined by the moon. He's panting, still gripping his sword in one hand. With his free hand, he wipes sweat from his brow. Then his face tilts this way, his gaze landing on Gammon's head.

"How nostalgic," he mutters. Then he kicks the head clean down the corridor. Blood sprays in its wake, and I wince. When I open my eyes again, he's right in front of me, staring down, blood still dripping from his sword, making a puddle in front of me, seeping into the grooves between the stones.

Using the tip of his bloody sword, he tilts my chin up. He smiles.

"It's been a while," Collin says. "Have you missed me, Nameless?"

As a child, Caighlan Smith loved to build and navigate pillow mazes. An adoration of Greek mythology soon followed. Canadian born and raised, Smith studied English Literature and Classics at Memorial University of Newfoundland. Her first novel was published when she was nineteen. Her name is pronouned KAY-lan.